One lone figure in the crowd . . .

Andropov walked through the crowd, his valise unmoving in his tight grip. His eyes, behind thick sunglasses, scanned and picked out the obvious undercover police and Secret Service agents.

What surprised him the most and threw off his planning were the people. The crowds behind him seemed a tangible mass that could not be swayed or moved. He edged his way to the back. Along the way, one blustering bulk of a man didn't feel like moving.

"Off my foot," he shouted at Andropov, who merely looked up to meet the man's eyes. They locked glances: Andropov's cool and hard, the other man's angry.

Suddenly, the other man's expression changed entirely. A trickle of blood flowed from his gaping mouth and he slumped forward. Someone shrieked . . .

During the melee, no one saw Andropov quietly slipping out, headed back toward a bus station. He was casually wiping a knife blade on a sheet of newsprint and already making plans for Berlin . . .

Ace Books by David Evans

TIME STATION LONDON
TIME STATION PARIS
TIME STATION BERLIN

TIME STATION BERLIN

DAVID EVANS

ACE BOOKS, NEW YORK

This book is an Ace original edition,
and has never been previously published.

TIME STATION BERLIN

An Ace Book / published by arrangement with
Bill Fawcett & Associates

PRINTING HISTORY
Ace edition / September 1997

The Putnam Berkley World Wide Web site address is
http://www.berkley.com

Make sure to check out *PB Plug*,
the science fiction/fantasy newsletter, at
http://www.pbplug.com

ISBN: 0-441-00473-3

ACE®
Ace Books are published by The Berkley Publishing Group,
a member of Penguin Putnam Inc.,
200 Madison Avenue, New York, NY 10016.
ACE and the "A" design are trademarks
belonging to Charter Communications, Inc.

PRINTED IN THE UNITED STATES OF AMERICA

10 9 8 7 6 5 4 3 2 1

This one is for my wife, Deb,
who kept me from getting lost
in myriad reveries and meaningless thoughts
when a good conversation was better.
She also kept me on course,
so this wouldn't have been done
without her love and encouragement.

Prologue

**Place: United Press International Offices,
West Berlin, West Germany
Time: 2:17 p.m., Sunday, June 2, 1963**

"Can you believe this garbage?"

Heads turned in the small set of rooms that comprised West Berlin's United International Press offices. The speaker's voice was loud, forceful, and used to being heeded. It belonged to Conrad Stein, a middle-aged journalist who had survived more news than any man should in a lifetime. After all, he began covering the news right out of high school, reporting war movements from what was left of Germany at the tail end of World War II.

Stein was beefy, with thick forearms always on display, since his starched white sleeves were permanently rolled up to the elbows. His patterned, wide ties were always loose around his neck, and no one recalled ever seeing him wear a jacket in the offices. On the other hand, away from the sound of Teletypes and typewriters, Stein was reputed to be a gracious host who knew his way around a menu and could spot a good new restaurant before the city's elite. As a result, even government leaders were known to call for advice on where to entertain, trying to remain a step ahead of their competitors. This afforded Stein tremendous access, which allowed UPI more than its share of exclusive news stories.

There was little question that Stein was in his element and would not be moving aside for any of the young crop of reporters, who were usually toiling away but were now hanging on his every word.

Stein had walked out of his private office, set back from the five desk main room and next to a small secretary/ receptionist's desk. Clenched in his right hand was a yellow sheet of legal paper, his black ink scrawl visible around the ripples.

"The Russian government has finally chosen to comment on Kennedy's visit," he pronounced. Seven sets of eyes remained fixed on him as he worked his way farther into the room. Choosing a spot toward the center, Stein looked around at his staff: reporters, secretary, Teletype operator, photographer. "The key word in the long spiel is 'provocative.' Provocative! Anyone want to explain to me why it's provocative?"

He stopped, inviting an answer from his audience. This was fairly typical behavior for the bureau chief, and everyone knew what was expected from them: commentary which would lead to a strategy for covering a major event. John Fitzgerald Kennedy's visit to West Germany later in the month certainly qualified as major.

"He's the leader of the Western world?" This from Eric Gruber, the photographer and rookie of the staff.

"Tell that to de Gaulle," cracked Peter Heinz, the key political reporter. It was no secret he preferred the idea of a European leader setting the pace for the free world rather than the Americans.

Stein smiled at the comment but nodded toward Gruber. The photographer's blond hair moved freely as he shook his head in acknowledgment. Where most Germans kept their hair clipped neat and razor-short, Gruber was of a newer generation that seemed to ignore most of the customs. Stein could not care less since the finished photographic work was highly acceptable. Gruber's reasonable youth was also an asset, since Stein could count on the kid day or night, saving him budget dollars on freelance assistance.

"Provocation is in the eye of the beholder," Stein observed. "They obviously feel threatened when the U.S. President comes to town, although there has been no attempt to prevent their completion of the Wall. And there won't be anything stopping them, since we all know how the Russians would react if anyone on this side so much as took a hammer to that monstrosity. Still, calling the visit a provocation this early means they're worried. Let's run with that." He began scanning the room, mentally picking his reporters as if choosing sides for a game.

"Okay, let's get all the standard previsit stuff settled. Spec, I want the itinerary with all the flowery details. You're American, so give me their side. Talk to some U.S. businessmen in town. Peter, let me have the Old One's reasons for wanting Kennedy here. Then contrast that with the Fat One's position—which is obviously against anything the Old One says. Katrina, can you get me a map of the visit from the U.S. Embassy? We'll use that for art. Oh, don't worry, Gruber, you'll have work to do, since I want you to accompany the tour from start to end. We'll need plenty of shots for everyone's scrapbook.

"No doubt about it, folks," he said, clapping those large hands together, "this is one visit we're all going to remember."

Footsteps echoed against the polished floors of the large, dim building. He was the only one in the wood-paneled hallway, convinced that no one wanted to be seen away from their desks. The figure also suspected that few fully understood their way through the labyrinthine layout, and getting lost was tantamount to career suicide. There was little doubt that they knew their way from the elevator to their office and to the washroom. Anything after that might strain their management skills.

Instead, he was confident of his course and moved

quickly around corners and deeper into the building. Everyone on the street knew the building's identity and purpose, but no one discussed it loudly, publicly on the streets or even in the privacy of their favorite pubs.

It was home to the KGB.

Since the agency's inception, they were the secret police, ensuring strict adherence to the dictates of Communism. While premiers would rise and fall, Russia would be safe under their shadowy, iron rule. To the world at large, the KGB were the feared initials and stuff of spy novels. The GRU, though, was the group that kept internal security tight, and there remained a rivalry and tension between the two that always threatened but never once erupted into a war.

A dark gloved hand gripped the metal handle on the door and pushed it open. The door moved soundlessly inward, flooding the hall with high-wattage light. The man quickly entered the room, closing the door behind him, certain no one would follow. Where a secretary should be stood an empty desk, devoid of even an intercom. The anteroom was off-white and without decoration of any kind, although tiny cracks of age could be seen in the plaster. The floor was wooden and scuffed.

Ignoring the barren space, the man crossed the small anteroom and walked through another door without pausing to knock.

He was expected.

In the larger inner room stood three men, all in handsomely tailored suits, cigarettes burning uselessly between their fingers. Beyond them was a huge mahogany desk, its surface covered with papers, file folders, and glossy black-and-white photographs. On the credenza behind the desk, dark hardcover books stood, creating the sense of a black void that would catch one's attention. The paneled wood walls had large photos of Joseph Stalin and Nikita Khrushchev as sole decoration, while a Russian flag stood limply on a floor stand in the corner. It was a typical director's office, totally without personality, available for any occupant the heads of state wanted in that particular job. Of the three men watching the room's new occupant, any of them could be the leader, any of them the servant. In Russia, this was an interchangeable government structure.

"Comrade," the center man acknowledged.

Heads bobbed in greeting, no one else speaking.

"Let us speak to the point, since we want you to have adequate time to prepare." This from the man on the left side of the room. He gestured toward the desk and its surface contents.

All four men stood before the desk, no one taking the lead, no one even attempting cordiality, staring at the photos of a man with a full head of brown hair, small eyes, and a bright toothy smile. He could have been an American movie star. He was, instead, President of the United States.

"We expect a great deal of trouble from this man when he arrives in Europe," the center man said. "He dislikes the Wall and he dislikes us. He is also in deep trouble at home and abroad. He will need to do something bold and that is what worries us.

"We would like you to prevent his boldness." The visiting man stood silently, seemingly expectant with questions that he chose not to ask. The men in the room took note of the look, and the previously silent one began to reply.

"Yes, there has been a great deal said about the possibility of some agreement. They call it a Nuclear Nonproliferation Treaty. Our government considers this quite suspect, and, even if it is signed, the French will ignore it like they do everything they haven't proposed first. Instead, we are acting on our country's sovereign behalf."

The man nodded, reached across the desk, and grabbed a folder and envelope. He silently handed it to the visitor and gave him a gap-toothed smile. "You are probably wondering why we are sending you instead of a local agent. Our counterparts in East Berlin have not proven trustworthy. They have, instead, allowed too many people to leave, including their own. We cannot rely on them from such a distance. We feel more confident in sending one of our own. You."

"Whatever you need, tell us. But do not fail."

The recipient of the material nodded once, hefted the

papers in his hands. It was a comfortable feel, a little heavier than usual but that made sense. There would be that much more to know about this new target. He had not failed his employers and was inwardly pleased at being the man chosen for the coveted assignment. Protocol prevented him from expressing any personal joy; he was merely doing a job for the state. Every soul did his part.

He left the room of nameless men and returned to his small apartment on the other side of the city. It would require at least a day if not more to sift through the information he had received. Another day or two for planning, and then a day for the equipment, cash, and documents he needed. No question he would have time to rehearse and perfect his work. No question was to be left unanswered, no contingency unprepared for. He was an artist at his work; it was just that his work was that of an assassin.

One of the nameless men walked down the hall, made three turns and entered an office, almost exactly the same as the one he had just left. The only difference was the arrangement of flags and plaster cracks. He sat behind the desk and carefully pried up a corner of the wood paneling. Beneath, fitted smoothly in a cutout, was a small, beige instrument with keypad and miniature screen. Two fingers went to work, and within seconds the screen lit up, casting a shallow light on his face. A woman looked at him with cold eyes and no emotion on her face.

"Report."

"I have successfully convinced these small-minded fools to take a chance. We have ordered the assassination of President Kennedy."

"Excellent. If you steer this right, then our holdings in 1975 will give us the leverage to seize control of the world financial markets."

"And from that, becoming new masters."

"Correct. Remember, you have begun a process that needs to be seen through to completion. Will this assassin get the job done?"

"I have been assured."

"Trust no one. You forget the prime rule."

"He shall not fail. Nor shall the plan."

With no other word, the dark-skinned woman blinked off the screen and left the man alone in the barren office.

1

**Place: United Press International Offices,
West Berlin, West Germany
Time: 11:47 a.m., Monday, June 10, 1963**

"What have you got for me?"

The two reporters stood awkwardly before Stein's desk, small pads in their hands. Heinz, the self-styled political scientist, seemed to have stepped out of his tailor's shop, looking crisp in a gray suit, white shirt, and sedate maroon striped tie. Next to him, Alan Spector seemed to have been peeled out of a dry cleaning machine, incomplete. His shirt was rumpled, top button undone, his green plaid tie loose. His charcoal-gray suit pants looked baggy, and there were scuffs marring his black shoes. They were effective employees, in Stein's opinion, each with their strengths. Where Heinz had the political connections and slick prose style, Spector seemed to dig up dirt no one else could find, as if he knew exactly which rocks to look under throughout East and West Germany. The bureau chief didn't know much about this man, except that he was a good reporter, a solid if uninspired writer, and the biggest baseball fan he had ever encountered. The mysteries of American baseball eluded

Stein, but he knew it was one of the most important cultural artifacts the Americans cherished. Each October, Stein knew, Spector was the first in the office to check the Teletype for incoming news on the U.S.A.'s fall classic, the World Series.

"Adenauer has decided he will accompany Kennedy from start to finish," Heinz chirped from his notes. "He sees the opportunities this will provide him in the press. And it's also his last major foreign policy detail, so he wants to milk this for all it's worth."

Stein chewed a pencil, considering the information. He made a face at the announcement, showing his displeasure with Konrad Adenauer, lame-duck chancellor of West Germany, the sole person to hold the title since the end of the War. While pleased "the Old One" was finally forced into retirement, Stein was also less than thrilled with the chancellor-elect, Ludwig Erhard, "the Fat One." The country had healed under Adenauer's stewardship, but it was definitely time for a fresher approach as the world moved further away from the horrors of the Axis threat. Intellectually, he understood how Erhard got the post—he was a skilled economist, and money was more and more the motivating factor behind politics.

"So, what do we do about it? I've already got Gruber covering each stop. Is there some angle we can run with?"

Heinz frowned at the question. While he was a sharp reporter, he was not a clear thinker off the story. Stein felt obligated to ask leading questions, forcing his reporters—his entire staff even—to watch the decision-making process in the hopes that they could eventually save him a few steps along the way.

"I don't see anything good about it," Heinz began hesitantly. "Besides, the Fat One is fuming over it. So is Mayor Brandt. They both see it as cutting into their time with the President. Especially Brandt. This is his city." Heinz thought a moment, seemed to like his conclusion, and offered it aloud. "They'll be awfully cozy in the limo here in Berlin."

Stein paused, staring expectantly at his reporter. Heinz didn't notice the attention at first and then the silence got to him, forcing his boss to cock an eyebrow.

"What?" Heinz asked.

"Think. You're a newspaper reporter and what did you just say?"

Heinz was flustered for a moment, and Stein was frustrated that the obvious should elude him. He smoldered while the political reporter rethought his words. Finally a small glimmer of life returned to the man's eyes.

"Brandt and Adenauer—they're going to be riding together. They hate each other."

"Right," came the clipped reply. "How did that happen? Who engineered it? That's today's story. Go. Run with it." Stein shooed Heinz away from the desk, allowing him to return to his office space, another fresh angle uncovered.

On his way, the bureau chief turned to his other top reporter and asked, "What about you, Spec?"

"No question, the car will be crowded." Stein's frown said enough and Spector referred to his notes.

"I've got a complete workup on the pressure Kennedy is feeling in the U.S. He needs a successful European trip because he's getting hammered at home from Congress and his competitors for next year's election. This trip has been growing just a bit out of control, and it seems everyone wants a piece of the President's time."

Stein nodded, soaking up the background, seeing how it could be shaped into a useful local piece for the smaller German papers that couldn't afford their own reporters for anything more than residential events.

"Prime Minister Macmillan is desperate and pressuring Kennedy for a London stopover. He needs some good press himself after all this Profumo silliness," Spector continued. "Looks like the State Department is trying to shoehorn in a quiet visit at the end of the trip, before or after Italy. As it is, Kennedy will start here, then on to Ireland for a family reunion of sorts, probably a day in England with no pomp or circumstance, and then Italy."

Stein paused in his pacing, thinking about the entire situation. "Aren't they crowning the new Pope right about then?"

Spector nodded in agreement and, without checking his notes, added, "He'll spend a full day out of Rome so the Pope can bask in his moment. Kennedy will fly up the next day."

"Will Jackie be coming with him?" Stein asked.

Spector shook his head. "She was scheduled to accompany him when the trip was first conceived, but then *she* conceived so she's staying home."

"Cute, Spec," Stein noted. "Okay, work that up with the chronology behind the trip. Give me the whole story and why he is making each stop. Everyone knows about us, but let's get into why he's on tour. Let's have the political trouble at home as a secondary piece. The papers can run them together or over two days. Let me have twenty-five inches on the tour and about thirteen on the politics."

"No problem," Spector replied and spun around, leaving the area. Stein concentrated on local political stories Heinz had to complete before Kennedy arrived in another two weeks.

Passing Katrina Beck, Stein's secretary, Spector barely noticed her gaze. She always seemed to be looking him over, and he decided it felt comfortable although he never encouraged her. He couldn't, despite the temptations.

Instead, the American went to the back of the small rooms and found Paul Urban, the UPI's chief Teletype operator, hunched over the keyboard, keying in a small piece about Germany's plans for the next Olympiad, coming the following year. Urban was a slight figure, with thin graying hair, a cigarette permanently affixed to his mouth, wire-rimmed glasses framing his oval sweaty face. There was an intensity to Urban's eyes that fascinated Spector.

"You look like hell," Urban muttered, not once taking his eyes off the typewritten copy clipped to a board on his right side. Spector was surprised; he never saw Urban notice his arrival.

"I've had a busy day."

"More Wall scavengers?"

"Yeah." Spector leaned against the office wall, watching Urban enter more words. He was impressed with how precise the man's work was, how few errors he made, and how quickly a story moved from typewriter to Teletype, letters transforming to electronic signals that moved along wires around the world. Such signals had helped sew the world together since the early telegraph efforts a century earlier. Technological advancements never ceased to amaze him, despite his knowledge that the evolution was far from over.

"This time it was a couple of teenagers, joysurfing the 'stream." The disgust was heavy in his voice.

"How'd they ever get access to something so amazing?" Here, Urban actually had a hint of admiration in his question.

"Parents were major contributors to someone's campaign. Asked a little favor for a birthday gift. Never occurred to the rich folk that their kids would cause any trouble. Or maybe get shot."

"Where'd you find them?"

Spector snorted. "Over by Shoneburg, right out in the open. Idiots say they forgot the *Vopos* were armed. I don't know what they teach these kids in school."

They shared a brief laugh, and Urban returned to his work, finishing the story and completing it with the journalist's universal sign-off: "30."

Spector looked off into the distance, ignoring Urban, who tidied the mass of paper he'd just finished inputting. There were a few moments of silence that stretched until the older German cleared his throat. It startled the American enough to make him refocus his eyes on his friend. They were tired, somewhat haunted eyes.

"This is definitely building up to something, Paul," he admitted. Urban looked surprised by the comment but kept silent. "Kennedy's coming is definitely an important event and may be the entire reason I'm here. Hope I'm ready."

"How could you not be," Urban said encouragingly. "You've been here three years and move through this city like a native."

Spector nodded briefly. "I like it here and can see why people get enamored of the city. It's a special place, more so these days because of what it has endured."

"Berlin has been the epicenter of a lot over the centuries," Urban said, giving the words some reverence. "I've come back just to see it rise phoenixlike. It's where I trace my family and it's gone uptime. Here, it's still vital."

The small apartment was dimly lit from two table lamps, flanking a small, worn couch. The assassin, Gregor Andropov, sat at the wooden dining table, his soup cooling, his beer untouched. Spread out on the table before him were a dozen black-and-white photographs of the famed Berlin Wall, each showing a different location along the American and British sectors.

His left hand held a black grease pencil, and he tapped it against the table's surface, ignoring the marks building up. Next to the photos were train maps, flight schedules, bus routes, and road guides. Under that pile sat a passport and train tickets, both under the name of Pavel Andreivich, importer.

On the man's right side was a small, walnut-brown case, the lid open. Inside sat two finely honed knives, gleaming in the dim lighting. They flanked a small pistol, its dark metal barely registering the light. Behind the case was a box of ammunition and a sheath with ties that allowed a knife to be strapped to a leg, much like the celebrated American cowboys.

The man's eyes reviewed the photographs, making black marks on the road map, noting each position. A question occurred to him, and he deftly reached to a different pile and extracted a newspaper clipping, the Cyrillic letters familiar to his gaze. The article, from *Izvestya*, condemned the American President's forthcoming European trip. Buried deep within the article was the necessary timetable.

The pencil crossed off Bonn, Hanau, Wiesbaden, circling only the Frankfurt and Berlin stops of the visit.

A smile finally crossed the man's lips, and he continued his work, well into the night.

2

Place: Berlin Wall, East Berlin, East Germany
Time: 12:04 p.m., Saturday, June 22, 1963

Gravel scattered under Spector's shoes as his feet pounded a path along the perimeter of the East Berlin side of the infamous Wall, near Unt. D. Linden, opposite the American sector. The sun was shining brightly, and he was feeling the sweat drip down his back. Also making him feel awkward was the Luger pistol stuffed under his belt, rubbing unhappily against his pelvic bone. His breathing came easily thanks to constant conditioning, but Spector knew he wouldn't be able to keep up the pace for more than another block or two.

His quarry remained at least another fifty meters ahead, totally oblivious to the stares and shrieks of the morning shoppers, their places on the tedious lines interrupted. The runner was at least as tall as the American, dressed in an olive-green jacket and khaki pants that were about five years ahead of European style. His hair was also longer than expected in Germany, auburn and flowing easily over his shoulders. He seemed much heavier than Spector, which made him hope the man was also in worse physical condition. The pursuer needed a break, since this was the fifth illegal action Spector had had to stop in the last few weeks.

The *Grenzenpolizei*, the Border Police, were bound to pay attention to the commotion first near the Wall itself and then along its path. Spector had no desire to get shot at or make crossing back to the West more difficult. In fact, it began to anger him, which propelled Spector faster, finally gaining ground on the man.

The timing could have been better, since just the day before the East German government had announced the toughest restrictions yet, designed to almost permanently separate the West and East Berliners from seeing each other except at a long distance. Before the chase began, he was distressed to see boarded or roped-closed shops, bars, movie theaters, and hotels. The announcement, just five days before the President's arrival, was surely no coincidence, and Heinz, back at the office, was making a big deal of the act. Sadly, overnight people lost their jobs or homes; students needed to register to attend schools in the new one-hundred-yard *verboten* barrier between the Wall and the rest of East Berlin. Newer special passes were required of the citizenry to be within this space, and privileges enjoyed for centuries such as swimming in the border lakes or fishing in the rivers were suddenly gone. Harsh violations brought on steep fines or automatic prison sentences.

Work had begun on erecting new nine-foot-tall fences with the intention of being done before the American President and his media entourage would arrive in the West. Already, green huts and red turnstiles were being added to the existing checkpoints at the perimeter of this new strip. Curious, this morning Spector had gone across the border, using a special pass that deleted any reference to his work as a journalist. It had the mark of a high-ranking East German official, so it was never questioned by the Border Police, even today, with the new policies hurriedly being put into place. He was fortunate to have had such documents with him at all times, especially in light of yesterday's second dictate that forbade any filming or photography that involved construction of the new barriers.

The East German government, and their Russian masters, were determined to sharply curtail the mass exodus of citizens during Kennedy's visit. There was no question that this new zone would be brutally effective, but not impossible to circumvent. His walking tour was cut short, though, when this out-of-place figure took advantage of a dozing East German officer, helping to install one of the new huts, and lifted the soldier's Luger from the unsnapped holster which was slung over a stack of concrete bags.

Spector watched in amazement as the souvenir hunter seemed ready to get away with his prize but recognized that this was in clear violation of the laws which required him to act. And so the chase was on.

Along the way, they followed the zigzagging edge of the new *verboten* zone, and neither seemed to pay attention to their direction. Nor did they stop to notice the couple furtively moving across the zone, obviously trying to get near one of the incomplete border stations. In a flash, Spector analyzed their actions and realized they were making a last-ditch attempt to get over the border before things clamped down behind the new wall and gates.

The distance dwindled as Spector concluded his mental analysis and the man loomed larger in his sights, which pleased him. The breathing was getting harder and the sweat flowed more freely down his neck and back. Both men rounded a corner and neared one of the checkpoints between the two Germanys. Three Border Police, a division of East Germany's famed *Volksarmee*—People's Army—looked up from their boredom and watched the race with mild interest.

One guard, the tallest of the trio, began to swivel his rifle up and shout for both to halt. The first runner seemed startled by the sound and skittered on the ground, his feet betraying him. He went falling over and over, landing finally near the unmoving, albeit amused, police.

As the Luger thief stopped, so did the couple, now a few meters away from freedom. They froze when they saw the guard, gun in position. In that instant it became obvious that nothing could be done to effect their escape. Whatever planning and hoping had gone into the attempt, it was doomed to failure. Spector stared hard at them, watching their faces; emotions going instantly from cautious hope to utter fear. His heart went out to them.

The guard twirled around, oblivious to the young couple loaded down with bags, aiming eyes and gun instead at Spector, who was moving too fast to stop in any manner. Suddenly old habits returned and he adjusted his momentum just enough to go into a slide, going under the gun and slamming into the fallen runner. The move was smooth to the eye and elicited laughter from the guards, but Spector felt shredded pants, small trickles of blood form around his right thigh. He'd definitely be sore for the next few days, nothing to look forward to.

Spector grabbed the lapels of the other man's jacket and pulled him close, covering his right hand's independent actions. The hand had slipped into a small pocket of the pants, withdrawing a small metal flask of scotch. While bringing the stunned man to his feet, the American quickly unscrewed the top and tried to discreetly spread the liquor about.

"*Was ist los?*" one of the guards asked.

"Sorry," Spector replied in perfect German. "My friend has been celebrating a bit much. He found out he's going to be a father . . ."

"Twins," the other man said, his first words since the chase began. Unfortunately, the word was in Peruvian-accented English and lost on the guards.

"He's very, very excited," Spector said, trying to maintain a light mood. He threw an arm about the seemingly drunk man, who was still regaining his senses. The guards watched warily, listening carefully and unsure of how best to react. Finally, the tall guard held out a hand and demanded to see identification.

Spector used his free hand to withdraw his proper documents, granting him almost unlimited access to the Germanys even under these new restrictions. The inspecting guard whistled at the authority represented by the credentials. He showed it to his colleagues, neither of which had ever seen the name actually in the man's own script, providing such free permission. To cover their awe, though, required them to be harsh in their actions and words, so they verbally abused Spector for another moment for letting things get out of control.

At no point did it occur to the guards to check the other man's ID.

Nor did they notice Spector's own hidden gun, which went to prove how lackadaisically the soldiers went about their work.

"Take him back to the gate you came from and remember, there's no more celebrating anywhere near us," the lead guard barked.

"*Jawohl*," Spector muttered, hefting the other man's left arm around his shoulders and beginning to turn back toward the Brandenburg Gate. The thief allowed his rescuer to shoulder plenty of his weight, exhausted as he was from the run. Both men exuded a great deal of heat, and the perspiration flowed freely, soaking clothes and ruining what was left of Spector's outfit.

About twenty-five meters away, Spector finally had enough and let go of the other man. "You do know you're under arrest," he inquired in unaccented English.

The man dully nodded and shook himself all over, trying to regain control of his body. Both of their breathing had returned to normal, but together they looked like a ragged duo.

"Are you a Beam Back?"

"No." The voice was thick, accented from below the equator.

"Okay, then we have a violation for unauthorized Beaming, a violation for petty theft—and that gun gets returned—and a few other misdemeanors along the way. And you go back today. Your sight-seeing trip has just been canceled."

There was silence between them for another few steps.

"Never expected to see you on this side of the Wall. What were you doing here?" the man asked.

"Checking things out. Do you know anything of this time?"

A shake of the head. Typical, thought the Time Warden. Most illegals were totally ignorant of the time they visited.

"Well, the U.S. President, John Kennedy, will be here in four days and tensions between East and West are boiling, potentially to explode. They won't, of course, but that's why I'm here."

"Why?" The thief was proving to be rather dull-witted, which further annoyed Spector.

"We Temporal Wardens are placed throughout the 'stream, protecting pivotal points from interference. It's okay for historians and scientists to Beam Back because they've been bonded. But once the general public got ahold of time travel, the Wardens were required. So, what brought you back here?"

The other man stuffed hands in his coat pockets and looked up at the bright blue sky. "I'm an antique gun collector. I also have built up a lucrative business fulfilling needs from other enthusiasts."

"Terrific," Spector muttered. He did not like this interloper at all.

"I was asked to retrieve a Luger from this era, and I used a friend's machine which seemed to have a defect. I was hoping to be here twenty years earlier or so."

Spector let out a sigh, about all he was good for, but not something he wanted to admit. "Just great. So, how long have you been breaking the law?"

"Why should I tell you?" The defiance began to make the Warden angry.

"Now that you've been caught, we can send an agent through the 'stream to track your moves. We can record your illegal visits and build up a really pretty case. We don't take morons like you lightly."

The man slumped his shoulders, defeated. "I'll be brain-wiped and consigned to the labor battalions. That's no life!"

"And your petty thievery may have affected time, or your faulty machine may be the reason Amelia Earhart's plane vanished or be the sky gods the Incas once believed in. Trust me, it's people like you who force people like me to spend our time back here, biting our tongues and keeping order.

"The exact process of history must remain unchanged," the lecture continued, "otherwise little ripples could turn into a tsunami and none of us would have a home to return to. You and your other 'collectors' keep me busy, but I don't do this for sport. Now let's go, back through to the West and your one-way ticket home."

He had made similar speeches to the others he had collared in the previous weeks. This one was an accident, but others had become real Germany-freaks, loving the country that no longer existed during the Temporal Warden Corps' era. When he was first recruited to the Corps and got assigned, he was curious about Europe, a continent he had never visited, which kept changing and evolving through the centuries. Countries and boundaries kept shifting, empires rising and falling, families rose to great power only to be eclipsed by the tide of time. By Spector's day, the borders had been so thoroughly rewritten, the result of both war and politics, that his Europe and the Europe of 1963 were thoroughly unidentical.

A European posting also kept him from being tempted to retry his hand at baseball, since it was not part of the fabric of European life.

That couple had rushed away from the melee and back toward the edge of East Berlin. Still in the new zone, they made their way directly toward one of the closed taverns, a sign announcing the Owl's Refuge's abrupt closing by order of the East German government. As they neared the door, it opened a crack, acknowledging that someone was still inside.

An older woman, her graying hair pulled back in a bun, wrinkles showing more suffering than age, studied the couple as they rushed through the doorway. With a shake of her head, the woman closed the door and waved them further into the bar, toward a back room which had the sole light on. Inside that room was the woman's husband, a bald man with a thick moustache and full sideburns, streaked with white. Both wore unexceptional clothing, muted colors that seemed to mirror the entire country.

"What happened?" the man called Wilhelm Hoyt asked.

"We were on our way and . . ." the young woman began. She seemed quite nervous and her hands were visibly shaking. The older woman left the room and returned with a dark brown bottle and two shot glasses. With practiced ease, the woman filled a glass and handed it to the other one. Carefully, the younger woman steadied the glass and sipped down the contents without pause. She proceeded to take a deep breath and continued. "Then we were passed by two madmen chasing each other, which caught the attention of a patrol. We were directly in their line of sight and couldn't have crossed without being shot."

The man, her husband, nodded his head in agreement as he finished his own shot. "Elizabeth is right. It was suicidal even to try."

"Not at all, Wolf," Wilhelm said. He reached into a vest pocket and withdrew a pipe and began fussing with it.

"If you really want out, then you should be able to go. No question about it," the older woman, his wife Gerta, added.

The young couple seemed thoroughly dejected and remained silent, contemplating the horrible prospect of a future spent in East Germany.

"What have we here?" Conrad Stein called out from across the main newsroom.

Spector had barely entered the ground floor UPI offices with the time thief, named Manuel Couto, when the bureau chief descended upon them. The crossing back into the West went without a problem, and along the way the Time Warden detoured long enough to slip the Luger back near the still-slumbering soldier. He would wake up wondering how his gun could have fallen on the ground but not once imagining that it had been taken on a jog along the Wall.

Couto remained relatively silent along the way, the awareness of his punishment settling over him like a plastic wrapper. As angry as Spector was for the flagrant misuse of the time column, Couto was morose with having been

caught and a profitable life ruined. Casual mention of a wife
and five children made no difference to Spector, who merely
stated, "Should have thought of that early on, bucko."

Just before entering the offices, nearly a kilometer away
from the Wall, Spector warned his prey, "You'll be going
uptime in just a few minutes. Don't think about spoiling my
cover, because either way you go back." Couto nodded his
understanding.

"You wanted the American angle on Kennedy's visit, but
I found this South American gent and thought it might round
things out," the reporter replied brightly.

Stein thought about it for a moment but couldn't see any
use to the interview and said so.

"Kennedy has done a lot of good work with the South
Americans, especially relations with Panama, so they like
him a lot. On the other hand, his detractors dislike the entire
stink from the Bay of Pigs fiasco. Just trying to keep things
in perspective."

"Well, you look like hell, Spec. Did you have trouble
convincing him to grant you an interview?"

Surprised, Spector looked down at his torn pants, sweat-
soaked shirt, and bare arms streaked with dirt. "Not quite,
but I did take a nasty fall. Sorry about that."

With a dismissive wave of his hand, Stein retreated to his
office, summoning Katrina with a wiggle of a finger.

So distracted, no one really noticed Spector leading
Couto to the rear of the offices, past the Teletype station and
the ever-present Urban, who stared in wonder at the new
face.

"Is he . . . ?"

"Yeah, and he's about to go home," Spector replied,
cutting his colleague off.

Urban put on a serious face, glanced toward the front of
the offices, and nodded once. Spector, in turn, led Couto
back just a few more feet to a room marked "Supplies."
Inside were wooden shelves with pads, pencils, paper clips,
and the like. But the right-hand wall also had a special
hinged doorway that just Spector and Urban knew about.
The Time Warden pushed gently along the seam, about two

thirds of the way down the wall, tripping the locking mechanism.

The entire wall seemed to swing inward, opening up into a vast room with pure white walls and a stack of gunmetal-gray equipment. As he reached his right hand inside a large inner opening, a spark seemed to go off and the equipment winked to life with a small beep sounding out. A wafer-thin card was removed from Urban's wallet and pressed against the side of the equipment which made red lights shift to green. Amber lights winked and after several seconds turned green as well.

In the room's center stood the Beamer, a large chamber festooned with controls, safety features, and lights. Plenty of bright lights.

The stack of equipment was composed of the directional controls, manual overrides for the Beamer, and a well-maintained Temporal Discrepancy Alert system. Unauthorized use of the machine itself, in this era, would set off the alarm which would trigger a subdermal implant called a Trac Link in Spector's left hand. It had a constantly updated, dated stream of data from the Institute, keeping an uptime link in perpetual use.

Urban set to work, a master at making the machine sing. His younger partner liked watching him at work, reminding him he wasn't totally alone.

A slow whine built up, and Couto watched Spector work in silence. A containment field started to take shape around the machine itself, adding an orange tint to the structure. After another minute or so went by, Spector removed a small cartridge from a cache set low in the stack. He popped it into a slot, hit three switches in sequence, and then began reciting the particulars of the case, noting time, location, name of the prisoner, his crimes, and the particular statutes involved.

The recitation done, Spector slipped the cartridge into a slot within the Beamer itself and then stepped back. Seconds later, the whine seemed to vanish as it moved beyond the human ear's ability to discern it. As that happened, there was a coalescence of light in the center of the chamber and the brightness turned almost solid and formed a shimmering pillar, shifting in tone from white to yellow to blue and back again, cycling through the colors almost faster than the eye could follow.

Automatic circuits continued to wink on, forcing the machinery hidden within the UPI offices to draw tremendous energy from the local power station. The locals added an additional transformer, thanks to the Time Warden's needs. His payments were large enough to keep matters private, cover the cost involved, and in the end made them a more efficient operation so everyone benefited.

The warp column took a few minutes to form. Once it did, the featureless room was flooded with its brilliance, yet not a single glimmer leaked through the hidden doorway.

"In you go, Couto," Urban commanded. The chamber door had slowly irised open, the light spilling out, painting wild patterns across the bare walls.

The condemned man hesitated, then slowly walked the short distance to the light source, stepped through the doorway, and was suddenly enveloped by it. Spector and Urban watched impassively as the door snapped closed and the criminal was rapidly deconstructed into molecular components and then thrust into a tachyon stream that returned him home.

In another year, fourteen months at most, Spector's time assignment would be done and he, too, would be able to go home. Until then, he recognized how much more vigilant he would have to be, especially in the coming days when Kennedy would be present. Some figures in time were madmen, others attracted madmen. Sadly, he knew which Kennedy was and what was to come five months away, in Dallas, Texas.

"Let's get some dinner, Paul," Spector said glumly.

At the small restaurant, each man ordered a sausage platter and two mugs of dark beer. Immediately, Urban lit up, the smoke mingling with the overhead lights. Spector felt comfortable with the man, even though they were far apart in age, experience and temperament.

"Do you ever get bothered by what these men face when they return uptime?"

Spector looked into Urban's tired eyes. "I never really think about it. They did, though, break the law, and my daddy always told me the law comes first."

"You miss him?"

"I miss everything. After all, I was supposed to die when my train derailed in Ohio eighty-five years ago. I should have been dead, like the other Red Stockings. Those were some good men, Paul—and I still, to this day, don't understand why I'm the one alive. Instead, after striking my head against that hardwood rack, I blacked out."

Urban sat back, listening, since it was the first time Alan had ever felt like discussing his odd transformation from second-string pitcher for the Cincinnati Reds to Time Warden. He felt contemplative, after all the time shenanigans he had been forced to confront. They had futures and squandered them while he had no future until he was supposed to die.

"When I next opened my eyes, there was a doctor checking some chart. I tried asking him some questions, but instead this bull of a man walks right in and straddles the chair."

"Mason, right?"

"Right." Spector recalled the first time he saw Bill Mason's rugged looks with his heavy jaw, large nose, and weary blue eyes. Running a hand through his sandy hair, the man introduced himself and began spinning a story the likes of which Alan Spector had never imagined.

The food arrived, heaped on the plates, and still steaming from the kitchen. Both attacked their meals with gusto. As he chewed, Alan thought back to those conversations that had reshaped his life.

Somehow, Spector was selected to join something called the Temporal Warden Corps. If he could survive three years of grueling training, then he could be posted to some point in the past, some era that needed protection. The concept made his head spin and he wasn't sure if it was a hallucination or something akin to heaven.

"Why can't I go back to the Red Stockings and keep pitching? Send me back to just after the accident."

"I can't do it, son," Mason said, true sympathy in his voice. "Instead, we're giving you a second chance at life and an opportunity to make a difference. Tell me the truth now, how good a career would you have had as a pitcher?"

Spector considered the question and his two-year stint with the team. Despite his love of the game, they were not easy years. He certainly wasn't a winning pitcher like his teammate Will "Whoop-la" White. Never could master a curve to complement his above-average fastball. Already he had heard rumblings earlier that fateful August day that he might end up being traded to Chicago or released.

"I was okay," he said slowly.

"Your final record was 14−30 after nearly two years, am I correct?"

Spector lowered his eyes. "Yeah."

"Make a bigger difference here. Our research can show you what became of the game. You can watch archival recordings of the greatest games or even attend some in person. And you can do some good."

"If I refuse?"

"I guess we return you to the train and . . ."

". . . and I die. That's my choice?"

Now Mason lowered his eyes for a moment and said, "That's the size of it. Look, Alan, I personally selected you because you have a good head on your shoulders. You have great work habits and take your job seriously. You are physically conditioned, educated, and a good team player. I don't meet a lot of people in your exact circumstances and I'll tell you, I work long hours to keep them all. Work hard and I'll find you a good spot in my division. Hell, I'm Chief of Operations for a five-century period that includes baseball's golden age. Join a new team and you won't be sorry."

Spector thought the matter through one final time and then looked into Mason's calm eyes. "Given the alternative,

I'll sign up. The training's going to be tough, isn't it? I guess I have a lot of learning to do."

Mason leaned forward and clapped the recruit on the shoulder and smiled. "We can bring you up to speed on world events pretty quickly. It's the training to think on your own and react to preserve the Timeline that's going to be tough. You'll see. Get better, and you can start with next week's classes."

Those next three years of his life were the hardest he ever experienced. Still, he was an adept student and worked hard at those lessons. As a result, he was equally well liked by his teachers and colleagues, which meant he graduated with honors and a large number of friends.

Of all the U.S. presidents he'd studied, Spector had developed a fondness for Kennedy. He was struck by the promise that was dashed by Lee Harvey Oswald's bullets. The hints of greatness intrigued him, and when the era became available for a posting, Spector volunteered, figuring it would allow him an unparalleled opportunity to witness some of that term in person. He might even get a better understanding of what made the man special. Words on discs were one thing, but witnessing the true man was something else entirely.

He used that argument when he lobbied Mason for the posting.

"You're a team player, Alan," Mason said that afternoon immediately following graduation.

"So what?"

"West Berlin in that era is significant but not enough to fully staff it. You'd be an agent with one non-field agent. Our budgets are tight and we have to be careful with materiel. What do you think about that?"

Spector didn't pause. "It's still a wonderful opportunity and the only place during Kennedy's term of office where you need a Warden. I think I can handle being essentially on my own for a five year stretch. After that, I'll switch to something fully staffed."

Mason snorted and smiled, making an odd combination.

"Let's not worry about your second posting quite yet. Look, it may be pivotal and then again it may be five boring years. But if you want it that much, you'll do a better job than anyone else. Make me proud."

". . . and I like being able to eat real sausage, fatty and greasy. All those chemicals they use to treat the animals today . . . tomorrow . . . whatever, they bred the taste right out of pigs."

Spector realized suddenly that he had missed Urban's entire diatribe about life uptime. He yanked his mind out of his past and looked down to see both men had completed their meals. Urban had already ordered coffee and was enjoying his after-dinner cigarette.

"Aw, you don't know good sausage," he said, trying to get back into the conversation. "I had an aunt, ran a farm over to Joliet—that's in Illinois—who took her granddad's recipe and made it even better. Never knew what seasonings she came up with, but I could remember begging my parents to go visit them about four times a summer."

The two argued over good German food versus the Americanized versions of the nineteenth and twentieth centuries. Their meal finished and paid for, the duo went out into the street and took a leisurely walk toward the part of the city where both kept apartments.

Once more, Spector lapsed into silence, thinking about being on assignment in a time and place close enough to his native era to make it seem painful. His work to date had been as unexemplary as his pitching the first three years. And the loneliness, despite the occasional meal with Urban, was beginning to gnaw at him.

The last number of weeks, though, he had been kept on his toes, and his work had been well regarded by the Wardens he spoke with each time an interloper was returned uptime. True tests were coming and he wanted to be certain to justify Mason's faith.

Faith was not something Spector had a lot of these past few months. He had to rediscover it now and use it to keep him going. As they moved farther away from the guards, and closer to the gate that would lead them to safety, Spector considered the couple and how he had inadvertently ruined their chances for success. Had he shattered their faith?

3

Place: West Berlin, West Germany
Time: 6:35 p.m., Saturday, June 22, 1963

Nearly a kilometer away, in the darkening shadows between two squat buildings, a spark formed in the air. Emerging from the brief cocoon of light was a blue-clad butterfly of a woman.

A moment passed and the rest of her form coalesced in 1963. She wore a striking, bright blue evening dress that had a plunging back, a skirt well above the knee, and stockings complete with perfectly placed seam. Her short, black hair had been sprayed into place so the bangs hugged her forehead. The momentary lights reflected off her frosted lips and then began to dim as the distant circuits began to cycle off.

The woman had a burgundy, compact, duffel-style bag over one shoulder, and she gently laid it against the ground, reaching into her small, black handbag. A well-manicured hand removed its sole content: a dull gray DA.

"You are now in West Berlin, West Germany, on June twenty-second, 1963," the Digital Assistant confirmed to its owner. *"There is a Time Warden stationed here, named Alan*

Spector." She needed to check in with him as protocol demanded, her mind recalled. The contact was required within the first hours within the new era but not immediate. With the DA she accessed information about Spector, including his local address, and decided to be forthright about her work and visit Spector before she moved on.

The lights had faded and the column had dissipated, leaving no trace of ripping a hole through time or the atmosphere. Like Spector, she carried within her hand a Trac Link that was preprogrammed to return her homeward at the end of her one-week stay. The woman was one of the privileged few Beam Backs who had the freedom to move through the era without restriction.

Slowly, she walked toward the entrance of the alley and saw a city street with narrow, round vehicles moving back and forth. A few boys ran by, one carrying a large red ball. She strained her hearing for a moment and heard many, many sounds.

Here she was, at last, in long-ago West Germany!

The city was louder than she'd imagined, with cars, trains, and people. Even for a dusky weekend afternoon, it had a sense of life to it that was vastly different than her home time. Buildings were lower, the architecture speaking of much longer ago times, mixed with then current architectural ideals. Few were more than ten stories tall and allowed the deepening sky room to envelop the city.

She noticed smells next and breathed deeply, getting a sense of the place. Mixed in with car exhaust were flowers from a corner stand and baking bread from a shop across the street. These were deliciously mixed for her, and she stopped to enjoy the moment.

People passed her by, most craning their necks to stare since she was dressed for a formal affair and there were none nearby. As a result, she stood out, the last thing she wanted to do right then. However, she boldly stared right back and took in the conservative cuts of the clothing, the length of the skirts—all but hers far below the knee. Men's clothing was mostly nondescript and unimaginative with neckties being solid colors or merely striped. Hats of dark colors covered most male heads, and for the women they were large, round, and fairly ugly to her futuristic eye.

Still, she enjoyed watching and even gawking a bit. It was one thing to watch holo records of surviving film clips or even pore through pictures at the university's Central Archives, but this was something else. This was the full breadth and depth of the German people for her to study. Not selections or random samples, but everyone wearing everything, eating anything, and exchanging those day-to-day mundanities that could never quite get captured by recording equipment. This was most definitely the opportunity of her short lifetime.

And here it was, while she was just twenty-five years old, just aged enough to fully appreciate the chance.

Up ahead, at the corner, was a uniformed police officer keeping an eye on the evening strollers. The woman walked over to him and immediately caught his undivided attention.

"I'm sorry, Officer, but I'm a little bit lost in this part of town," she began in perfectly accented German. A year of study and practice paid off right then and there.

"No problem, my pretty lady. How can I help you?" Already he was ready to flirt and pay her lots of attention. It made her feel slightly giddy, but she kept to her business.

Pulling a piece of paper from her small handbag, she handed it to the older policeman. He moved closer to a streetlight and read the address. Smiling, with creases deepening around his mouth, he returned his attention to her and gave her the series of turns required to find Spector's apartment. No doubt about it, a little jealousy slipped into his voice.

"Well, after all this, I hope he's home," she said with a broad smile.

"Yes, a real shame to waste such a perfect night and you in that fetching dress. Will you need some help with that bag of yours?"

"Why, no, thank you, Officer. It's rather light," she replied with a little laugh. Rather than stay and continue to tease, she thanked him again and made her way toward the apartment building.

• • •

Spector was deep in concentration. Instead of enjoying Berlin's active nightlife, something Urban had made into a sport, he was settling in for a night with Richard Hofstadter's *Anti-Intellectualism in American Life*, one of the spring's most talked about books. Halfway through, he thought Hofstadter's position was full of crap, but then he wondered if that just proved the author's point by being anti-intellectual toward the scholarly work. Or maybe he was still an Ohio hick despite all his reeducation and conditioning. Maybe he'd know better when he completed the thick tome. If he could stay awake.

Suddenly, there came a knock at his door.

Putting the book down, and yawning deeply, he walked over to his kitchen cabinets and withdrew the official pistol he brought with him from uptime. Unlike the bullets fired in 1963, this gun unleashed electrostatic charges much like the tasers introduced about two decades further uptime. Keeping it out of sight, he opened the door and was taken aback by the sight of the attractive young woman.

"Mr. Spector?" Her voice was a delight to hear, soft and friendly. He noted immediately, though, that they shared the same accent. His suspicions were aroused.

"Can I help you?"

"I hope so. May I step in, please?" She seemed perfectly ordinary, that is, if every ordinary woman were so pretty.

He turned serious and narrowed his eyes at her. "Who are you?"

She smiled and began. "Angela Chance, from the University of Edinburgh, class of eighty-eight."

The narrowed eyes flew wide open. "When? Wait, come in here before you say another word."

With that, he ushered Angela into the small apartment, carefully closing the door after scanning the dim hallway to make sure the arrival was unnoticed. So far so good. He turned about and watched the striking woman put down her duffel and carefully scrutinize the unimpressive surroundings.

"Which eighty-eight, please?" he asked, picking up the conversation.

"Sorry. Twenty-six eighty-eight. I'm a grad student, here on a class grant."

He held out his right hand, instantly recalling all the procedures. "Your authorization, please."

She withdrew the DA from her handbag and placed her thumb against the sensor. Once it winked to life, she handed it to him and stepped back. Spector's hand nearly dwarfed the more modest version of the DA she had brought with her. It was not Institute-issue but most definitely within specs showing she came from a monied background, just not spoiled like his other recent visitors from uptime. He scrolled through the forms issued from the University, the Scottish government, and the Institute itself. There were also records of the cover story fabricated for her by the University's chronal studies department: a complete life in miniature. A bonded representative had made a quick trip back, prior to her arrival, to plant the details at the University to authenticate her cover story. The papers used for the era were chemically manufactured to dissolve into irreplaceable fragments within thirty days. Everything seemed fine, which was a relief after all the illegal activity he had recently suffered through.

"You know," he admitted, handing the DA back to her, "it makes sense that someone would genuinely be here to witness Kennedy's visit and famous speech. I actually expected several, so I'm surprised to see just you." Maybe another Warden would encounter more when Spector's subjective five years were over.

"I agree," she said, a smile readily on her lips. "John Fitzgerald Kennedy remains one of the most oft-studied presidents from America's past. The researchers either demystify or canonize the man, depending upon their point of view."

"I guess it's better to be witnessing him here rather than in Dallas."

She shook her head sadly. "His brutal assassination, in another five months, helped give his life some special aura.

Funny, but most people look at his entire life as one always striving for something better and always having it snatched away."

"I admire the man," Spector said. "Those feelings have only grown and I deeply appreciate Kennedy's effect on America and the world after arriving in this time."

"Where are you from?"

He shook his head with a smile that didn't seem mirthful. "Sorry, classified."

"Right."

"All right, welcome to 1963, Angela," he said, handing back the device.

She smiled again and walked into the living room, noting the view from his window.

"So, you're a Beam Back, I presume? Here for holiday?"

A shake of her head, sending only small portions of her black hair back and forth. "Really, just Kennedy's speech. My thesis is on 'Political Gestures and Their Effect on History During the Cold War.' The Berlin Wall was one gesture and Kennedy's visit another kind. I'm trying to contrast them, since this is the hottest part of the Cold War between Capitalism and Communism."

Spector took his place on the love seat, gesturing for Angela to take the wing chair. "Sounds like a good approach. How was your trip through the 'stream?"

"Now that was a rush," she replied with a laugh.

"Feel ill when you came through?"

"No, should I have?" Her look was one of both interest and surprise.

"Most don't feel anything but some do get sick. At least you didn't ruin your outfit. Quite nice for the time, but why so formal?"

She laughed again and leaned back, brushing smooth the outfit, seemingly proud of the curves described by the material. "I had no idea how well I'd travel and thought I'd better wear my best outfit rather than keep it in my luggage. It certainly has attracted some remarkable attention."

"You wear it well," Spector said, resisting any form of attraction he might feel. She was, after all, younger, and scheduled to be here for just a week. He'd have his work, she'd have her research. Despite the temptation, he'd keep this relationship, like all his others these past three years, professional. "So, what's your plan?"

"I'm taking the train to Bonn tonight so I can watch Kennedy's arrival," she began. "From there, I want to follow the entourage. As I understand it, his 'I am a Berliner' speech was written during the tour, not something prepared in advance, right? I want to see what formed those ideas."

He nodded, approving of the sense behind the agenda.

"I'll see you back here in Berlin when he arrives, then?"

"Sure," she agreed. "No problems. I'm programmed to stay here through at least Thursday night. Is the train station far?"

His advice was to take a taxi to the station, and they completed the visit moments later. She seemed eager to be on her way, and he suspected the busy week was just beginning. At least it was just the one time traveler to worry about.

At the Berlin rail station, Angela had no trouble reading the train board and then secured a ticket on the next train leaving for Cologne, about an hour later. Just enough time to buy a magazine and a snack for herself using replicated money she had packed. Crossing the tiled station, she was continuing to study the people passing back and forth, trying to cope with the concept that she had traveled centuries downtime. Better than a VR suite or even the experimental cortex discs. Nothing from her real time could capture the full sight and sound and smell of the era, rich with variety and filled with possibilities.

She may have been paying attention to the sizes and shapes of people, but she was not careful on the details. Even if she were, there was no way she would have recognized the man directly behind her at the magazine stand. His grip was tight on the small leather case in his right hand and his smile was even tighter.

Gregor Andropov was already in West Berlin and was ready to begin his mission.

"I am in Berlin," the voice said over the telephone connection, which was poor.

In Moscow, the man was once again in his private office, staring at some information crossing the tiny screen of his electronic device. "Good. Security matches our intelligence?"

"Yes."

"Good." Of course it would, given the access he had to America's military data from the Kennedy Library, before its unfortunate destruction in the twenty-second century.

"I must catch the train."

"Good luck." The men hung up, and the illegal time traveler stood alone, contemplating the mission. He had worked hard to infiltrate first the GRU and then the KGB itself. It had been time-consuming and painstaking, but he knew each day suffered in that unpleasant era meant he was closer to pulling off a time crime of magnificent proportion. The payoff would more than make up for the years spent surrounded by paranoia, fear, and incredibly poor cooking.

4

Place: Air Force One, West Germany
Time: 9:50 a.m., Sunday, June 23, 1963

"Are you sure we've got everything covered?"

The speaker was John Fitzgerald Kennedy, current President of the United States and weary world traveler. Air Force One was completing its final approach to Wahn Airport, and the cabin stewards were busying themselves from fore to aft, trying to leave the presidential entourage in peace.

Kennedy was forty-six and in perpetual discomfort from chronic back pain that in many ways kept him the most incapacitated world leader since Franklin Roosevelt. Cushions helped a bit on the longer flights, but he needed to stick with a regimented exercise program and be constantly checked by his personal physician.

None of the pain, though, kept him from enjoying life to the fullest, and he remained the vision of the rugged American: playing touch football with his brothers or being seen with glamorous women, starting with his lovely wife Jacqueline, but his private appetites stretched well beyond her alone. Many of his closest friends and official aides spent nearly as much time covering for Kennedy's amorous adventures as they did briefing him on Communist activities throughout the world.

"Captain says there's a crowd waiting down below," came a call. It was Pierre Salinger, his press secretary, who came into view and leaned over to look out one of the small windows.

"At least someone still likes me," Kennedy cracked. "After the Berlin Wall, the Bay of Pigs fiasco, and the Cuban Missile Crisis, I wasn't sure if Europe wanted me to come."

"Trust me," Salinger said gravely. "This trip could only help. You'll get acres of good press for this. And there's nothing Goldwater could do to match it."

"Hell, he's not even Irish," quipped Dean Rusk, secretary of state. He had joined the men, and in a moment the three were rehashing all the reasons this was still a good idea.

"Yeah, but he's back home pointing out that the reasons behind the trip vanished months ago, so I'm wasting my time and the taxpayers' money," Kennedy complained.

"It's a wash, Mr. President," Rusk responded. "Okay, so your host in Italy got bounced out of office."

"So did Adenauer," Salinger added.

"No, he was pressured into retiring, not bounced," corrected Rusk, who rarely concealed his distaste for Salinger's manner.

"At least in Germany you get to spit at the Wall and meet with the heir apparent. And in Rome, you get to meet the new Pope. In fact, you'll be the first world leader to pay a visit, so the timing works to our advantage."

"Too bad Jackie couldn't make it," Kennedy noted. "She would have loved meeting Paul VI. She had such respect for Pope John XXIII, you know."

"You have no one to blame for Jackie's condition but yourself," Salinger said, letting out a loud laugh. Kennedy watched, noting how Rusk barely concealed a wince at the sound. In many ways, he agreed with his chief diplomat. On the other hand, Salinger was right: her pregnancy, due to end in September, was something he was eagerly acting upon.

"You will get to play the Great Statesman in four key countries, successfully avoiding de Gaulle all the way."

"You have my undying gratitude for that, Dean," Kennedy said, joining in the light laughter.

It was going to be a grueling schedule, but he needed the publicity, the goodwill, and most of all, a chance to stick it in Charles de Gaulle's eye. The French president had been his rival for Democratic power, and as Europe was struggling with its economic woes, France was suddenly the strongest voice. Kennedy and de Gaulle disliked each other over matters pertaining to tariffs and Communists. The President also had his problems with the Old One on the same issues, especially since Adenauer was such a vocal critic of America's lackluster response to the Wall. That very issue had eaten away at Kennedy ever since the word reached him at his Hyannis Port home two years earlier.

Looking out the small round airplane window, Kennedy gazed at the lush, green countryside. So much healing had returned the luster to Germany that it was hard to imagine an ugly concrete snake divided the place into twins. It was a harsher beauty than Ireland, his next stop, which retained its magic over the centuries. Germany, though, had spent its life rewriting its borders and waging wars large and small so it prospered in fits and starts. Once it was a world power and now it was a whipped patch of land that was trying to find its strength once more. Perhaps its best days were to come, he mused, wondering what the chancellor-elect Erhard was like.

Behind him, friends and colleagues were checking their notes and itineraries, making sure they knew where they were going. Kennedy didn't care too much about the stops in Germany before Berlin on Wednesday. He did know, though, he would have to endure three straight days with Adenauer and that could make anyone testy.

"What's first, Dean?" he asked his head of foreign affairs.

Rusk adjusted his thick, black frames and checked a binder in his hand. "We have a parade through Cologne today and mass at the great cathedral. Tomorrow it's Bonn, Hanau, Frankfurt, and Wiesbaden. We'll fly to Berlin tomorrow night and then Wednesday you'll see the Wall and make your key speech at Town Hall. Word from the ground is that they've been lining up since dawn."

"Told you," Salinger stated.

Kennedy smiled at the concept and showed off his perfect, white teeth. "Do they know it's me and not Elvis Presley coming to visit?"

Polite chuckles all around greeted the joke.

Minutes later, the plane touched down and the airport was jammed with police officers on motorcycle; a motorcade of at least a dozen cars was lined up, drivers at the ready. A crowd of nearly a thousand citizens was held back behind rope barriers with more police keeping order. Dark-suited men were clustered here and there, some no doubt local politicians while others had to be the omnipresent press.

The cabin was finally cleared of aides and Kennedy was left alone for a few minutes to gather his wits, run a hand through his thick brown hair, and take a deep breath. For a moment he allowed his mind to wander back to the earlier presidents. It wasn't until Teddy Roosevelt that presidents needed to cross the oceans and seek political help, and fewer still had yet to reckon with a growing global media that seemed intent on tracing his every step.

Clearing his mind, he checked his reflection, decided he was ready for his cue, and strode forward toward the doorway. A ribboned gangway had been positioned from the ground, and with the door open, he could hear the cheers without recognizing the words. The emotion was positive and it made him smile naturally. God, how he loved the crowds.

Passing Rusk and the others, he framed himself in the doorway and waved. The cheering went louder, and police had to physically restrain the throng from surging closer. He waved another moment or two and then began to descend the stairs.

"Elvis has nothing on me," he said to no one in particular.

• • •

The motorcade started up and left Wahn Airport and his jet. It would be cleaned and refueled over the next few days, preparing for the next leg of the journey. Meantime, Kennedy would suffice with ground transportation and was satisfied. German-made cars had a terrific reputation, and he liked having a chance to check that out for himself. Sadly, being President prevented him the luxury of trying out a Volkswagen or Mercedes-Benz on the legendary autobahn. Still, he could dream.

Once on the ground, he had been steered toward the local pols, all of whom deferred to Konrad Adenauer. The gnarled, older man was nearly bald, and the years in office showed in his eyes. Kennedy had learned long ago to read much from a man's physical condition and acts more than his words. For example, he knew his rival Nikita Khrushchev was mostly bluster but was essentially a bully until someone stood up to him. De Gaulle, on the other hand, was a man of solid convictions and had earned his current position. While an ideologue, he remained consistent, and at least the president could respect that.

Adenauer had been to the United States three times previously—another reason Kennedy needed to be in Germany—so he had a sense of the man. The Old One was a skilled politician who had lost his way when the country was split asunder. He was a people person, not one to fuss overly much on things beyond his understanding. Economics was one such area, and as the nations of the world became more dependent upon one another for trade and currency, such gaps in education would prove the downfall of more than one politician.

Standing beside the Old One was Robert Lochner, head of Germany's RIAS radio and assigned as Kennedy's interpreter for the duration. Lochner, nearly as tall as Kennedy and a bit older, stuck a hand out and greeted the President in English. As he tried to do the formal introduction between leaders, Adenauer jumped the gun and thrust a liver-spotted hand forward.

"Welcome to Germany, Mr. President," he said in heavily accented English.

"It's good to see you again, Mr. Chancellor," Kennedy said, his political smile firmly in place. The Chancellor nodded, understanding the intent if not the actual words.

The two men were rapidly introduced around to the other suited officials from Bonn, America, and a few points in between. Lochner proved to be an adept interpreter, keeping up with the sometimes rapid exchanges. He and Kennedy had met previously and was easily approved for the job during the visit.

"Our tour of Cologne will be brief, but we will spend more time in Bonn tonight," he explained to Kennedy as the motorcade started up. In the lead car, Kennedy, Adenauer, and Lochner chatted amiably about nothing in particular, feeling each other out and making sure tensions were kept away from the public.

The crowd seemed endless to Kennedy. They lined the roads and city streets at least five deep, often closer to ten. Hands, handkerchiefs, and small American or German flags waved frantically. Kennedy took it all in, pleased and surprised by the depth of emotion on display. He leaned over to Lochner and asked in a whisper, "I thought this country preferred France to the United States."

"The politicians do," Lochner admitted. "These are the people."

Kennedy nodded and smiled knowingly.

"What's Erhard like?" he suddenly asked.

"A good man," came the reply. "He's a little bullheaded at times, but cares deeply about the condition of his country. He wants to beat the inflation and negotiate away the tariffs."

"Sounds good," Kennedy admitted. He had grown weary of Adenauer's harping on America for constant public support while seeming to prefer de Gaulle's standoffish approach to the Berlin crisis. There had also been a flurry of correspondence between the world leaders with about half the content concerning itself with complaints over tariffs on exported chicken. In Kennedy's opinion, Adenauer should have been concerning himself with improving the efficiency of the farming so they wouldn't be so reliant on such exports. They were a notoriously high cost producer of goods that did not serve the people well at all. He also knew such efficiency would improve the economy and check an escalating inflation.

The very question of Germany's involvement with the Common Market and continued working relationship with America had been thrown open for debate. Overall, it exasperated Kennedy, who on more than one occasion would have preferred telling Bonn and Paris to shut up once and for all. Of course, presidents couldn't do that.

He stopped worrying about chicken and studied the people and surroundings. "What lessons have been taught to the generations that followed?"

"Excuse me, Mr. President?"

"I'm sorry, Herr Lochner," Kennedy said. "I'm looking at all these faces. The young ones are full of promise for tomorrow, but the older ones, they've suffered terribly, haven't they?"

"Some certainly have."

"The War cost us lives, but it cost you lives and land. Crushed their spirit, didn't it?"

Lochner looked thoughtful for a moment and then nodded. "It has been a long time coming back and then the Wall stomped down hard."

"Damn that thing," Kennedy muttered, almost too softly for Lochner to hear. The youngest children along the line, some not more than three years old, he realized, were suddenly being cut off from half their heritage, half their family, and perhaps half their future. It angered Kennedy, who wanted to do more than just visit. He needed to leave something behind for these people.

"We need to talk later," Kennedy confided in Lochner. "I want to brainstorm about my Berlin speech. It needs to be something beyond words." The radio manager nodded in agreement, and the men exchanged brief smiles.

It was a sunny warm day, again, perfectly pleasant and a

promise of a nice summer for Germany. Alan Spector ignored such niceties entirely as he worked at his desk within the UPI offices. Stein had long ago declared Sundays optional days for staff since they were generally slow news days. However, since the Wall was erected nearly two years ago, it also meant the entire staff was on alert and could be summoned at a moment's notice. Being near the office or a radio was a must in Stein's mind, which prevented casual countryside drives or picnics by the beautiful lakes. To the Temporal Warden, it was a small price to pay, but for a secretary like Katrina, he imagined, it put a serious crimp in her social life—whatever that was like.

Spector considered his coworkers for a moment, ignoring the notes he was reviewing for an article on the memorabilia being prepared for Kennedy's imminent arrival. Stein was a perfectly capable leader, a tough newsman that had lived through enough real news to have a sense for what was important and what was chaff. While gruff at times, he was also a good leader who preferred doing things by example rather than pontificating. During some of the biggest news in the last three years, Stein was out there, pressing contacts and getting important perspectives that helped propel UPI to the forefront of international news gathering forces during the Cold War.

With all that, though, Stein seemed totally unaware of the modifications made to his own bureau, including the power lines Spector had ordered installed in the rear room. Every month he paid a handsome sum to the local power authorities to provide the source of extra energy, and the local officials never questioned why so much intermittent power was required. In fact, most of his meager budget went to the power bill. A small stipend was split with Urban, and he kept a petty cash box filled with all manner of European currency from punts to francs. Too, Stein seemed ignorant of Spector's real skills as a reporter. All for the best, the Temporal agent thought, since he had another two years to endure.

His five years in the past would be enough for him.

After all, it prevented him from forming serious emotional attachments, forcing him to settle for one-night stands or paying for a prostitute. Neither were options he liked, but circumstances forced him to remain cautious. In other eras, Spector knew, Time Wardens had entire crews that could be counted on and they performed admirably. They also provided friendship and council, where his own situation forced him to keep things close to the vest, which meant he confided only in Paul Urban.

Urban rarely spoke of the past, and Spector had opened up the night before mostly to try to coax his older colleague into sharing with him. They had worked day by day for three years and not once did Urban say much about his life prior to being posted in Germany. His pride in the country and land of his ancestors was admirable, but Spector yearned to know more. Now at more than the halfway point in his assignment, the silence was becoming overwhelming. His attempts to befriend Urban were always rebuffed, so he kept their evening meals to a minimum.

Forming friendships was difficult, and after the first year Spector stopped trying. Fellow reporters had commented on Urban's sprightly nightlife habits, but it only served to annoy Spector that he was never invited along. Obviously, Urban wanted to stay by himself, and he had to respect those wishes.

Looking around the offices, taking in the ambience for perhaps the thousandth time, Spector continued to marvel at how people managed to get along so well without so much. Typewriters rather than voice-activated digital assistants, analog clocks rather than microwave-synchronized chronometers, gas-guzzling automobiles instead of magnetically propelled people movers.

Just amazing.

Cracking a few knuckles to loosen the fingers up, he then rolled a piece of crisp white paper into the well-oiled manual typewriter and tried to think of a clever lead.

He banged out the story quickly and left it for his boss, who normally checked in late Sunday afternoons. It was right after the Stein family had their Sunday dinner. His children would clean up and Stein would check the offices to make sure all was calm and quiet. Otherwise, weekends were for the family and he seemed to guard those days religiously, another admirable quality Spector liked and realized he had come to long for.

As Spector struggled with words, the other people affected by his most recent Warden action took stock of their lives. Still in the small, shuttered pub, they met with a small cadre of friends. Most had thought of fleeing to the West, but with each level of barbwire or concrete, their will was sapped. And for every story of a successful escape, there were five of disastrous attempts.

No one knew for sure how many of the stories were true—did people really balloon over the Wall or tunnel under it? What about those who tried to swim across some of the rivers? No doubt bribery and sheer audacity worked as well as months-long planning but neither guaranteed success. For Wolf and Elizabeth Krause, their act the day before was one of desperation, and now they were uncertain how desperate they truly were.

At a table near the rear office, the Krauses were surrounded by Peter, son of the owners; the older couple themselves; and Hilda Steinbach, a neighbor. Six people sitting, thinking, and not daring to speak out loud. Whatever joy was in their lives was crushed with the announcement two days earlier that their street was unavoidably contained in the new *verboten* zone and they would have to seek out new livelihoods.

Draining the last of his drink, Wolf looked into the tired faces. He sought out hope or inspiration but found nothing but despair.

"Was that our final chance?"

"That's what Walter Ulbricht would like," Hilda answered.

"Why should he care," Elizabeth wondered, speaking for the first time in hours.

"He runs this country the way Russia wants it run," Wilhelm said with disgust. "It shall remain that way for the rest of my life but hopefully not for the rest of yours."

"Such thoughts," his wife clucked.

"*Es ist mir Wurst*," the elder Hoyt said. The words literally translated to "It's my sausage" but meant "I don't care." "I've lived my life, served my country, and now this is the reward for such duty. Why should I not speak my mind? It's about all I have left. The *Vopos* out there aren't even allowed to help us load a truck to move the stock to some new place. You don't just open up a new tavern. People have their loyalties and are wary of interlopers."

"You're just a businessman trying to do your job," Elizabeth protested. She was waved off by Hoyt, who was lost in thought about his missing place in the world.

Wolf watched the exchange, having fallen silent again. His mind tumbled around the concerns of the Hoyt family, and his heart went out to them. They'd been friends of his family for decades, and in his own hour of need, they gave generously. Both had plenty to consider in the coming days.

"You know I used to do magic tricks as a little boy," Peter Hoyt began, leaning over toward his boyhood friend. "Wanted to be famous like America's Houdini, I guess. Anyway, the one thing it says in all the books is that misdirection is as important as the trick itself. In the coming week there is going to be plenty of misdirection just a few hundred meters away."

Krause thought about it for a few moments and shook his head. "What, am I supposed to ask Ulbricht for permission to go over and watch President Kennedy?"

The other man swatted Krause's closely cropped head. "No, sausage-for-brains," he said. "Everyone on both sides will be paying more attention to Kennedy. That's your next chance."

"You really think so?" asked Elizabeth, hope suddenly returning to her bright hazel eyes.

Wolf Krause thought long and hard about the possibilities.

All of the German crowds were much the same to Kennedy. With clouds diffusing the sunshine, the people looked a little less colorful but just as forceful. Chants and cheers echoed from beginning to end, which was why he enjoyed the idea of stopping within Cologne. To his constant surprise, almost every other person en route to the Köln Cathedral was waving an American flag. There were quite a few German flags on display as well.

Adenauer leaned across the car, bundled up in overcoat, thin wool scarf, and leather gloves. He pointed to a structure approaching in the distance. "Köln is one of our treasures you missed when crushing my country," he said. "It's our cathedral and I would like us to stop there."

Kennedy understood the translation and nodded in agreement, even though he knew a mass was already on the official schedule. His back ached something fierce after last night's flight so the walking about would do him some good. Lochner passed the instructions on to the driver, who got on a car radio to relay the information to General Ted Clifton, who was taking responsibility for the President's security arrangements.

A few minutes later they stopped before the grand structure, its spire set off against the darkening clouds. Köln Cathedral had been constructed back in the fourteenth century and was a remarkable example of German excellence from that long-ago era. Most everyone poured out of the motorcade, except the drivers, who took the break as a chance to smoke. The cars with the international media had pulled over, and photographers jockeyed for position with Gruber from UPI elbowing his way past some veteran from Associated Press.

Kennedy twisted left and right, trying to loosen up his back, and then walked around the car to get a closer look at the building. He tried to tune out the cheering crowds and avoid making eye contact. On the one hand, with the press present, he could make a splash and plunge into the crowds, but he wished to please his host and bask in the glory of the spiritual structure.

"Where did the flags come from? Don't tell me these families just happened to have American flags in their homes."

Adenauer smiled broadly at the translation. "Oh, we

arrange things as you do in your election campaigns. But we didn't arrange this huge crowd. The cardinal is wishing right now that he could attract this many people to the cathedral for one of his regular masses.

"Come, let us pray," Adenauer prompted.

Here, in their church, Kennedy could say a few private words for the people who had come to move him almost immediately. All too often he saw a country as represented only by the politicians and statesmen. A trip like this, much like his campaign swings through America, reminded him of the people that made up a country's true character. While he might dislike Adenauer, he wished him no ill will. Instead, he imagined what the man endured to keep his country together while forces beyond his control tore apart an entire society.

Together the men walked into the cathedral and strode toward the front, near the altar. The priest in residence greeted them warmly and then disappeared into the back to allow these two great men private devotions before the public mass was to begin.

In the distance Angela Chance watched the goings-on with rapt interest. She used a traditional camera of the era to snap pictures, trying to blend in like a tourist. With each step, though, she inched her way toward the front, nearing the American contingent. Chance could see tan-colored military uniforms, black-suited Secret Service Agents, and gray-suited aides. Her mind briefly stopped to consider the paucity of women in the mix but recalled how it was decades before their representation increased in Washington. Something for a paper in the future, perhaps, but today she was watching pieces of history pass before her eyes.

Every so often she got a glimpse of Kennedy himself and she beamed at him, despite his inability to single her out. She, like the others, could not attend the mass within the cathedral for security reasons, but the time traveler was determined to get as close as possible so she could get even closer that night in Hanau.

• • •

Also outside, as the leaders prayed in relative privacy, Andropov walked through the crowd, his valise unmoving in his tight grip.

His eyes, behind thick sunglasses, scanned the crowds, picking out the obvious undercover police and Secret Service agents. They had carefully positioned themselves around the cathedral so no one could get near.

The land around the building was too flat and open to allow any chance for setting up his rifle and scope.

What surprised him the most and threw off his planning were the people.

The crowds behind him seemed a tangible mass that could not be swayed or moved. The stream of well-wishers was found at Wahn Airport, and they seemed to be everywhere along the route. There was no break along the roadway, and the map indicated there would be no opportunity this day. He needed to revise his planning, mentally deciding on concentrating his efforts on Berlin.

To remain anonymous, Andropov edged his way to the back of the crowd, people being only too happy to get a little bit closer, hoping for a better view. Along the way, one blustering hulk of a man didn't feel like moving.

"Off my foot," he shouted at Andropov, who merely looked up four inches to meet the man's eyes. They locked glances: Andropov's cool and hard, the other man's angry.

Suddenly, the other man's expression changed entirely.

A trickle of blood flowed from his gaping mouth and he slumped forward, falling atop other spectators. Someone noticed the blood and shrieked, setting off a loud commotion, which summoned some of the German police officers.

During the melee, no one saw Andropov quietly slipping out of the crowd and heading back toward a bus station. He was casually wiping a knife blade on a sheet of newsprint and already making plans for Berlin.

The article finally complete, Spector glanced at the wall clock and decided enough work was done to justify his UPI salary. Now he would have a few hours to complete his

Warden duties and still have time to catch another solitary dinner at a restaurant. Tidying his desk, he noted a new story was just coming over the ticker, so he wandered a circuitous route between the other desks and glanced at the headlines. A piece about Kennedy's departure from Washington was coming across. He had flown first to spend some time with his children in Massachusetts before the ten-day foreign trip was to begin. As Spector liked that about Stein, he also admired that about Kennedy. Somehow the President, more than most of his predecessors, placed a high level of importance on his children, Caroline and John Junior. The article went on to identify the sizable contingent accompanying the President. Four officials from the State Department plus assorted flunkies, then a handful of special councils and special assistants, a press secretary, support staff, three military aides, and his sisters Jean Smith and Eunice Shriver, who would act as official hostesses while Jackie stayed home. Critically, he scanned the writing style, deemed it acceptable, and left the office.

The walk to his home was short, just a few blocks in the American sector of West Berlin. Even though the country was West Germany, Spector was interested in how the Allied partners had so carefully carved Berlin into three sectors so everyone could keep an eye on the seat of power. No one wanted the rise of another Adolf Hitler, least of all the Germans. War atrocity stories continued to surface as more war criminals were brought to trial around the world. The greatest drama of the last decade might not have been the Cold War, but the Nuremberg War Trials. What humans could do to one another never ceased to surprise Spector, who had spent three years training to defend himself against most of those indignities.

Being a Temporal Warden was a lifelong commitment with at least half the training time spent learning enough detection skills to best blend in with a society—but retain an edge. For example, he was a black belt in martial arts, good skills in a country that seemed to rely on fists. He was also armed with his pistol that looked like any other for the 1960's but was manufactured with a more durable design and offered energy charges over bullets, which one day might mean the difference between success or death.

Normal training involved the injection of RNA samples to help reprogram the brain. Where Spector accepted it for the German language, he eschewed additional doses in favor of six months' intensive learning about Germany and Europe in the 1950's and 1960's to make sure he knew the idioms, customs, and mores of the society. Drug abuse, for one, was not prevalent until years later and the sexual revolution from England and the U.S.A. would not get to repressed Germany for quite some time.

When possible, Spector also indulged his baseball passion and studied up on the great players of the era, hoping for a chance to vacation in America and catch a game. It was one thing to hear about these men, but to witness them live, that was to be savored. He often tried to guess which year, which game would be the most satisfying. Alan concentrated mostly on the pitchers of the era, marveling at how the role, once the low man on the totem pole, was suddenly the centerpiece of the team. He had two okay pitches: the fastball and an ineffective slow curve, but the arsenal some of these men brought to the mound was astonishing. Should he see one of Sandy Koufax's no-hitters? A Bob Gibson masterpiece in St. Louis? Or watch Roger Maris break Babe Ruth's single-season home run record?

Circumstances, though, had prevented Spector from vacationing anywhere the first three years, so his opportunities were getting limited.

He did, though, make a point of reading extensively, making certain he kept up with the American and European best-sellers. Sampling rock and roll was also a joy, and he was in the small Hamburg club the night a group called the Silver Beatles performed some scorching rock riffs. Some things were not to be missed.

Arriving at his apartment building, he walked up to the third floor and immediately took off his tie, white shirt, and jacket. While working, he preferred the "uniform" of a reporter but now he could relax. Putting on instead a blue cotton pullover, he settled onto the love seat in his tiny living room. To his left was a square table with a simple lamp its only decoration. Spector never entertained so he didn't have to make his home a showcase. He preferred the simplicity as a reminder of the time he was visiting.

Underneath the table, though, was a small false panel that contained an object about twice the size of his palm. It was a navy metal, about fifty millimeters thick, and had a space for thumbprint activation. This device alone would simplify his work at UPI tremendously, being a recorder, computer, word processor, and data storage system. Instead, he used it for completing his regular reports, which were then sent uptime to his superiors at the Institute.

Before going downstream, Spector had acquired a complete archival reference on 1950–1970 so he could verify information which he limited to Warden-only business. He enjoyed exercising his training and did all his reporting without such help. To date he even avoided double-checking his facts with the digital assistant, nicknamed DA.

Spector had little to report after yesterday's busy morning, so he made some general observations about the tenor of the times, texture to go with the facts the historians extracted from their temporal observations. There was a great deal of anticipation over Kennedy's arrival, much expectation, too. He was roundly criticized when America had only tepid protests to offer when the Wall went up seemingly overnight. His vice president, Lyndon Johnson, had come to Germany months after the Wall and made pretty speeches but offered nothing substantial. Now there was speculation the President might make a demand of Khrushchev or use the Wall as a bargaining chip of some sort. Of course he knew there would be a rousing speech that would help further unify the West Germans and solidify Kennedy's political position back home. The Wall would remain until the Germans themselves tired of it and would take it apart in another twenty-five years.

His commentary complete, the tired traveler idly flipped around the 1963 database, looking at more detailed reports than anything he could find in Berlin newspapers. If they seemed primitive, their attempts at television news were positively barbaric, and he avoided watching to the point of not having a television in his home.

For a Sunday well into the baseball season it was an uneventful day. He looked a little bit ahead and read up on Juan Marichel's no-hitter, due to occur the following month. While respected within the game, Spector knew the San Francisco pitcher would be underappreciated by the general public until well after his death. He then gave the most dominant team of the past decade a careful look. The Yankees' stars were aging, failing, and fading. Maris never displayed the same power after hitting those sixty-one home runs two years earlier. The great Mickey Mantle was hobbled with a broken foot and would miss the All-Star game, just two weeks away, and catcher Yogi Berra had been reduced to part-time outfield play as Elston Howard eased into the role of everyday catcher and slugging star in addition to being the first black in pinstripes. Of the Yanks, Joe Pepitone would do the most creditable job during that All-Star game which the National League would win on just six singles, two of which were hit by Marichel's teammate Willie Mays.

Maybe that was the game to see: go to Cleveland, visit Municipal Stadium, and watch a close game. Mays would be amazing, and Spector could see a parade of terrific pitchers such as the feisty Don Drysdale, rookie Jim Bouton, and Jim Bunning. No Koufax, though. And it was too early for Gibson or Seaver or Palmer or McLain; too late for the best from Ford, Shantz, or Spahn.

He shut off the DA and postponed his travel plans— again. Instead, he stared out the window, watching the day slip by, knowing full well it was a calm day before a stormy week.

"I have everything the papers have printed about the visit," Peter Hoyt said as he entered the bar area.

For the last few hours, the Krauses repaid the Hoyts' kindness by helping them take inventory and begin packing the supplies. Wilhelm kept muttering about not knowing where he would go or where to even begin looking for a new location. No one from the government had offered to help, and he was feeling his age.

Every time he said anything aloud about retirement, his wife made negative sounds that resounded throughout the empty bar. "You know perfectly well that you'd drive me to an asylum, you stay home all day. Better you put your energy into making a new place for beer."

Peter chuckled at his mother's comments while the Krauses exchanged smiles. The neighbor, Hilda Steinbach, had returned home to gather boxes and valises that could be used for moving.

Wolf, his sleeves rolled up and dark vest removed, handed his wife three bottles of vodka and stepped toward his friend. With a curious gaze, he studied the sheets of newspaper that Peter held out. The reports were scattered over several weeks and were filled with Communist invective against the United States, President Kennedy, Capitalism, and just about everything else. Still, piecing the reports together, the younger Hoyt had fashioned a crude schedule.

With a long reach, he pulled down a small picture calendar that hung behind the bar and slapped it on the bar top itself. A long finger ticked off the days as he repeated the itinerary: "Kennedy arrives in Bonn tomorrow. He will then go to Frankfurt and on Wednesday come to Berlin. He will meet with Mayor Brandt and then make a speech. He leaves that night."

"So we'll have until Wednesday to plan, *ja*," Wolf said, seeking reassurance.

"Plenty of time, my woodenheaded friend," Peter replied affectionately.

"They've put gates in the sewers, searchlights by the rivers, and raised the Wall steadily so now we cannot ever touch the top. Even if we could touch the top, we'd slice our fingers on glass or wire." Elizabeth finished packing a box and walked over to study the calendar as if there were already plans laid out. She frowned for a moment before saying, "We have three days, but what do we plan to do? That's three more days to solidify the new zone. How could the American President provide us with that much of a distraction?"

Her husband imitated the frown.

5

The UPI offices were bustling with activity that cloudy morning. Stein had arrived earlier than usual, having breakfasted with Mayor Brandt to confirm details over Wednesday's guest of honor. He was filled with good spirits and a desire to nail the coverage better than their competitors: the other wire services, Associated Press or Reuters; the major papers such as the *Times of London*, *The New York Times*, or even the revered *Herald Tribune*. Everything had to be right, and he drilled instructions at Katrina, who furiously scribbled notes. As soon as his rapid-fire delivery was completed, she was already dialing the phone, setting up interviews and arranging prime spots for their photographer. She loved moments like this, since it kept her busy and challenged rather than stuck taking dictation and watching the world go by her. Today she was in the thick of it, making her realize there was more to working at UPI than getting Stein his fifth cup of coffee.

It was nearly nine when Spector walked in, suit coat slung

over a shoulder, hat tilted at a funny angle. He seemed just as happy as the bureau chief but for no apparent reason. Perhaps it was the caressing sunshine or the color of the sky. She couldn't tell, but she liked that about him. The simpler things in life seemed to delight him, and she found it enormously appealing.

He preceded her stay at the wire service, Katrina having arrived eight months after him. Alan had always been polite and friendly but never forward despite his awareness of her being single. According to her parents, twenty-seven and single was wrong. Yet no one had proposed nor had any of her relationships seemed the right one. Her marital status was the subject of too many conversations at home.

She had tried dating someone at the service once. The photographer before Gruber was a dark, swarthy Italian named Bianco and they went out to dinner twice, dancing once. He was colorless, two-dimensional like his pictures, and in the end seemed interested only in finding a way to expose her like a roll of film. After throwing him out of his own car, she vowed never to make that mistake again.

Still, Spector had such pleasant eyes.

He waved from across the room, and she barely had time to acknowledge the gesture before a voice at the other end asked a question. And then she was off, making arrangements in a flurry of activity. When this presidential visit was over, Katrina was hoping to persuade Stein to give her even more to do and maybe see if she had what it took to be a reporter. Perhaps personality profiles or reviews. Something inconsequential so if she stank, no harm was done.

Scribbling confirmations on her pad, she watched Spector walk past his desk and whisper something to Urban, who was already inputting Spector's piece from the day before. She realized Stein was a quick reader and rapid editor, so the copy turned in was edited and back out within an hour. If something took more than an hour, the reporter invariably was sent back to rewrite the piece.

Urban and Spector seemed such odd friends, given their age differences and backgrounds. Urban was said to have been a general assignment reporter for years before choosing to retire behind the Teletype. Stein continued to cite Urban articles to Heinz on how best to cover Mayor Brandt or the Old One's proclamations. He was a private man like Spector; neither seemed to ever date—that she knew about. Spector was a fine reporter, she knew, but he didn't seem to share Heinz's drive to succeed and advance. There must be something more to him, but she'd be damned if she knew what it was.

"All done, Miss Beck?"

Startled, Katrina dropped the pencil and looked up at the slightly amused expression on her boss's face. It was a broad, round face with slicked back, thinning dark hair. His features were a little on the blunt side but the overall package made him ruggedly handsome in her mind.

"Sorry, sir, almost done," was the hurried reply.

"Good, good. You know," he continued, walking toward his office again, "there'll be a reception or two coming up. Maybe I can fix you up with a Secret Service agent or something. How 'bout that?"

Oh, great, she thought, now he had it in his head to play matchmaker. Fortunately, Stein dropped the line of thought when he glanced down at his desk and saw Heinz's latest article. He reappeared in his doorway, the sheaf of papers clenched in his big, beefy fingers. "Heinz! Do you know what we do here?"

The political reporter seemed stunned to be addressed. He looked up from his notebooks, uncertain of how to respond. Katrina kept a phone cradled near her ear to give the impression of being busy. She ignored the dial tone and listened.

"We're a wire service," came the lame reply.

"What does a wire service provide?" Stein prompted.

"News. . . ."

"News! That's right. And can you tell news from fiction? Because if you can't maybe we need a new political reporter. This certainly can't be news. Our masters like news because the client newspapers pay good money for information. Take this fairy tale back and put some meat on it! We'll need it by the noon deadline!" It meant the piece

would be available to American publishers in plenty of time
for their afternoon editions.

Heinz slowly rose from his desk and walked along death
row, the short matter of meters between his desk and Stein.
Taking the papers back, he saw the black pencil marks
turning his prose into a Rorschach test. Without a word, he
turned and headed back toward his desk, while Stein
returned to his office and picked up the next item, a contact
sheet with photos Gruber left before taking a train to Bonn.

The entourage stopped in Hanau for the night and was
housed in a grand hotel. There was, of course, a state dinner,
hosted by Adenauer, which stretched well into the evening,
further tiring the President. All day he had waved at people
in the towns of Bonn and Hanau, spoken at length with the
Old One on a variety of matters, and toured around a slew
of facilities whose distinctions had already blurred. Instead,
his mind increasingly turned toward his room, a hot shower,
and a lot of sleep. He was finding the jet lag of six hours to
be tougher than he last recalled and it was wearing on him.
Kennedy's back pain hadn't let up despite a good night's
sleep after arriving. It continued to force him to move
gingerly, and at times he longed for the crutches he used in
the privacy of Hyannis Port or the White House. In public,
though, he needed to project the image of a firm, fit
president, ready to take charge and lead his country forward.
The talk was polite for the press with toasts and smiles but
without substance. Kennedy later met with top aides:
National Security Council honcho McGeorge Bundy, General
Ted Clifton, special assistant Ken O'Donnell, and Rusk.
Lochner was freed from his obligation and retired to the
lobby for a smoke and some rest before turning in.

Seated in a plush chair, Lochner idly watched people
come and go through the vast lobby with its ornate carvings
and appointments. Uniformed employees scurried back and
forth, carrying luggage, messages, or pets. Men in expen-
sive suits and women in evening dress strolled back and
forth, many chattering on about the dinner and how handsome Kennedy was—especially compared with the Old

One. There was a general sense of excitement in the air, and Lochner was pleased.

His own reporters were covering the motorcade, and they confided that the people were nearly euphoric over Kennedy being there, as if the President's presence alone could uplift an entire nation. Lochner mused over the comments, wondering just what Kennedy might be able to say or do to justify such blind faith. He couldn't dismantle the Wall by himself nor could he negotiate with Khrushchev or Ulbricht over the Brandenburg Gate. It would have to come from the speech, and he wished the President and his colleagues well as they revised the text.

Such thoughts were immediately banished when he spotted a woman walking through the wide metal and glass doors at the entrance. She seemed to command attention, with her short, black hair and striking emerald-green dress that was at once elegant and sexy. The young woman couldn't have been at the dinner; he would have remembered someone who stood out so. Kennedy would have noticed, too, especially since he had commented that the German women seemed to like their bratwurst a bit too much.

While he couldn't help but notice her, she seemed to notice him and wended her way through the crowd in his general direction. Moments later, she was approaching, obviously intending to speak with him. Good manners took over and he rose to greet her, a smile coming easily to his lips.

"Good evening, *Fräulein*," he began.

"Good evening, Herr Lochner," she replied, in German no less.

His face betrayed his surprise. "You know who I am?"

She giggled a moment and said, "Sure. You're the President's interpreter. I saw that earlier today. It must be a thrilling opportunity to hear the intimate details between leaders."

"It has its moments, yes," he continued. "They are both good men with a common goal of improving our lives."

She rolled her eyes and smiled even broader. "Oh, please.

They dislike and distrust each other. The chancellor feels let down over America's reaction to the Berlin Wall, and Kennedy has no use for a lame duck."

Lochner felt himself staring a moment too long and regained his composure. "My, that's quite an observation from someone so young."

"Is twenty-five too young to follow politics?" she asked, her duffel now on the floor beside her.

"No, not at all. I guess I just don't meet too many people your age who have such firm opinions on politics. You know, you do have me at a disadvantage. I don't know your name."

"Oh, sorry." She put out a hand. He noticed no jewelry at all, but the fingernails were painted an interesting shade of pink. "I'm Angela Chance, a graduate student from the University of Edinburgh." He noted she gave the name the soft Scottish burr it required but her accent was distinctly American.

"An American studying in Scotland now here in Germany. How odd, don't you think?"

"Not at all," she said. "School is over for the semester, and I liked the idea of traveling the continent. There is so much to see. Right?"

Lochner gestured to the seat beside his. "Please, join me. Tell me, where have you been?"

Seating herself, she didn't seem to notice or mind the way Lochner studied her exposed legs.

"I arrived in Berlin yesterday and took the train to Bonn to follow the President. I thought it would be fun to see how he handled the situation here, what with the Wall and all."

Lochner was amazed by the woman's good looks and sharp mind. She seemed to be a true political devotee. She must want something, his experienced mind warned him, but there was little hurry getting to the point.

"All of Europe is suffering at the moment, right?" she asked.

"There are a lot of concerns—some political, some social."

"And a lot economic, right?" she went on. Moving a

minute bit forward, she continued, "There's inflationary fears from shore to shore. In Germany alone inflation is up to what, three or four percent?"

"Actually, I heard it was just two point eight percent," he replied.

"Is that all? But it's got everyone worried sick, right?"

"Well, yes," he conceded. "The tariffs are quite disconcerting to everyone as you might imagine."

"De Gaulle started that one, right? And America followed, socking it to everyone along the way."

Lochner nodded with a knowing smile. "That is one way to look at things. But, of course, as bad as things may seem here, they are far worse on the other side of the Wall."

"Do tell," she prompted.

"Well, for example, I have heard that while we pay something like twenty cents for an egg, they must pay closer to forty cents. And wages are far worse for the same kinds of work, so the standards of living over there are abysmal."

"But both sides have to stand on long lines for their purchases."

"My dear, the only country that successfully avoids that is America. I suspect it has something to do with all that land you possess."

She laughed and plunged on about other differences between the Germanys.

Their conversation ranged through a variety of topics, all of which were political. She displayed a keen intellect that fascinated the interpreter, and they engaged in short debates on any variety of topics. Her knowledge of German politics was excellent, and despite studying the subject in Scotland, she was equally up-to-date on American doings.

They moved from the lobby to the small bar within the hotel for some wine. The conversation was going on an hour, and Lochner's initial suspicions had faded. She never asked anything of him but seemed to be going from topic to topic, almost seeking confirmation that her remote sources of information were accurate. He relaxed and went with the flow, especially after the second glass of wine.

"So, tomorrow you go to Frankfurt, right?"

"Yes, we do. And from there to Berlin. You'll be following all this?"

She sipped from her glass, the first. "I wouldn't miss Berlin for the world. I bet he'll be brilliant there." Angela placed her glass on the wooden table between them, leaning in. "What's he like?"

"Kennedy is pretty much what he appears to be," Lochner said. He knew to be cautious despite feeling expansive. This was the President of the United States after all, and he was currently in the man's employ.

"You know," she said, running a tongue across glossy lips, "I'd love to have a chance to meet the man. He seems so charismatic. I bet you feel that even more up close. Right?"

"Oh, yes, he exudes a charm," Lochner replied.

"Do you think there's any chance? I'd be ever so grateful if you might be able to . . . arrange something."

For the first time since they met, there was a long silence between them. Lochner weighed any number of facts in his mind. Security immediately came to mind—was she really a political buff or was she stalking him like prey? It was natural, though, for any American to want a chance to meet their president. It was also natural for a young woman to find the man appealing. If she knew this much about politics, might she know, too, about the President's private reputation as a ladies' man? Then he considered Kennedy. He had been away from Jackie for several days and was no doubt lonely at night. Many traveling men were like that. Would Lochner be doing the man a favor? And the woman? If it backfired, what would happen to his position?

Friend? Foe? Assassin? The thoughts swirled through his mind, colliding against each other like balls on a pool table. No clear idea was coming through.

Then he noticed her eyes. They were inviting and longing. What form of gratitude was she hinting at? American girls had a reputation for being freer with their bodies than those here in Germany. Could she mean that? Was the wine helping him misread the signals? Too many questions and a headache rapidly took up residence between his eyes.

"Tell you what," he said, just to say something. "Let me go see what the full schedule looks like and if there is some way to arrange a meeting. Nothing long, mind you, but a chance to say hello."

She grinned at him.

"It may take a while and of course we'll need to establish your bona fides," he continued, rising from the seat and putting down several marks from his pocket to pay for the drinks. "Why don't you check in, and I'll leave word with your room."

"Sure. And you'll check out my story in the meantime." He gave her a surprised look, which made her giggle a little. "Thanks ever so much, Herr Lochner," she said, crossing and placing a lingering kiss right on his lips. He hoped she didn't notice the sweat now on his face.

As Chance checked in with the front desk, smiling her way into a room that was normally reserved for a traveling politician, she did not notice the man checking in parallel with her.

The man carried a small black valise, a tight look on his face, and constant suspicion in his eyes.

Major General Chester "Ted" V. Clifton, military aide to Kennedy, was stretching his legs in the hallway by the President's suite. Secret Service agents were positioned by both sides of the doorway, looking passive rather than menacing given the late hour. The entire floor was quiet with few lights seen from underneath doors.

Lochner emerged from the elevator, having used the ride up to take stock of his situation. While he had gotten along well with Kennedy, he had no idea whether or not the President would like an available companion or not. Instead, the interpreter would sound out the officer and see if he was making a fool of himself or not.

The explanation came out in a rush, Clifton nodding his head in weary confirmation. Once Lochner was done, he felt better and more than a little foolish. He did omit the fact that there was the possibility Angela would bestow similar acts of gratitude on him. That was another moral problem for later, given his marital status.

Clifton's oval face seemed weathered from service to his country and the hair was thinning and going gray. His watery blue eyes took in the information and processed it, keeping silent, making Lochner wait and sweat again. The headache spread from between his eyes to stretch from temple to temple.

"Ah, I believe the President has mentioned how much he misses Mrs. Kennedy," Clifton commented. "He's still up, wrestling with the speech. They finally got a framework started, but he says it's missing the heart of it. Maybe he needs a distraction, a good night's sleep."

He called into a walkie-talkie, asking Agent Segui to quietly look into the information Angela Chance left with the front desk. "If that checks out," Clifton began, "we'll then make quick calls to Langley and the Bureau, which should then clear her. We've, ah, done this sort of thing before. I'll also have someone ring the University. Any idea what time of night it is over there?"

Lochner nodded, feeling relieved he had read the situation properly. Having supposedly done his duty, he had passed off the situation to a military commander who could best assess the logistics involved. He said his good nights to the general and returned to the elevator and his room below.

Clifton, he noticed, had already gone back into the suite, no doubt passing along the suggestion to his commander in chief.

6

**Place: Hotel restaurant, Hanau, West Germany
Time: 11:06 a.m., Tuesday, June 25, 1963**

Robert Lochner met the presidential entourage for breakfast the following morning in the hotel's banquet room. It had been set aside for the President's exclusive use, and the hotel had spared no expense in making it a pleasant if not remarkable experience.

His head hurt. Too little sleep, too long a day, and too much intoxication—more from Angela herself than the wine. At least the headache was more manageable, although it seemed to elude the aspirin he took even before brushing his teeth.

He was waved through the door by a Secret Service agent that recognized him from the previous day. Walking toward the group, clustered at tables near the front of the room, he slowed his pace as he spied a familiar head of hair.

"My God," he muttered to himself as he got closer. Before the President could notice him, General Clifton walked briskly to his side and drew him toward a side table.

"America thanks you," Clifton said in jest.

"What, what happened?"

"Well, she checked out clean as a whistle. Good grades. No record of any sort. Family has money from oil, near as we can tell. All on the up-and-up. She certainly charmed the pants off you, and then he charmed the skirts off her, I guess," Clifton said.

Lochner nodded dumbly.

"What amazes me is that she's here for breakfast. Kennedy introduced her to Bundy as a student he met the night before. This is a new one on me."

"Did we make a mistake?"

"Only if this blows up in our faces. So far, he's in good spirits. He has ordered her special VIP privileges so she can continue with us."

Lochner was stunned. "You mean, she'll be here for the whole trip?"

"Looks that way," the general confirmed.

Outside the hotel, Andropov studied the lineup of cars and motorcycles. He mentally counted them, comparing the arrangement with the previous day's. Then he measured the space between vehicles, judging how much room there would be between the people en route and the vehicles themselves. At most, there would be two, two and a half meters from one side of the road to the other. The limousines were a bit over two meters wide, then space between the cars and cycles, and then cycles to the people. Getting between any of those layers would be tough, impossible.

Any thought of standing within the crowd and taking the bold chance with a rifle was dashed yesterday as he noticed the writhing mass. Too much chance of the shot going wide and then being gunned down himself by the police.

He might do better finding a building to hide in and strike while the President was making a speech. There would be the stop at a church later in the day or tomorrow at the Wall itself. His masters made it clear that the symbolic gesture might go either way: shatter the hopes of the so-called Free World or galvanize them against the Soviet Union and precipitate a war.

Better to strike away from the most protected spot. Yes, the hotel offered more possibilities.

In his overcoat pocket was a map of Berlin, and he would study it and be there ahead of the motorcade. Today would be his date with destiny and he would not fail.

The trip through Frankfurt seemed twice as long as Bonn, but the crowds were just as enthusiastic. Kennedy tired of so much enthusiasm and goodwill, but he gamely waved and smiled and did not mind being pelted by the occasional flower. Well-wishers actually broke through the barricades on more than one occasion and made their way to the lead car. Kennedy, to the Old One's astonishment, actually reached out and shook hands, greeting his newfound fans. To him it was much like the senatorial campaigns of the fifties where actually connecting with the people was possible. Sadly, being President now meant only staged opportunities to meet with people, and they were more and more local heroes, national figures, and fewer Joe Publics from around the fifty states. Later that night he would be informed that a woman was in such an emotional state that she triggered the labor process and gave birth along the parade route.

Along the way, he was finally introduced to Ludwig Erhard, the Fat One, and heir apparent to West Germany. He was significantly younger than eighty-seven-year-old Adenauer and had a keener grasp on world politics. Balding with gray hair, a jowly face, and a double chin, it was obvious how he had earned his nickname in the press. Kennedy's policy boys, though, had come up with a great deal of background on the chancellor-elect, and Kennedy appraised him of being a good public servant.

"Mr. President, this is indeed a great honor, a great honor indeed," Erhard began in thick English.

Kennedy smiled, showcasing those bright, white teeth. "I've heard some good things about you, Mr. Erhard. . . ."

"Ach, it's just a man serving his country, you understand all about that. Although I may have been serving while you were still in diapers." He chuckled at his weak joke;

assistants or other hangers-on laughed as well. Kennedy kept the smile plastered in place. Erhard certainly wasn't cuddly and revered like the gnarled chancellor, but Erhard also was more decisive in his actions. His political future was assured when, just a month earlier, he'd successfully negotiated the end to a potentially crippling metal workers strike.

"I'm not so sure about that, sir," Kennedy said, pressing on. "However, we do share many common goals for Europe and democracy, and I hope we will enjoy a solid working relationship in the years to come."

"Expect to win again, eh?"

Kennedy's eyes narrowed a bit at the mention of the election and reminder of the grueling campaign that was already being mapped out. Keeping things light, he joked, "I certainly wouldn't want to miss out on the exciting changes you have in store for the country."

The chancellor-elect nodded sagely, winking in response to the comment. "Plans I have. Getting the people to swallow them, that's the trick, my new friend. That's the trick."

To Kennedy's delight the conversation soon showed that, where the Old One preferred de Gaulle's take on the world, Erhard leaned more toward America, and it made Kennedy hopeful that the countries would prosper together.

And finally put arrogant France in its place.

The flight from Frankfurt to Tegel Airport was uneventful, which pleased the worn-out Kennedy just fine. They had crowds of people littering the roadways between the airport and Berlin proper, and the entourage waved heartily. There was no doubt that the outpouring of affection for the President was being deeply felt by the politician.

Once in Berlin, they were greeted by Mayor Willy Brandt, a short, stocky man with a broad grin that Kennedy liked immediately. The men had briefly met before, but they seemed more like old friends than political allies. And even though Adenauer and Brandt had been harshly critical of the United States' lack of action when the Wall went up two years earlier, there were no rebukes or harsh words. Still, Brandt was nursing wounds inflicted when the Wall went up and John Kennedy had done nothing. Since that day, the mayor had hoped for something far more substantial.

On the other hand, tough words were awaiting the President at his hotel. Once ensconced in the largest suite available, Kennedy was meeting with General Lucius D. Clay, originally the deputy military governor of Germany immediately following the Allied victory. The general returned to Germany at Kennedy's request when the Wall was erected. He easily represented a strong American presence, and his original role of calming the public's fears worked to a degree. Still, Clay was deeply concerned over the President's presence in the country and the hard emotions it stirred up on both sides of the Wall. He had cabled Washington back in February that he felt the trip was a mistake and could be a disaster.

Rather than wait for an appropriate moment, Clay used his reintroduction to the President as an opportunity to press his point in person. "Mr. President, while it is good to have you visit the German people, I would like to remind you that things here are tense and have only gotten tenser these past few weeks. The East German government has tried to strengthen the Wall at the expense of its people. Much of that is due to your very presence on West German soil."

Clifton, a military peer to Clay, although a few years younger, bristled at the tone in the man's voice. Kennedy, who loved absorbing as much data on all military matters as he could, leaned in and appraised the general.

"My policy people back in Washington think these steps would have happened sooner or later. So they did it to make me look bad. It's an old Republican trick," he joked.

Clay remained in command mode and did not react to the comment. Instead, he plunged on. "Sir, if things boil out of control, we do not have armed personnel in the vicinity to deal with it. I urge you to tread carefully in word and deed."

The President listened intently but seemed disinterested in the advice and said so.

"I've reviewed the security arrangements and there is a

risk of someone being able to shoot you. Twice in Berlin you will be very exposed."

Clifton, in charge of those arrangements, felt angry enough to cut in at that moment. "Mr. President, I assure you that the work I did with the German army is the best available given the geography. There's nothing to fear."

Kennedy looked over at both men, watching two hawks circle each other, protecting that which was most precious to them. To Clay, it was a responsibility to the German people, an assignment he himself had given the soldier. To Clifton, it was the President himself being protected, and both were willing to argue until their points prevailed.

"Gentlemen, I am satisfied with the status quo. Should something change, General Clay has the Berlin advantage and I will defer to his opinion . . . should that be necessary. Now, let's move on to other matters."

Later in the day, the President met with his fellow travelers in the suite, which had been rapidly transformed into a miniature White House, complete with staffing, a bank of phones, briefing books, and typewriters awaiting a call to action. Soft drinks and hard candies were placed every few feet around the living room, and people indulged regularly, already weary after just two days of touring.

The conversations with Konrad Adenauer had also taken their toll on Kennedy; Lochner, too, who had retired to his room.

A few hangers-on, Angela included, remained nearby, keeping more to themselves. Some were close aides to Rusk or Bundy, but there was at least one official secretary, ready for the President's immediate needs.

Before O'Donnell, Rusk, and Clifton were copies of the incomplete speech for the following day. Kennedy had read it through at least once already, unhappy with the way it sounded. "Hollow," he declared. "It needs something classic, something for the ages."

O'Donnell, a longtime personal friend, offered a Shakespearean quotation.

"No, everyone quotes Shakespeare," Kennedy grumbled. He was clearly stressed and irritable and disliked displaying this side of himself, especially so far from the familiar confines of the White House.

More conciliatory, he added, "But you are right, it has to be something memorable. Theatric. Now wait a minute, wait a minute. What was the proud boast of the Romans?"

His aides looked at him blankly, not certain of where he was going, and Kennedy was surprised that his mind was moving faster than theirs, or their education was that lacking. The Harvard grad continued to be a voracious reader, devouring the classics of western literature along with the modern potboilers.

"I have it," he said with remarkable clarity. "'*Civis Romanus sum.*' It means, 'I am a Roman citizen.' I can adapt that but need to do it right, in German. Send Bundy up here. He'll know how to say it in German."

The secretary reached for a phone by her side and dialed the room number for the National Security Council chairman. He heard her ask Bundy to come up, and it was a matter of moments before the chairman walked into the suite.

Taking a soft drink for himself, Kennedy explained what he needed and why. Bundy nodded and the President watched expectantly.

"What about something like this, Jack: I am a Berliner. Not a German citizen but something specific to the city, the Wall, and the unification of the people."

Kennedy broke into a smile. "I like it. A lot. Okay, so write it out for me, let's see what it sounds like." Bundy began scribbling on a legal pad, using a pencil handed to him by the efficient secretary, whose name Kennedy had trouble recalling.

"*Ich bin Berliner*," Bundy said, handing the paper over.

Kennedy frowned for a moment, hating having to use German. He may have mastered Latin as a student but was pretty bad when it came to using other languages. Still, he needed this to finish the speech and was running out of time. If it meant practicing a lot for a day, so be it.

He said the three words but his accent made it difficult to comprehend. Bundy tried to talk him through it again.

"You're getting it, Jack," O'Donnell said cheerfully.

"Yeah, thanks. I'll have to keep at it. Good work, George. We'll add it to the heart of the speech, but I think it needs more. Your themes are right, but what if I add, 'Let them come to Berlin.' Use that as a rallying cry."

All immediate heads nodded in agreement, which pleased the President enormously. He noted even the heads around the room seemed to bob affirmatively.

"Great. Okay, let's work this stuff in. Ken, give me a phonetic German version to practice with. I want to get this one right tomorrow."

O'Donnell agreed and began writing on his own pad. The secretary began annotating her master copy of the speech which would have to be retyped for tomorrow's event.

Looking at the words, Kennedy made a face and tried it aloud once more. The German pronunciation was even worse the second time, and the room fell silent. After a moment, though, Angela let out a delighted laugh.

Kennedy stared at this young woman, this enchanting person who made a long day wonderfully longer, and tried to imagine what was so funny. He realized it was his own mangling of the language that elicited the sound.

It did sound pretty bad. Awful even.

The President joined in the laughter and realized it was okay to laugh. It just meant he had work to do. He appreciated having this youthful face and point of view. She was amazing—great sex but also an active, inquisitive mind that seemed to fully grasp the facts for the global picture. He was used to avoiding politics with his occasional bedmates but not Angela. She was one for the books.

7

Place: Hotel, West Berlin, West Germany
Time: 9:45 p.m., Tuesday, June 25, 1963

Andropov purposefully walked through the lobby of the hotel, this time without his trench coat, dark glasses, or valise. He was nattily attired in a pinstriped suit that was Italian in cut, projecting an image of his being a successful businessman. Part of his prolonged success was in deflecting any suspicion by blending in with his surroundings. Most of his expenses were a direct result of maintaining an extensive wardrobe that allowed him to pick and choose for any locale, any environment. Fortunately, he had a conditioned physique that allowed him to look right in about any outfit.

Posing as a traveling salesman, he arranged an impromptu meeting with the hotel's catering manager.

"I will need a good hotel to host a meeting for fellow salesmen," Andropov said convincingly. "I have a new line of dry cleaning equipment that I think will be a big success and I need space to show it off."

Deter Knacht, the hotel's veteran manager, had already begun totaling up the profits such a meeting would bring to the hotel. He was therefore rather eager to provide this Pavel Andreivich with a full tour of the facilities. They began with a review of the banquet facilities: several large rooms all connected to a recently refurbished kitchen setup.

"This is all very nice, very nice indeed," Andreivich/Andropov said, admiring the griddle and hood near the kitchen's center.

"*Ja*, it's all under a year old. Our chef can prepare anything custom you need or we have a variety of menus you could prearrange," Deter continued, a nervous hand pushing imaginary stray strands of hair behind his left ear.

"I am very fond of veal," the Russian assassin said casually.

"We have six or seven wonderful veal dishes," Deter said in a rush.

"I'm sure," Andreivich replied. "What sort of food is the American president enjoying? Hot dogs and fried chicken?"

Deter was flustered at the insult directed at such a great leader, a fellow guest in the hotel. A hand mopped at sweat forming on his upper lip. "We don't actually, ah, prepare such fare. Nor has the President ordered any food as yet."

The tour of the facilities continued, lasting an hour or more. Andropov played the salesman, probing as matter-of-factly as possible about this and that. Deter was so involved in netting the sale—after all, two or three dozen salesmen staying two nights plus round-the-clock meetings meant six meals plus bar service, which began adding up to serious profit for the normally dry late summer season—that he answered every question with more detail than was necessary. Along the way, the KGB agent noted the state of repair of each exit door, where the fire suppression equipment was kept, what the security and medical arrangements were, and the service corridors for the meeting rooms.

When the meeting was completed, Andropov returned to his room, suddenly provided on the house as an investment against future business, and took a short nap. Refreshed, he then began to wander the facilities on his own, slowing in spots where he wished to examine certain windows or doorways. Since the staff had just seen him being shown around, no one bothered to stop or question him. This afforded him relative freedom, and he took advantage of it for the next hour and a half.

He ordered room service and ate lightly, as he always did before an assignment's climax. Andropov eschewed the veal and consumed broiled fish, wild rice, broccoli rabe, and a dry white wine. Black coffee and no dessert.

Methodically, he checked the sharpness of his throwing knife, the components of his sound-suppression pistol, and his fabricated identification. Should something go wrong, he would be known as a Russian importer for a fabric manufacturer. Agents at the listed address in Kiev would confirm the identity then relay the fact that someone had checked on Andropov's cover to the KGB in Moscow. The smooth working of his plan and support operation made him feel good and confident.

Slipping the knife into a shoulder sheath, he returned to the lobby and established his presence.

Secret Service agents mixed with German police officers throughout the lobby and on the street for a block in each direction. Being a June evening, the night was cooling rapidly, and Andropov walked through the main doorway to feel the briskness of the air. Strolling, hands in pockets, he moved down one block and turned, going around the entire area, counting off official vehicles (marked and unmarked) and personnel. His eyes also sought out fire escapes, alleyways, manhole covers, and other potential escape routes. While his success rate had earned him this assignment, he had also had a small number of failures that taught him to be carefully prepared for every contingency.

Returning to the hotel forty minutes later, the assassin sat in the lobby glancing at a newspaper, once again making himself an accepted part of the scenery.

Glancing at his watch, he saw it was nearing eleven. It would soon be time to act.

"I think we've done enough studying, Wolf," Elizabeth Krause said.

"*Ja*, it's almost eleven," Peter agreed.

The two folded up their papers and stored them in a small leather bag. With a yawn, Hoyt stood and stretched his arms over his head, fingers brushing the low ceiling. Inside the bar, the group had discussed new escape plans and argued for hours on what should be done. The elder Hoyts kept preaching caution and had played referee between the more impulsive Peter and the brooding Wolf.

"We'll never get over, whether Kennedy's on the other side or not," Wolf muttered.

"You will if you want it enough!" Peter argued, anger mixing with fatigue. "Everyone is going to be listening to the President, everyone is going to be watching the West. All you have to do is get through one of the checkpoints. We've got plans, we've got—"

"No money! We'll have to bribe a guard," Wolf countered, his face getting red. "Maybe several guards on both sides. We spent nearly everything just to get here at all. If your parents hadn't agreed to house us, we'd be sleeping on the street!"

"But, Wolf, sweetheart, we couldn't have stayed home anymore," pleaded Elizabeth wearily. "We agreed on that. We've reached our limit here and our future has to be in the West."

He stretched out, comforting her in his large arms, his head resting against hers. "I know, I know, *Liebchen*," he said quietly.

"Let's sleep and then tomorrow try what we can. Opportunities can be made," she said, attempting to buoy both their spirits.

"You seem jumpy," Urban said, putting his stein of beer back on the table. He picked up a deck of cards and dealt.

"Just nervous," Spector replied. He picked up each card as it was dealt, placing them in some order. It forced him to concentrate on something specific instead of worrying about everything.

"Ever since the tourists began descending on this place, I've been afraid they were right to station me here. The temporal alarm hasn't sounded, so I must be doing something good, right? I keep expecting it to go off, though. Not that I'm afraid of doing my job—I've been doing it all along. Instead, I'm afraid, with JFK here, I'm going to be really, really needed. And that will be a first."

"Look, I was trained to support the Warden, run the Beamer. Heck, I even maintain supplies and money, balance your checkbook. But these temporal mechanics can make my head hurt. Couldn't one of these tourists have altered time dramatically if you hadn't performed your function?" the Teletype operator asked. He finished dealing and looked at the hand and frowned.

"No luck again, eh," Spector teased. "Yes, any of these actions could have messed up time. That tourist the other day just lifted a Luger. No big deal, right? Well, let's suppose that this guard was on duty and someone managed to get across the border because he didn't have his weapon. The person who should never have gotten West got there, and his presence sets off a chain of events that could alter all of history. Or the couple I interrupted trying to escape. Were they supposed to have gotten over? Who knows?"

"And who knows if the couple gets across and starts a successful bakery and lives happily ever after with no change to history."

Spector nodded, drank from his own stein, and smiled. "That's why we have the Temporal Discrepancy Alert Computer. It stays in constant contact with my time just in case. The couple gets across and opens a bakery. No big deal. The computer stays quiet. The couple gets across and starts the Fourth Reich. The alarm bells could be heard out here."

"Okay, I get the idea. Now, can the temporal whatever computer predict the outcome of our game?"

Spector smiled and finished his beer. "Only if your winning means the end of time as we know it. Come on, let's finish. It's almost eleven and tomorrow's the big day."

Time: 11 p.m.

General Ted Clifton was used to keeping state secrets; in fact he liked keeping them. The tall man wore his uniform proudly and enjoyed exchanging salutes with his subordinates. While some of the grunts were on the far side of the world, fighting in the jungles of Vietnam, he had all the perks that came with his title: a choice assignment with the President, traveling to the world's capitals, and presiding over the créme de la créme of the armed forces. It made him feel safe, secure, and just a tad smug.

No job was perfect, and for Clifton that meant handling the fun secrets, the important secrets, and the dirty secrets. For some time now, he had been keeping some very big secrets from the nation. John F. Kennedy liked women. Everyone knew that. After all, he'd married a beautiful woman and had already produced some attractive children. What the public did not know was that he still liked variety among women and was frequently seeking out new conquests. Most were anonymous, but some were well-known, including the movie star Marilyn Monroe.

With very few exceptions, the women were onetime dalliances, there to satisfy the President's desires and little more. He never sought them out for their companionship; Jackie more than provided that. Few were her intellectual equal, and none were quite so graceful and stately. There was no question for Clifton that John loved Jackie.

What always confused Clifton was how Kennedy managed his deep love for Jackie when he was in his second year of a well-concealed affair with Mary Pichot Meyer. Kennedy had used Clifton's services to help keep things obscured from prying eyes at the White House. Jackie must have known about Jack and the artist—hell, half the journalists on Capitol Hill must have had an inkling—but she never said anything about it to anyone. She kept things to herself, and Clifton always admired that poise that came so naturally to her.

The President had clapped a hand on his shoulder earlier that day, drawn him away from a handful of Secret Service agents, and whispered thanks in his ear. "She's amazing," he had said. "Wherever did you find her?"

So he knew he had done his commander a favor. The trip was definitely taking a toll on him, and the President was tired, just bordering on cranky, what with the time changes and constant demands on his waking hours. With Jackie back in Washington, Clifton knew Kennedy needed a recreational break, and going to the movies was not going to be the answer.

What did surprise Clifton, though, was that Kennedy was so taken with this attractive young woman that he had credentials issued in her name and she was coming along for the full ride. He thanked himself that after the first night, he had had her double-checked. Everything still came through clean, convincing him her story was true. She was the fine upstanding American she appeared to be. There would be more than enough people in the entourage that no one would think of her as anything but a traveling secretary or administrative aide. The media tagging along would probably never notice, and the ones who did would keep quiet. The President enjoyed good enough relations with the beat reporters that their silence was virtually assured.

With the day's visiting done, Kennedy had concentrated on finishing his speech, and he had come up with the elegant phrasing that would endear him to the German people. Clifton knew a winner when he heard one and figured Kennedy would get past the atrocious pronunciation problem with practice. Still, he would need his rest and back exercises, and it fell to O'Donnell or Clifton to get him back to the suite.

Kennedy had asked Chance to stay through the evening, including dinner and the speech deliberations, so it was obvious to Clifton that despite having her own room in the hotel, she was going to stay in the suite tonight. It fell to him to make the event as discreet as possible, which meant repositioning the Secret Service agents further down the corridors and keeping one man out of the suite itself. There were more than enough German police down in the lobby and out on the street that the President's life was secure.

For all of a minute Clifton paused to consider Angela being a probable threat. However, she seemed exactly as she presented herself: a grad student with a keen interest in politics. Robert Lochner's praises still resounded in his ear from the previous night, and throughout the day he'd caught Angela engaging Rusk or Press Secretary Pierre Salinger in conversations that probed nothing more than American or German policy. She was certainly sharp, attractive, and the kind of companion most people would desire. Still, he'd instructed one of the agents to check her room during the day and nothing was found amiss.

Kennedy was completing a conversation with Bundy, so people began to stretch and make their good nights. Clifton silently gestured to the agents still in the suite and they followed him to the empty bedroom, the one not being used by the President.

"We'll need to redeploy our night watch," Clifton began, choosing to avoid the truth behind the order. He outlined where he wanted the men, and for which hours the coverage should be highest and lowest. Everyone nodded while one took notes on a map of the floor, marking the changes with red ink. No one questioned the moves, although Clifton suspected the veterans could guess why. These were highly dedicated Treasury Department men that were trained to protect the President at the cost of their own lives. To date, no one had been asked to make such a sacrifice, but the understanding was there and presidential detail work was highly coveted, especially with the gregarious, friendly Kennedy.

"At last," Kennedy said upon closing the door to his private bedroom. "Feels like I did nothing today but wave."

Angela sat on a chair in the far corner of the room, watching the great man unwind. With a grin, she waved at him only to receive a grimace. He liked the undemanding companionship and her smile; it was simply reassuring and friendly.

"I'll tell you, Angela, two days with Adenauer is enough. At least tomorrow I can share him with Brandt and Erhard. Ever see Brandt in action? Now there's a politician—a guy with ideas and with the fire in his belly to get them heard. He may be a mayor today, but I can see him running this country after Erhard. He's got the goods."

Kennedy removed his tie, draping it across the dresser's mirror. Fingers quickly undid the first two shirt buttons and then he sat at the foot of the bed to remove his shoes. He felt tired all over but also felt like chatting with Angela since she was so smart and well-informed. Looking over, he studied her oval face: the high cheekbones and bright eyes, skin a little pale, makeup light but well applied. The outfit was beige, with a high collar, wide brown belt, and sandal-like shoes he could not easily identify. On the other hand, his wife was the fashion expert, not him—all he knew was that he had never seen shoes like that before and they accentuated the outfit nicely.

She was sitting passively, enjoying just being in the room with him. Angela had yet to make a demand of him and had acquitted herself well throughout the day. There wasn't much time to speak with her, but getting in and out of the motorcade or at the luncheon, they'd exchanged glances and smiles. Angela definitely made him feel good about being there, and he was reassured that he was projecting the right image.

"I'd like you to stay tonight," he began, almost halting in mid-sentence. She made him feel good, but also a tad nervous. Maybe it was the intensity with which she watched him.

"Sure," she said softly. Rising, she walked over to sit beside him on the bed. Her hands interlaced with his, and her head found a place on his shoulder. They sat there, just resting for several minutes in relative peace.

8

Place: Presidential Suite, West Berlin, West Germany
Time: 12:43 a.m., Wednesday, June 26, 1963

Kennedy's suite was on the eighth floor of the ten-story hotel. During his walk around the block, Andropov noticed that in their naiveté, no one was positioned on the roof. There were no flybys that he could tell, so there was a higher degree of confidence than there should have been.

Nor was there anyone in the elevator area checking room keys to make sure the people belonged there. Far too civilized. Too trusting. Barely anyone could get through when Premier Khrushchev stayed away from Moscow, even if they did have business in the building.

It was therefore child's play for the careful, well-armed Russian to make his way up to the tenth floor and then across the floor to the service staircase in the rear. The assassin was wearing a dark gray shirt, buttoned to the collar, black slacks, and rubber-soled black shoes. His knife handle and sheath were also dark, so he was able to play with the shadows to a degree. His weathered hand gently tried the knob, finding no resistance, and pushed the steel door open. The access way was dim with low-wattage lightbulbs burning every three meters or so. With careful moves, he closed the door and made his way down the stairs. Every so often he paused, listened for hotel personnel also using the access way. Not a sound, so he was fortunate.

At the eighth floor doorway, Andropov placed his right ear against the door, listening. Silence. He tried the left ear to be certain. Still nothing, so he eased the door open a crack. No trip wires noted, no guard in the mirror set against the far wall, above a half table. The assassin knew he had to go down the corridor, turn right, and then make another right to get to the wing with Kennedy's suite. There were probably guards down each of the corridors, but from this way he could bypass the elevator bank and surely miss a handful of security people.

Still silent, Andropov slipped into a pair of tight leather gloves. A hand reached for the knife and clutched it. The metal blade was sharp and matte gray, not reflecting any light. It was a hunting knife that was balanced for throwing, but the wielder rarely used it in such a fashion.

"Got a cigarette?" a voice called out.

"Yeah, come on," another voice replied.

Andropov froze, mentally placing where the men would be, based on the hotel's floor plans the compliant manager had showed him that afternoon. One would be near the elevators, the other—the man moving off position—was coming from the juncture where to the right was the President, and to the left were other rooms used by the American party.

He quickly moved across the carpeted floor, careful not to make a sound. Hurrying a bit, he got past the juncture and turned right, hugging the wall. Slowing his breathing, Andropov listened as the guards chatted, a lighter going off.

Inwardly, Andropov was amazed at how easy this had been. The Americans and Germans were so trusting that it had never occurred to them someone would try to get close to their precious president. He had had much harder assignments.

To guarantee immediate response time, Kennedy's room was not locked—another surprise to the assassin. No one by the door—most unusual—he'd fully expected to have to kill at least one guard to access the President.

Slipping in the room, Andropov listened for the soft click of the door catching. Scanning, he noted that no one else was in the living room. A small lamp against a sideboard was on, giving the room a small amount of illumination which let the Russian get a sense of his surroundings. The living room was in the center of the suite with two bedrooms branching off in the rear and a small kitchen area to Andropov's left. Windows gave the room a sense of size, and during the day it was probably well lit from all sides.

He would have to guess which room contained the President and presume he would not encounter a slumbering guard.

Choosing the left room, Andropov walked over and laid a hand on the knob, trying to sense if there were any safety features. Instead, the knob turned freely, emboldening the Russian. From here it would be easy to strike and stab the President in his sleep. His fame was assured.

Looking into the room before crossing the threshold, Andropov was surprised to notice two forms in the king-size bed. All right, he thought, two deaths for the price of one. He wondered for a moment if it was some noteworthy woman or a common whore. Some leaders were like that, he knew. On more than one occasion, his work led him to discover his targets involved with call girls (or boys) of one kind or another. The tastes of some of these people—men and women—never ceased to amaze him, and in a remote way fascinated him. His preferences were far more conventional.

Hefting the knife, Andropov moved quickly toward the bed, figuring on making a quick strike to the President, then the woman. With just a short distance to cover he paused to make sure both were still sound asleep.

The knife raised higher, the man moved right to the edge of the bed.

With a sudden intensity, the arm swung down, making a swooshing sound in the air.

The swoosh was replaced with an electronic crackle, the

likes of which the Russian had never heard before. The knife met some resistance in the air, sparks of red and yellow lighting things up. Andropov was astonished, unsure of what was happening.

Sparks continued and the President stirred, eyes fluttering open. At seeing a figure, the eyes went wide, Kennedy's expression going from sleepy to angry.

It was time to run and Andropov knew it.

He spun on his heel and bolted for the door as Kennedy rose from the bed and tried to get out. The last thing the failed assassin heard was the electronic crackle again and a curse in English. Whatever kept his knife away from the President also kept the man trapped on the bed.

Hastily, he bolted from the room and into the hall. The Russian realized the door was opened too quickly and rebounded off the wall, making a sound that, in the silence, was clearly heard by the Secret Service. Gripping the knife, Andropov knew escape would be difficult, but not impossible.

Footsteps alerted him, and the inevitable confrontation came closer. The first agent emerged into view, gun raised, barrel toward the ceiling. Upon seeing Andropov, the agent began to lower the weapon but then looked down and saw the knife already protruding from his chest. Blood seeped quickly into his starched white shirt.

The man fell with a gurgle, and Andropov savagely ripped the knife free just as the second agent came upon the scene.

Andropov whipped the knife upward, cutting deeply into the agent's gun hand, slicing open skin and veins, gun and blood dropping to the carpet. The agent tried to kick the KGB assassin in a vain attempt to protect his president. Instead, the knife swung down and sliced open the man's neck, effectively letting him bleed to death in a rush.

More footsteps indicated one more agent on his way, and a voice called into a walkie-talkie, alerting the entire security force. He would have to move quickly to effect any kind of escape. Swiftly, he gripped the knife and charged further into the hallway, heading back toward the access stairway. The third agent leveled the gun at Andropov, and there was a moment of stalemate.

"Hold it!" barked the man. "You're under arrest, so just stand there."

Instead, Andropov inched closer to the American, still holding the knife.

"Stay there or I'll shoot!"

Andropov tensed and watched the man's eyes. They were clear but just hinting nervousness.

Instantly, he hurled the knife and dove to his right, going into a forward roll. As the knife imbedded itself in the agent's right shoulder, forcing an errant shot, Andropov regained his feet and stomped the agent into unconsciousness.

With no choice left, Andropov moved to the window near the elevator bank and opened it. Sirens were already going off and chaos would soon fill the nearby city streets. Fortunately, he had planned for this level of catastrophe. As the window opened, he stuck his head out and looked to his left. Dangling carefully was a thick, knotted hemp rope that came down from the roof.

Hands grasped the rope and he climbed out the window and began scaling the two stories to the roof, figuring he would have at most five minutes before police floodlights started checking the upper areas. All he had to do was jump to the next roof, enter the office building, and emerge the next morning when he could blend in with the crowd.

His breathing was hard when he reached the roof, but Andropov was almost free. At least two agents were dead, but somehow the President survived. He had never encountered such an electronic force, and he was puzzled by its nature. However, he had seriously underestimated the Americans and would not do so again.

Deep within the offices of the UPI, a computer system snapped to life and a small alarm chirped, lights blazing around it in the gloom of the dark, hidden room.

"Damn it all to hell, what just happened?"

Kennedy was painfully sitting up in the bed, naked and

alert. Angry. Angela had yet to see the famed Irish temper flare up in the man, and the intensity fascinated her. Here was a man filled with incredible charm, poise, and charisma but with a dark side that she had heard only bits and pieces about. This was something amazing to watch.

Another part of her mind, the more rational part, also recognized that something significant had just occurred. Someone had managed to get into the President's suite and almost succeed in murdering the world's greatest leader. A thousand questions rushed through the brain synapses while she tried to remain calm and supportive of her bedmate. There was no question that she had done the right thing, but it was something she would never be able to reveal to the man. After all, how do you tell a partner, after having just had great sex, that you saved his life by using a force emitter that was set into motion just as the lights went out? The device, issued to students to avoid unwanted physical confrontations in her time, was clearly not something found at the local E. J. Korvette. Set to personal biorhythms, it was deemed a fail-safe protective device.

"I woke up when I heard something, a squeak maybe, and saw this man. I think his seeing me frightened him off," Angela said, sounding as strained as Kennedy.

As they stared at each other in amazement, neither bothering to cover their nudity, they could hear the sounds of fighting in the hallways, uncertain of who was victorious. After a moment more, Kennedy seized the phone on the nightstand and summoned help. Being President had its advantages and that included an operator awaiting his line at all hours so response would be quick.

"Ah, Angela . . ." the President began.

She was already up, reaching for her clothes, an unsteady smile on her face. "Don't worry about it, Jack," she said, using his name for the first time. "I'll be dressed in a sec and then fade into the night."

Kennedy's anger softened for a moment, and he looked at her. The expression flooded her with a warmth she had yet to feel with any man from her time. Truly there was something unique about this man, and the experience was something that would add an extra layer to her thesis. She could feel herself rising to the top of her class even as she rushed into skirt and blouse, tucking hose, brassiere, and panties into her pocketbook. While reaching in, she thumbed off the protection device remote and prevented an embarrassing moment when the President attempted to get off the bed.

Kennedy was busily fumbling for pajama bottoms and bathrobe so he never noticed her actions or thought twice about her explanation. This was just fine with her, because it was a flimsy excuse for why a trained assassin would be frightened away. She hoped the explanation would hold long enough for events to propel him and the security agents past the moment of discovery.

Seated in the bathroom, she couldn't stop trembling. Somehow, a simple visit to the twentieth century had grown incredibly complicated. No, she hadn't fallen in love with Kennedy, nor was he the best lover she had had. But there was a force, a magnetism to him that drew her close and now she realized that like a moth to the flame she was burned. But what had she done to history?

Perhaps two minutes after the attack was thwarted, Ted Clifton came rushing into the suite. He was out of uniform, wearing an unbuttoned white shirt, black trousers with no belt, and socks with no shoes. It was clear he was terrified of anything being amiss, since security was his responsibility and Kennedy was both his president and his friend.

"Mr. President, are you all right?"

"Furious but fine, Ted. What the hell happened?" Kennedy was standing in his robe, hands in his pockets to control the rage beginning to build within him. Sirens were already audible through the old brick and mortar walls, and pounding footsteps and shouts were coming from another direction. Sheer pandemonium was threatening to take hold.

Clifton looked ashamed at failing and stared more at the bedroom's area rug than Kennedy. "Someone came in and tried to kill you but ran away before going through with the attack. He killed two men on his way out and escaped through a window."

Kennedy began to pace to work off the angry energy that had built within him. Clifton continued to watch the figure pick up speed along the way. "Who was it?"

"We don't know," Clifton admitted. "Could be any of a couple dozen explanations. I have Brogna taking facts from Hundley, the agent left alive."

"Be damn quick about it," Kennedy snapped. "I want to know who it was, why he wanted to kill me, and most importantly, how he managed to get into my room!"

The general stammered a moment and finally said, "That was my doing, sir."

"What!"

"When it was obvious Angela Chance was going to be here tonight, I thought it wisest to redeploy the men, giving her greater ease in and out of the room. Not once did it occur to me someone would even get onto the floor, let alone into your room. You don't know how sorry I am about this."

Agents, German police, and members of the American traveling party gathered on the floor. Clifton had regained his sense of authority and issued orders to keep the suite clear. McGeorge Bundy and Ken O'Donnell had been admitted several minutes earlier and were sitting with the President, a room service tray of tea and coffee at his side. Noises out in the hall indicated medical personnel were dealing with the remains of the agents and moving Hundley, the injured officer, off the floor.

Dean Rusk knocked on the suite's door, slightly ajar already, exchanging glances with O'Donnell to gain admittance. In his hand was a small pad of paper, and the expression on the secretary's face was one of dire consequences. Whatever he had learned was obviously not good for anyone.

"Hundley got lucky, I think," he began. "First, he'll live, which is more than I can say for those poor bastards out there. Second, he identified the man as a known KGB assassin. Thing is, we don't know his name."

"Russian!" Kennedy said the word like a curse and

resumed pacing the room. His colleagues watched mutely as he worked off some of the adrenaline and seemed ready for additional information.

"It's not the first time anyone's tried to get you, Mr. President," O'Donnell said grimly.

"But the closest, right?" Kennedy asked the room. No one dared respond.

"The German police have done the usual: stationed people along the highways, sent officers to the airports, docks, and rail stations," Clifton announced. "If this son of a bitch tries to leave, we'll nail him."

"Just like they found him getting into the country," Kennedy muttered in disgust.

"Sir, it's very different—"

"Bullshit!" Kennedy cut him off. "That bastard Khrushchev wants me deader than I want him. All right, well, this time the gloves come off. He wants me, we'll just have to make it worth his while."

Everyone watched the leader of the Western World continue to stalk the living quarters, as if trapped in a cage. No one attempted to speak or guess what the man meant. Dire thoughts occurred to most of them, though.

"Everyone clear the floor and get back to bed. Grab some sleep and be ready for me at 0630. I think I need to give my speech a bit more punch than rhetoric, and I need to figure out how to achieve that. Go on, everybody out. You, too, Ted."

Clifton leaned over toward the President's left ear. "We'll resume normal security precautions but with double the men for the rest of the night. You'll be alone, right?"

Kennedy paused, staring at his friend. The anger had clearly taken hold of him and rational considerations such as continued security or Angela's whereabouts hadn't occurred to him. For a moment the image of Angela, still sitting in the bathroom, appeared to him. His heart went out to her for a moment and then he returned the look at Clifton. "Yes, that'll be fine, Ted. Good night."

The general turned to leave, took three steps, and then turned at the doorway. His face was a mask of sorrow. "I never intended for this to happen. If you want, when we reconvene, I will tender my resignation. I failed you, Mr. President."

Kennedy waved at the air. "You were doing me a favor and we had no inkling something was amiss. I thank you for looking after my, ah, needs. But this can't happen again. I want to sleep peacefully the rest of my presidency. And, boy, I'd rather kick that Commie's ass than yours any day."

Clifton left the room, locking it, and could be heard issuing orders to the guards on duty. No doubt he would barely get any sleep, dealing with German officials, media in two languages, and other matters that reminded Kennedy of just how glad he was to be above such matters. Instead, Clifton's efforts were to free him to ponder loftier goals such as how to respond to such an attack.

And the alarm bells resounded on the other side of town, louder than before, if that were possible.

9

Place: Temporal Warden Spector's apartment,
West Berlin, West Germany
Time: 3:44 a.m., Wednesday, June 26, 1963

A loud sound shattered Spector's dreams of race cars and cross-country driving. Whatever they meant would have to be put aside. In the years Spector had spent in the past, this was the first time the Temporal Discrepancy Alarm had gone off. As a result, he was instantly alert and moving from his bedroom to his small living room with determination. Quickly, he brushed off magazines from an end table and reached underneath it for a small, dark green case. He placed his thumb against the locking mechanism, designed to resemble luggage of the era, and heard a click. The top was off in an instant and the remote access to the Proximity Alarm was already engaged. Two fingers jabbed at the dark red alarm cutoff control, and then he focused his attention on the readout screen.

"Stand by, Warden Spector," came a faceless voice.

Moments later, Bill Mason's thick features filled the small screen. Those watery blue eyes looked like they lacked sleep, and the expression was of tight concern.

Without preamble, Mason launched into an explanation. "We have a Priority Two alert of an exceedingly perilous nature, Alan. An event in your time just occurred which, if uncorrected, will create one of the fastest moving temporal wave displacements we have ever measured. It's moving with such force that the destruction it could leave in its wake will be devastating."

"How many subjective days do I have?" Spector inquired.

"Sixteen hours."

Spector's mouth dropped. He had never heard of such a thing and yet they were still giving the incident a Priority Two. He knew intellectually that Priority One problems were so rare that he had personally never met an agent involved in such a mission. Still, if the wave speed estimate was right, this surely would qualify.

Mason turned to face three people Spector could only see pieces of, and they had a hurried conversation punctuated by Mason grunting a lot. "Details are just about ready. We've gone to a high-alert status here, and I'm assigning Warden Dianna Basehart to monitor you from here. She'll be right behind you on the information flow and can time hop in should something go wrong. She's experienced in mid-twentieth century."

Spector considered Basehart, a year or two senior than him and a Warden with an impressive record. Without having met before, he gave her a vote of confidence. His grin at the screen was all Mason needed to see.

"Good luck, Alan," he said simply and then moved out of camera range. A moment later, Basehart, who also looked like she had just woken up, said good morning. She had jet-black hair, just below her ears, with bright eyes and full lips.

"According to telemetry from your system, whatever you do, you need it done in just under sixteen hours."

"Understood. I'll set the implant for fifteen hours to give me a little breathing room. That means . . . about 6:30 p.m. my time."

Basehart frowned at the calculation. "That's awfully

short, Alan. If it's moving with that kind of fury, minutes may mean years altered. Please be careful."

Spector nodded just once, then asked for the report if it was ready. Moments later, the computer banks at Temporal Warden Headquarters, centuries uptime, had correlated data from probability histories and actual histories. He read through the report twice and then slumped back in the chair.

A minor incident involving a KGB assassination attempt against John Fitzgerald Kennedy was supposed to fail. Kennedy was never to know of the incident and the would-be killer was captured by the Secret Service. Instead, the assassin got close enough to scare Kennedy and, as a result, the American President unleashed a war far too early in the nuclear age for mankind's maturity to match mankind's destructive nature. In short, Spector had less than sixteen hours to stop the President of the United States of America from launching World War III and irrevocably altering time as it should be.

For just a brief moment, Spector wished he had stayed on that train in Ohio.

Grabbing the phone, he dialed Urban's home and counted seven rings before the groggy voice answered.

"We're on Priority Two alert," Spector said without hesitation. "I need you at the Beamer."

"What the hell's going on?" His voice was not only sleepy, but he may have been sleeping off another wild night out.

Briefly, the Time Warden condensed the events and repeated them to his colleague. "It's going to get bumpier from here," Spector said and hung up. Mentally, Spector commanded: *Implant chronometer activate, time fourteen hours forty-five minutes*. That would give him just a few more minutes' leeway, more to satisfy Basehart than himself.

It was a sleepless night for Kennedy. He may have dozed here and there, but the anger kept him agitated. Anger and more than a little fear. He had often been said to have had a death wish or a desire for danger, and in some ways he agreed. Tonight proved that: risking his life for sex, okay, great sex, but still why do that? Thoughts washed over him and he allowed them to beat at him, pounding his conscience and moral fiber.

In the final analysis, Kennedy recognized that he was angry at both himself and at the Russians, but he was more than a little scared that he had come perilously close to death. He didn't want to die anytime soon, since there were many unfulfilled plans. There were great issues of his day to deal with such as civil rights, the conflict that was starting to get out of hand in Vietnam, the entire Communist issue, the state of welfare, the space race, and so many other things. He knew it was the dawning of a new age for America; he could see the tangible signs of the people shaking off the torpor of the 1950's and getting passionate all over again. The passions were a mixed bag, but they were emotional voices and he liked much of what they had to say.

The days of reigning for sixteen years, as Franklin Roosevelt attempted to do, were long gone, but he knew he had eight good years to give to the people and lead them forward. If he could beat the Republicans in 1964 and have until 1967 to enact his plans, he knew he would leave America in far better shape than when he inherited it from Dwight Eisenhower. Congress was mostly behind him, and much as he personally disliked Lyndon Johnson, the Vice President was very effective in twisting arms and maneuvering votes. Together, they would be the architects for a new society, a great one at that.

But first, the President knew, he had to send a clear message to his counterpart, Khrushchev. He could not allow an assassination attempt to go unanswered. Of course, he couldn't be public about the attempt, since it spoke ill of American security and planning and would reflect badly on his German hosts. Instead, his signal had to be clear and unmistakable.

A knock at the door interrupted his thoughts and brought him back to the immediate situation. Kennedy called the visitor in and was pleased to see Clifton back in full uniform. His colleague always seemed at his best in full dress, and it made him focus on the task at hand. In this case, it was damage control over the KGB spy's mess.

"What have you got, Ted?" Kennedy asked without preamble.

The general took a seat and opened a manila folder filled with white and yellow sheets. It took a moment to find the right note, and he began, his voice full of control as opposed to the self-doubt exhibited short hours earlier. "We have a name. Hundley gave us enough, and the boys at Langley have pegged him as Gregor Andropov, a known KGB employee. He's been implicated in a number of high-level assassinations over the last five years. He's got a good track record with few misses so you, ah, were lucky."

"Where did he go?"

Clifton shook his head. "Can't say. He left no trail at the end of the rope, which led him to the fifth floor. He broke a window in a room he had already reserved. Smart guy; he had everything all figured out. The other room he had was bare of any personal effects, and you couldn't tell anyone was there. He paid in cash so there's little for our men to track."

Kennedy nodded his head in disappointment but was hoping for better luck in the future. Then he forged ahead.

"What about the press?"

"Ken and I got them calmed down. We gave them a story about a cigarette starting a fire in an adjacent bedroom. Everyone thinks you nearly burned and our fictitious smoker, an unidentified Secret Service agent, was injured and taken to the hospital. They bought it and are busily filing stories about your close brush."

"Close indeed," Kennedy repeated humorlessly. "Anyone suspicious?"

"Not at all," the general said. Kennedy nodded and continued brooding for several long moments.

"Where are the nearest naval vessels?"

Surprised, Clifton had to pause and consider. After several seconds he finally responded, "We have several stationed in the Atlantic on NATO maneuvers. I guess we have more on call at our European bases. Do we need them?"

"Perhaps. What about our local jet fighter capability?"

"General Clay would have the details, but I believe we're fully stocked here in Germany."

"Full missile capability?"

"Why, yes, I think so. What do you need . . . wait a moment. What are you thinking about?"

"Those sons of bitches have got to pay for this. It will only escalate if we don't stop them cold. Now. They snicker as we make speeches and let the Wall be fortified. They try to kill me. Well, I'm drawing the line. Today. Better get Clay in here.

"Also, get the staff in here and rolling," Kennedy suggested, thinking about getting dressed. It would be a long day and he wanted the little things out of the way.

"You did say 0630, sir," Clifton reminded.

"And it's six-fifteen, I see," the President replied. "All right. I'm getting dressed. Order up a full breakfast: coffee, rolls, fruit, whatever for the staff. You know what we'll need." He returned to his bedroom, the first time he had been there since he quietly escorted Angela from the room a little while earlier. She had been rather nervous and concerned, he recalled, but was a real trooper about the entire melee. With luck, he'd have time to see her alone before he had to fly the next day, no, tonight. By then, though, events might take on a life of their own, and Kennedy might not have any time for anything but ending the Cold War in a very hot way.

Within minutes, Kennedy had gotten dressed, and the first secretary, a brunette with big eyes named Buford, had arrived. Clifton was on the phone again, speaking in hushed tones with someone. The President greeted Buford formally and then asked for his schedule. As she ticked off the items, he returned to pacing the living room, eager for the food to arrive to get started.

"You have a breakfast with the wire services at eight, and then you have a meeting with Mayor Brandt at nine, and a session with Ludwig Erhard at nine forty-five. The motorcade begins at ten-thirty and is expected to last two hours. You'll stop first at the Brandenburg Gate and then make a stop at Checkpoint Charlie before arriving at the City Hall and public ceremonies with the mayor."

Kennedy nodded without pausing the wandering around the room. "Who's in the car with me this time?"

A quick glance at her papers and the reply was, "You, Willy Brandt, and Konrad Adenauer."

"Where am I?"

"You're on the right, the chancellor is on the left, and the mayor is in between."

"Change it." A simple, direct command, delivered with anger.

"Sir?" The young, not terribly attractive secretary seemed surprised by the command.

"I don't want them bickering for thirty-five miles. Put me between them."

"Sir, that can't be," the secretary managed to say.

"Why not?" the icy voice asked.

"German protocol demands you be on one side, closer to the people. There was a great deal of jockeying between Mayor Brandt and Chancellor Adenauer over the other two seats. Both wanted to be next to you. The chancellor won out on the protocol issue of being head of state and therefore needing to be on the outside of the car, closer to his people."

Kennedy imagined the bickering that entailed and smiled at the realization. "That means Brandt is between us and is furthermost from the people. But, between us, I like that. Okay, we'll follow diplomacy."

Buford nodded, scribbled, and turned to a phone to find Dean Rusk, who confirmed the motorcade arrangements.

Within the next several minutes, people drifted into the room, tense, more than a little nervous, and edgy from lack of sleep. Bundy arrived first, then O'Donnell, two more aides or secretaries, then the room service waiters, followed in briefly by the Secret Service. As the room filled, Kennedy paused and considered two things: first, it resembled the classic stateroom scene from the Marx Brothers' *A Night at the Opera*, and second, what was Angela up to? Safe and asleep, he hoped.

As soon as everyone served themselves, seats were taken, pencils poised and all eyes on the President. This was his moment to get things settled once and for all, and it was an opportunity he did not want to squander.

"Later today, I'm going to face the German people. It's going to be tough to look them in the eyes, with the Berlin Wall behind me, and make a speech with lots of nice words and empty threats. Last night proved that it is time to put some teeth behind those words. Last night proved to me that the Russians have crossed a line.

"That bastard Khrushchev must learn he cannot treat me like a peasant."

"That bastard Khrushchev cannot get away with this again."

Everyone nodded and remained tensed, unsure of what was coming. Kennedy knew what he wanted but needed their support to accomplish the impossible. He measured his words, tried to temper his boiling anger.

"The last decade was one that split the Allies apart. Stalin lied to everyone during the peace talks, starting in Yalta and going through one atrocity after another. He bullied his people after bullying Roosevelt and Churchill. No question that we were taken.

"France under de Gaulle has been difficult at best and annoying at worst. Their policies have been disastrous and harmful to Europe and have kept the countries rattled.

"The British have finally recovered, but they've had their own internal troubles and Macmillan is on the ropes politically. None of these Europeans have managed to do more than condemn the Wall. Any attempt at economic or political sanctions have not worked since de Gaulle has scuttled us.

"For two years the Wall has existed and been strengthened. For two years it has stood as a symbol of all that is wrong with Communism, and we have allowed it to remain. There's no question that something must be done.

"Yesterday I thought I had the right words," Kennedy

continued. He paused to check his speech where the phonetic spelling awaited. "*Ich bin ein bear-LEAN-ar*," he pronounced slowly. "*Lassen sie nach Berlin kommen.*" He recognized the pronunciation was lousy and needed work, but the point was made.

"Good words but clearly not enough. Do you agree?"

Everyone hesitated, eyes darting one way or another, checking to see what the others would do. The aides and secretary Buford knew they weren't included so remained silent. This was directed at his inner council of the moment. Normally, brother Robert would be there, but he had missed the trip, keeping an eye on things back in Washington. His time to tour Europe would come, but the attorney general had plenty to keep him occupied back home.

"Mr. President, what do you have in mind?" O'Donnell asked, hesitation in his voice.

"I hope you're not thinking what I think you're thinking," Bundy said.

Kennedy remained silent, his eyes searching out support. Praying he didn't have to act with impunity. The four gentlemen before him shifted in their seats, holding cups and saucers in their hands, looking extremely uncomfortable.

Finally he decided to speak out. "Yes, McGeorge, I want the Wall down. Today."

With the words in the air, the four seemed thawed out and filled with opinion. All four spoke at once, their words merging and blending but the tone consistent: they didn't approve. Kennedy was not surprised all that much, disappointed maybe. He let them get the emotions out of their systems and then waved for silence.

"All right, let's do this by the book. General Clay, can we do it? Today?"

Clay reluctantly but firmly nodded. "I started practicing to rip down that Wall two years ago until you stopped me."

Kennedy looked at him in surprise. "I did, didn't I?"

Clay looked stiff and uncomfortable, reminded of his preparations, only to be told to stop so his actions weren't misconstrued by the East Germans. He looked away from Kennedy at that moment.

"Dean, what do you predict the reaction would be?"

"The West Germans will canonize you," Rusk replied.

Kennedy smirked at the comment and then gestured for him to continue.

"The Russians will not stand for it. They can't. After Cuba, they won't stand down on the world stage again."

"I think they will take it because world opinion is against them," Kennedy said.

Rusk shook his head. "Opinion didn't stop the Wall from being completed or the checkpoints from going into operation. You're deluding yourself . . . sir."

Kennedy turned his attention to Bundy, who, as head of the National Security Council, had the big picture always in mind. Bundy had been fidgeting the most and now he was expected to comment.

"It's World War Three, Mr. President. You strike that wall down, Khrushchev will go nuts. He'll launch their missiles, you'll launch ours, and we'll all go down in flames."

"He won't go nuclear over Europe. He can't," President Kennedy protested, sounding genuinely bewildered for a moment.

"He might. Khrushchev is a volatile man and given to quick bursts of anger," Bundy observed, not pointing out the similarities. "You've taken a lot of shit before this decision. It's been a mountain of shit starting with the entire Iron Curtain and now last night. The President has taken it on the chin time and again and never reacted badly. You knock that wall down, he'll do something rash. Nuclear is worst-case but not out of the question."

"As long as it is possible," Rusk added, "we shouldn't provoke him."

"Do you have a better idea?" Kennedy challenged.

"Not immediately. Go on the road, make your speech, and plan something coolly. You're hot and I don't blame you. I can't. But don't escalate this into something you're not prepared to deal with."

Kennedy's pacing returned, at a stronger speed. "I say we

do this swiftly. Today. And give them no time to react. Send in the jets, blow the Wall from one end to the other, and we declare a stroke for the free world. The press will eat it up, and Goldwater withers up and goes away."

The men brooded, considering the bold plans being considered. He saw that in their guts they wanted to do it; they hated the Russians and the Wall the same way he did. That's why they were all on the same team. However, none of them were almost killed and didn't see things with the same intensity as he did.

The men argued around and around the issue for the next hour. Coffee went cold, hard rolls went uneaten, and the voices grew shrill or hoarse. Nothing seemed to sway the President and that began to deflate the men. He knew they would follow his orders since he was the commander in chief and had the option of calling in the armed forces at will.

Finally, the men stopped arguing. They remained steadfast in disagreeing with the President, but no one could convince him otherwise. His anger remained a hot coal in his belly and it urged him onward.

"I've got a meeting with the press I want to keep," Kennedy concluded. His tone was positively bouncy and jubilant, laced with the anger that seemed to be giving him renewed vigor despite lack of sleep. He stood before his colleagues and gave them his sternest look. "Call in the air force. I want a coordinated strike this afternoon, right after Free University. Scramble those jets and have them in the air by the time I make my speech. There'll be no way for the Russians to intercept them, and the Wall will be history before dinner. I want the German police briefed only as far as keeping the people away from the Wall the minute the motorcade leaves that stretch. Do it in kilometer stretches or whatever it takes. I want a plan of action and an executive order drafted within the hour."

The words hung in the air, and the men drooped their heads, resigned to carrying out orders they disapproved of. Sometimes that happened, Kennedy knew. Sometimes, the President must make the unpopular decision, but he suspected the historians would view this one of the most dramatic gestures a president had ever undertaken.

"When will you tell the chancellor?" O'Donnell asked.

Kennedy stopped to consider the question. "I think it best to tell him in the car," he answered. "Then I won't put up with the arguments while waving to the people. Also, it means others won't be there to hear it earlier and leak it. Let's go, gentlemen. Today is going to be a big one."

He strode out of the room, leaving the men to their work and their own private thoughts.

10

Place: Presidential Suite, West Berlin, West Germany
Time: 12:45 a.m., Wednesday, June 26, 1963

A wink of light allowed Alan Spector to step through the rift in time and space. The sensation was odd to him, considering it had been over three years since he'd last made such a trip. Tingling left his hands and feet almost immediately, and he snapped his eyes back and forth, getting a sense of the corridor Urban had sent him to. It was shadowy, a far corner of the eighth floor of the hotel with John Kennedy just a few turns away.

Straining his ears, he could make out the shifting sounds of two guards, at the opposite end of the floor, talking. From his quick scan of the details sent down from Dianna Basehart, he knew that Andropov had used that distraction as his chance to make a move.

Reaching into his coat, he withdrew the standard-issue stun gun and thumbed off the safety, using his fingerprint to confirm identity. With catlike steps, he maneuvered closer to the first turn and, with each footstep, could make out more of the conversation. The topic was nothing lofty like the purpose of the President's visit or the significance of the role they were playing but a lament that the TV series *The Naked City* had been recently canceled by ABC.

He tried to avoid letting out a laugh and continued sneaking, probably following Andropov's very footsteps. The second turn was just as easy as the first, and then came one final corner and Alan Spector was presented with an unimpeded view of the President's suite door. He approached it with some concern; after all this was the President of the United States, a man he had studied and come to respect. His parents had also taught him to respect the office and the man who held it, like him or not. Spector liked Kennedy and wanted to do right by him.

Silently, he opened the door and Spector suddenly got the sense that he was near another person. It made him stop in his tracks and listen, afraid of being discovered. After a few moments he realized he was being silly and the feeling was from Andropov and Kennedy being so nearby.

Tensing for a call to action, the Time Warden crossed the main room and went for the door, which Andropov must have left ajar. That meant the assassin was just a few feet away and ready to make his attempt.

He took a deep breath, then another, and finally rushed forward, using a leg to smash the door open and startle the Russian.

Sure enough, there was the large man, dressed darkly, with a knife in his hand, swinging it from a high arc to a defensive position. The noise startled the slumbering body—bodies—and they began to stir. With a low growl, Andropov rushed forward, ready to dispatch the American, probably guessing him to be an extra Secret Service agent. His movements were swift enough to throw Spector off guard, and the stun gun was suddenly in too close range to be fired.

He ducked, allowing Andropov's momentum to carry him over the Warden's body. By then, the people behind him were awake and starting to ask questions.

Andropov righted himself and stabbed toward Spector, who dodged out of the way, falling against a table lamp, which went crashing to the carpet. The Russian approached, hefting the knife in a tight fist, obviously ready to make a killing blow.

That dull gray knife moved toward the staggered Spector when suddenly an ashtray smashed into the Russian's arm. The Warden spared a moment to look at the person throwing it and was stunned all over again to see a half-naked Angela Chance sitting up in bed, next to an equally half-naked John Kennedy.

Oh, great, he thought, she's gotten deep into her research.

Andropov shrugged off the distraction and hurled the knife forward, burying it in Spector's thigh, forcing him to scream in pain.

By then, the sounds had alerted the Secret Service, who came rushing in, guns at the ready. Chance screamed at their sight, and Spector heard curses from Kennedy. He knew this was going badly and he immediately activated the emergency recall signal, forcing himself a few hours into the future and where he was supposed to be.

Place: UPI Offices, West Berlin, West Germany
Time: 4:12 a.m., Wednesday, June 26, 1963

"Nice scratch, nick yourself shaving again?"

All Spector could do was moan softly as his colleague cleaned the wound, tending to him more like a battlefield medic than a soothing nurse. The wound was nasty to the skin but at least seemed to have left delicate tissue and muscle alone. Still, he knew full well that this would complicate the next day.

"Damn it! I nearly died!"

"Could have told you that," Urban muttered.

"What do you mean?"

"Right after I Beamed you, Basehart called back with the first three dozen scenarios from the computers. Someone dies in each version of you going back to stop Andropov. Usually it's you and Kennedy dies anyway. Sometimes it's Kennedy and you get arrested as an accomplice."

"Great. And how many postulated that our student-observer would be in bed next to the President?"

Urban paused, drying the wound with a clean cloth. "I'd say about ninety-five percent of them had her there."

"Lovely. So going back won't solve anything."

"Nope, now stay still." Urban began bandaging the injury with compact, tight movements, proving he had had some experience at this before. But of course, if asked, he would most likely not volunteer the information, so Spector bit his lip, mostly to control the pain.

"Okay, if that means we work in real time, I've wasted about thirty-five minutes subjective time and just cut my mobility by maybe a third."

"That sums it up," Urban agreed.

"Shit."

Time: 8 a.m.

In the seven years Peter Heinz had been covering German news, he had met with the great leaders of his own country. This morning was to be a first: speaking with another world leader. He liked that it was Kennedy, who seemed far more interesting a leader than Macmillan, de Gaulle, or any of the others on the continent. He supposed Marshal Tito might be fun to speak with or Mao Zedong, but he had little interest in communist issues. No, he was firm in letting the people elect their officials and policies. Communism hadn't made people's lives any better, especially with the Wall as an example of what it must take to keep people in line.

Seated in the hotel restaurant, in his best dark suit and blue patterned tie, Heinz was accompanied by Reuters's Waldo Von Erich and Associated Press's Lothar Shenck, both in gray suits and carrying large pads and pencils. Heinz preferred to work with an antique fountain pen, one his great-grandfather had used and passed down through the generations. It was smooth and never splattered, allowing his crisply kept notes to remain legible.

Their conversation was muted, each avoiding the kind of questions they had for Kennedy and none bringing a photographer, preferring to illustrate their interviews with pictures from the day's tour of Berlin. Although it was just eight o'clock in the morning, people were already lined up the entire thirty-five-mile stretch of the parade route. Police and army officers had set up the barricades two days before, and the first people had arrived yesterday, preferring to camp out under the early summer stars than miss a chance to see the great Kennedy close-up.

After a few minutes' wait over a cup of coffee, Robert Lochner arrived and greeted the journalists. He was blissfully unaware of what had truly happened seven floors above the restaurant and seemed joyful of the day's upcoming events. The journalists peppered him with questions about the President and how he got on with Adenauer or Erhard. Heinz had had the chance to interview the Old One privately the day before so had some idea what his opinion of the American was.

"Kennedy is a funny man," Lochner admitted. "He makes some nice jokes along the routes. No one knew who I was, seated in the car with other American officials, but if they saw me wave, they waved right back."

The banter kept up as time ticked off and the President was late in arriving. Waiters were pouring third cups of coffee when there was an increase in the volume of noise directly at the restaurant's entrance. It was easy to hear, considering the dining room was empty of people, cleared out by seven-thirty to make the room secure for the President. Secret Service agents were positioned by the entranceways in a larger than expected number. Heinz had some awareness of trouble in the hotel the previous night, but another journalist filed a report with Stein and he thought nothing about it, concentrating instead on the great leaders and their great thoughts about one another and the world they ruled.

Kennedy strode into the room, all smiles, his eyes bright and the crow's-feet around them making him look distinguished as opposed to aging. He was in a black suit, white shirt, and red striped tie, somber and serious for the day ahead; just right in Heinz's opinion. His Secret Service contingent remained by the entrance, keeping people from getting close and ensuring privacy during the interview.

Lochner made the introductions in English, and fortunately, all three journalists knew enough of the language to
keep up with the back and forth chatter, double-checking to
make sure Lochner didn't adulterate Kennedy's responses,
sort of acting as a censor on behalf of the German
government. Once the President and the others took their
seats, waiters arrived with fresh glasses of orange juice and
a truly American breakfast: sliced fruit, eggs over easy,
potatoes, two crisp strips of bacon, and a large basket full of
German breads and rolls. No one's opinion was asked; but
someone had arranged the meal in advance and everyone
was served simultaneously.

Since they were all seated at a table for eight, but were
just five, the journalists had room enough for their notebooks not to get in the way of their meal. Kennedy attacked
his plate with obvious hunger and asked questions of the
journalists so he could eat first and concentrate on answers
afterward. On the way downstairs he'd been quickly prepped
by Press Secretary Pierre Salinger on his inquisitors so he
seemed knowledgeable.

"Tell me, Mr. Heinz," Kennedy began, buttering a slice of
brown bread, "enjoying your tutelage under Stein?"

"Why, yes," Heinz began, a bit surprised, "Conrad Stein
is a fine editor. I'm surprised you know of him."

"With all that has happened here the last two years,"
Kennedy replied, "the wire reports from Berlin have kept
me informed. I think he does terrific work."

"I'll be sure to tell him, sir," the reporter added. A few
minutes later, he discussed his schooling, his wife Gretchen,
and his love of soccer. Similar details came from the other
reporters, all met with nods and polite comments from
Kennedy. He certainly gave the impression he cared at least
one whit about these three men, but no doubt it was a skill
Kennedy had developed in America. Politics in Germany
were still very staid affairs with none of the coast-to-coast
campaigning required by the democratic system. Debates
and policy speeches were more the norm, and the idea of
actually getting out and meeting the people was something
never done at the high levels of government. Erhard got to

be chancellor more for his accomplished works than the number of babies' cheeks he had kissed. Heinz was uncertain which manner of campaigning he preferred, given the somewhat colorless men holding office in Germany compared with real spitfires in America.

A few months after the Wall went up, Vice President Johnson had come to Berlin for a quick inspection of the monstrosity and to pledge America's support for the West German people. Heinz was there for the speech, which flooded the square with thousands of people and helped restore some measure of confidence in America. Johnson was nowhere near the skilled orator that Kennedy was, but he was a better raconteur, keeping the flock of reporters entertained with many wild stories about his version of America and politics. Ever since then, Heinz had always considered Kennedy and Johnson one of the oddest pairings of leaders he had ever encountered.

Pushing away his empty plate, Kennedy signaled a waiter to collect it and then looked directly at Von Erich. "Go ahead, fire away," he invited.

At first, Von Erich was thrown by the odd combination of words, but Lochner helped translate and he smiled. "Mr. President, what will happen after you leave?"

"You mean, what will happen to the German people? Well, I would like to think they will see a real display of American commitment to your happiness and freedom. No question, after today, some very clear signals will be sent that will be unmistakable."

Kennedy nodded toward Heinz. "Chancellor Adenauer told me yesterday that you two had engaged in much correspondence over the last few years. What sort of subjects did you discuss?"

"Chicken." At the quizzical expressions from the reporters, Kennedy indulged in a short laugh. "I would say about half the letters were discussing the tariffs issue, especially as it affected chickens. It seems the tariffs have helped fuel the European inflation that every country seems to be suffering under. The other half of the correspondence dealt with the issue of the European Community and whether or not the

EC really wants to do business with America. We certainly didn't start the debate."

"Anything else?"

"Well." Kennedy smiled, a twinkle in his eye. "We spoke so much about chicken, I had him send Jackie a few of his favorite recipes for when he came to visit." The men laughed politely.

"Has England or France been any more cooperative with you on the matter of the Berlin Wall?" asked Shenck.

Kennedy shook his head and said, "Not really. For the last two years we have had many meetings and discussions from the ambassadorial level through to the president and prime ministers. While we all condemn East Germany's actions, our varying opinions have prevented us from presenting as united a front as I had hoped back in the summer of 1961."

"We've heard rumors that the Americans had been told about the Wall years earlier but ignored the warnings," Heinz commented.

Kennedy shook his head once again. "Now that we have learned that American military command ignored warnings about the Japanese plan to bomb Pearl Harbor, many people believe we've been warned of every major event and allowed them to happen anyway. Trust me that we had no inkling the Wall was going up when it did. Had there been obvious signs, as there were in Cuba, we would have prevented the work from ever starting.

"I would like to think we will help slow down the Wall's buildup by just being here and rallying the German people. In fact, I hope to arrest the process entirely."

"Have you heard that they just tightened the restrictions in the last few days?" Heinz asked, probing further.

"Yes, Mr. Heinz, I was briefed on this before I arrived in Germany. I think it means the East German government or their Soviet masters are justifiably concerned. No one seems to like living in that city, under those barbaric conditions, and they seem to just harden the people's resolve to expect freedom."

"But how can they ever achieve it with the Wall getting

taller and the number of guards increasing?" Von Erich asked.

"What goes up must sooner or later come down, they tell me," Kennedy answered. Heinz thought the reply flip, but there was something in the man's eyes that belied that amused tone. "Premier Khrushchev cannot wall up the people in every city in every country under Soviet dominance. He could never erect a real Iron Curtain separating East from West. His actions will betray him one day, and the people will eventually rise up and demand control of their own destiny. I hope to see a day when Ulbricht will say no to Khrushchev and chart a fresh course for the German people."

"Then you believe in the unification issue?" Von Erich asked.

"I very much believe that if the German people, on both sides of the Wall, want to be together as one country, then that is their right. But people on both sides of the Wall must demand their freedom and joint destiny. America can be encouraging and we can certainly help when things get dire, as we did during the airlift a decade ago, but I ask you, is it our place to remove the Wall for you?"

"I wouldn't mind," Shenck admitted.

"I wouldn't either," Heinz concurred slowly. "But you're right, maybe we need to rise up with one voice and if we need help, have one people ask for your help."

"But would you give it, if asked?" Von Erich wanted to know.

Heinz watched the President's eyes seem to gaze on a point on the wall over Von Erich's shoulder. The expression on his handsome face was one of deep thought. Finally, after about a half minute's silence, he replied, "If a unified request came, I think I could commit America to helping take down the Wall. We never wanted it there in the first place and have long been criticized for our inaction. In fact, our commitment to your people has been called into question for allowing the Wall to go up. And I think it's a fair question and easily asked of all the Allied nations. But

I think our actions ultimately will have to speak for themselves. Trust me, you won't be disappointed."

Heinz had the impression Kennedy was testing out some phrases for his speech later in the day. Adenauer had admitted to him a day earlier that Kennedy seemed troubled over the speech he would make at the Wall. He needed it to be something different than what Johnson had said and something powerful. Heinz wondered which portions were being rehearsed for the reporters and what the final words would be. This was certainly one event he did not dare miss.

The cup of coffee had long since cooled and Chance didn't care. She sat curled up on a plush straight-back chair by the window of her hotel room. She had eaten a few bites of toast and sipped some orange juice but couldn't manage much else.

Her mind was aswirl with conflicting thoughts and images. A simple visit to the past with the hope of meeting Kennedy started off so well. She'd charmed the great man and got to see him at work and at play, confirming her fascination with the President. All along, a portion of her mind concentrated on drafting her paper, worrying about how to footnote such intimate experience.

Things shattered when the Russian showed up and nearly succeeded with the Soviets' plans. This was unexpected and certainly not in the research she'd so carefully conducted before coming back to 1963. Did she have anything to do with it? Probably. And where was the spy? Would he be back?

Angela tucked her feet back beneath her and idly watched cars move back and forth on the street before the hotel. There was virtually no trace of the mayhem visited upon the hotel just a few hours earlier. Typical German efficiency, she mused.

Her options seemed limited. She needed to be near Kennedy, one, because she liked him and wanted to see him deliver the famous speech. Two, she felt obligated to watch over him, ready to use her personal protection device to again keep him safe from Andropov. But she recognized that things were not going right at all. Seated in the bathroom, she'd heard enough of Kennedy's rants and the argument that followed to understand that he wanted to tear the Wall down. He was forging ahead, ignoring the advice from his most trusted friends and officers, and once again nearing the brink of war.

And none of this was in the history texts.

Something had changed and she most definitely had had something to do with it. The realization had hit her before, but this time it struck her with enough force to feel as if she were punched. Her legs dropped from beneath her and she felt more than a little short of breath. *Oh, great,* she thought, *I'm hyperventilating. That's not going to help Kennedy either.*

Her options seemed limited given her desires. In the back of her mind Chance knew she had to speak with Spector, warn him.

Seated in the private room behind the UPI offices, a dejected Spector connected with the Temporal Warden Corps to track the temporal wave. He was relieved to see his uptime counterpart Dianna Basehart look as tense as he felt. Her raven hair hung limply, and exhaustion crept into her cobalt eyes.

"Research shows that Gregor Andropov was captured and ultimately exchanged in an unpublicized swap of spies in 1968," Basehart reported.

"If he's loose, are the captured American spies significant?"

She shook her head in frustration. "We haven't tracked that yet, but it's obvious the nuclear path is what's causing all the trouble."

Spector swallowed hard. "I need to know so I have the terminal option."

"I understand, Alan," she said softly. While a more experienced Warden, she had yet to take a life, a point of pride among their peers. "We'll have that information shortly."

"So I have no choice but to act here and now in real time," he sighed.

She nodded in weary agreement. "We'll keep the computers humming, checking for anything else you need to know. Will your man Urban be there?"

"I'll have him check in frequently. I'll be in touch with him through the DA."

"Good luck, Alan. I can't remember a tougher case with more restrictions."

While she tried to sound encouraging, that last bit of news was of no comfort to 1963's potential savior.

"Aw, the Mets lost again," Spector said in mock amazement. The Time Warden was returning to the office, slipping back into character. The offices were humming along in typical big news fashion. Stein was on the phone, bellowing at Gruber the photographer for getting one key shot out of focus. Katrina Beck was typing away at something, a letter most likely, for her boss. Urban was already inputting stories for international consumption, just about all of them involving Kennedy being in town.

Once fully inside the offices, Spector went to his desk and looked at his blotter for phone messages. None awaited him, but the printout of American baseball scores was there for him as always. He always appreciated Katrina's kindness at that; scanning the constant roll of Teletype stories received for any news regarding America's national pastime. Little did the pretty secretary realize that Spector occasionally used his own computer from the future to monitor ball scores from his apartment. Still, it was a nice touch from a sweet kid. Looking over at her again, and paying attention to the curves for a change, he altered the thought, kid becoming a woman.

Urban, sweat already beading around his forehead, a cigarette going in his mouth, looked up in mock surprise at the comment. Everyone at Berlin's UPI office had gotten to learn more than they needed to know about the game. When Spector finished scanning the report, he leaned down, knowing full well this was to be a private conversation.

"Anything significant?"

"Nothing at all. The major change is still coming."

Urban looked extremely worried. "What if the change occurs before you can do anything about it?"

"I want you to keep an eye on the Teletype. Check everything as it comes across, and if anything at all surprises you, flag it for me."

"Does that include anything like the Mets winning a game?" Urban cracked.

"While surprising, it's unlikely Andropov's escape made any difference to the National League," Spector replied, heading back toward his desk.

Before he arrived there, Stein beckoned him over, still talking on the phone to Gruber. He stood patiently, listening to the fatherly advice delivered in hellfire and brimstone tones. The pain in his thigh throbbed, but he ignored it and did what he could to minimize any sign of a limp, which would only raise unnecessary questions. If Gruber was as good a listener as he was a photographer, he had a chance of becoming even better with Stein's help.

"Okay, fine, get to the Gate and be ready. I bet the crowds slow things up so be patient. Right. Uh-huh. The deadline is four so make sure you're in the dark room by three, got it? Okay. Good luck." Stein finally hung up the phone and passed some paper toward Spector.

"That's the official police report on the incident at the hotel last night," Stein began. "What do you think of it?"

Spector scanned the document with its official terms and language, mentioning the fire in the bed and the smoke conditions and the like. He knew it was a page full of lies but couldn't admit it. He had to play dumb.

"A simple fire in a hotel room would, at best, summon an ambulance and one fire company, right?" Spector nodded in agreement.

"I was told there were fifteen police cars, seven ambulances, and two fire companies jamming the streets. What does that tell you?"

"It means there was extra concern since it was where President Kennedy was sleeping."

Stein nodded but snatched the paper back. "No one else

bothered to follow this up, but I did because it felt wrong. Seems I'm the only one with a sense for news anymore. Of those seven ambulances, Spec, three left the hotel immediately and the others remained awhile and then quietly returned to their stations. Those three ambulances went to a hospital and now there's a security clampdown. Fire in the bed, my ass."

Once again, the Warden had deep respect for Stein's skills as a journalist and realized his years behind the desk hadn't diminished those instincts. He hoped he'd be so lucky in the years to come.

"Heinz and Gruber the wunderkind have the Kennedy visit covered tightly. I want you to nose around the hospitals and see if there's a real story hidden behind the official statement. Dig deep and pray for gold."

Spector returned to his desk and thought about the freedom the assignment provided him. He had already used the computer to double-check the names of the agents killed by Andropov and their lives didn't make any cosmic difference. If he could figure out the entire Andropov business, he would have a story of some sort for Stein that would justify his time out of the office. It left him free to pursue the wrinkle in time once it made itself apparent.

As he considered the next step, there was a burst of noise, and he looked up to see Heinz rush into the offices. Without stopping at his desk, he went straight into the bureau chief's domain and began reading aloud from his pad. Stein seemed to be paying great attention to the words and nodded a lot. Obviously the interview with Kennedy had gone well, and Heinz would have some time to get it in shape before having to run out and cover the motorcade. It was scheduled to begin its slow march in just another hour.

"That's terrific stuff, Peter," Stein said, ushering the man from his office. "If he's asking us to speak in one voice, then the people have a right to know that he's ready to stand behind them. Or at least printing the promise may mean we can hold him to it."

Heinz paused and turned to his boss. "He's a politician,

Conrad. American politicians never seem to live up to their promises."

"Kennedy hasn't failed us yet, Peter. Go write it up. This stuff beats the crap out of the puffery the *Tribune* ran today. Go. Go."

"No doubt about it, Kennedy is up to something," Heinz said airily as he returned to his desk, diagonally placed from Spector's. Both had identical old wooden desks, with typewriters, telephones, and used coffee cups. Spector never managed to keep his as neat as Heinz's and suspected the man came in at night to polish the wood to keep his just a bit shinier than everyone else's.

"What do you mean?"

"Well, I'm not entirely sure," Heinz admitted, looking at his notes once again. He selected a crisp white sheet of paper and rolled it, along with a worn sheet for backing, into the typewriter. "Kennedy made it out that he wants German unification. He even pledged support to bring down the Wall if the people on both sides wanted it." Heinz seemed to be typing an article he had mentally written since the flow of typing sounded rhythmic.

Spector, though, considered the admission from America's president. It didn't sound right, making that kind of an offer, through a journalist. Why volunteer to help raze the Wall when that would likely lead to greater troubles?

Still bothered by the train of thought, Spector slowly strolled back to where Urban was completing a story. The operator had stopped sweating but had seemed to develop a new habit of chain-smoking.

"Paul, can you get into the room unnoticed?"

"I've got a break coming up, why?"

"Scan the military frequencies for East and West," Spector said grimly. "Heinz got some juicy quotes from Kennedy that have me concerned. Make sure everything is calm on the channels and let me know."

"Sure, but why military?"

"The way that alarm sounded, if something was amiss, I'm afraid it might be a big problem, and in this day and age, that usually brought in the military somehow."

He hated to waste any precious time but needed to clear his thoughts and assess the situation beyond just Kennedy. That meant waiting for Urban to check the military radio, so he tried to at least present the image of a reporter digging for facts. The next hour moved slowly for Spector. He made routine calls to the hospital, innocently inquiring about patients matching the names of the dead Secret Service Agents, and was not at all surprised when he couldn't make a connection. The American Embassy was so involved in the parade that he had to leave a message and someone would call back tomorrow. The ambulance company said they never went near the hospital in question last night, furthering the cover-up.

Heinz was furiously typing away, forgetting all about copy length and just getting the Kennedy quotes into black and white for Stein's blue pencil. He had barely let up, stopping just once for a bathroom break, allowing Spector a chance to glance at the other quotes. All appeared harsher toward the Communist Party than Kennedy's other interviews since arriving in Germany. So last night's event must have angered him considerably. The question began to concern him, how angry?

The voices came through the static in short bursts, using terminology that threatened to give Urban a headache. For the last fifteen minutes he had given up the Teletype watch to eavesdrop on the armies from both Germanys. The uptime computers were sophisticated enough to allow him to monitor whatever he chose, and he made idle adjustments to fine-tune the reception. During that time, he tried to imagine Kennedy plunging Europe into a war. When did mankind learn to use the atom only for benign matters? History should have been a stronger part of his makeup, but he had had other things to think about and never gave it much priority.

When a rogue Time Warden tried to abolish the city where the corps was headquartered, Urban was severely injured. He recalled the blinding pain as a flash bomb went off, obliterating his home, his wife, and their pets. How he survived, trapped for three days under the remains of a ceiling, still mystified him. Just as Bill Mason knew which buttons to press to persuade Spector or any of the others to join up, Urban, too, succumbed to the man's gruff charm. While he didn't have the psychological or physical makeup to be an active agent, he still possessed enough engineering know-how to man the Berlin station.

In anticipation of someone being posted to West Berlin, he was sent back eighteen months earlier so he could get acclimated and start converting the unused portion of the building that housed UPI into an operations center. He had installed the Beamer and computers and was busily stocking supplies such as currency and costumes when Spector was Beamed in from uptime.

Using some discarded Teletype paper, Urban jotted down notations on the location of American jets being scrambled in other countries to mask the ultimate goal of the President's plan. As he did so, he considered his colleague, taking a moment to reassess him. Spector seemed like such an idealist to the scared older man. At first he was filled with enthusiasm for being alive and living in some other time and place. Within a year, though, when he had yet to be needed, despair began to color his manner. It was subtle and had been missed by the respected Stein. Urban noticed it, though, but had no way to find a common ground with him. They were too different, something Mason should have taken into account when the Warden's posting was made. Urban was out to stay alive, and he found such refuge by going out and dancing, drinking, and sampling the entertainment Germany had to offer. He did this to remind himself regularly he was still alive and functional. How he justified his life also forced him to exclude Spector except for the occasional meal, which was necessary for the two to be reminded that they were in this temporal business together.

Minutes flew by as Urban watched with complete concentration as the exchange of Western messages increased in volume and intensity. The scrolling data went by faster and faster, being stored in a buffer for retrieval and study as the

Teletype operator understood it. Finally, a bank of lights flashed red and the screen went blank. He stopped staring and went closer to the computer and hoped he could distill the information down for his colleague.

Urban finished reviewing the information and read it slowly. He scrolled back and read it again, his eyes growing wider.

"Oh, shit," he said and ran for the main offices.

"Where are you going to watch the speech from?"

Heinz had just about completed his article and paused long enough to look up at Katrina Beck. Spector watched with silent amusement. Heinz rarely noticed people when he was deep in his writing and usually snapped at those who broke his concentration. The sole exception was Katrina, and he never understood how she managed.

There was a lot about her he realized he didn't know.

That train of thought was derailed as he saw Urban briskly walk into the main office and make a beeline for his desk. The expression already told him things were not going well, but he needed details.

"What happened?"

Urban wiped at the sweat on his forehead, gathering his thoughts. "They've called in a squadron of fighters and summoned all available naval vessels from the Atlantic. They are on a complete military alert with leaves being canceled, men assembling at their bases, and a lot of cross talk. What is Kennedy up to?"

Spector thought hard about the flood of news and then heard Heinz rip the last sheet of paper from his typewriter. Things began to sickeningly fall into place.

"I think," he said in a hoarse whisper, "Kennedy intends to bring the Wall down."

Urban gaped.

"He wasn't supposed to do that," Urban said. "That Wall stays up for some time to come. Damn! What happened? What happened with Andropov? Was that girl there?"

"Listen, Paul," Spector urged, "I need to get out there and dig. Keep the computer monitoring the radio lines and I'll call in for updates. Don't say anything to anyone because now I have to stop World War Three."

11

Place: East Berlin, East Germany
Time: 10:28 a.m., Wednesday, June 26, 1963

"Ach, the lines are just terrible," Gerta complained, walking back into the shadowy tavern.

She had been gone nearly two hours, much longer than usual for milk and bread. "With so many people moved out of the new zone, you would think the lines would be shorter instead. Such is my luck."

"Did you see anyone you know," asked her son Peter.

"*Nein*," she replied. "But the talk is gloomier than ever. They're saying the prices of meat are expected to rise again next week and petrol is up as of today. Moving is going to be harder than we thought."

Peter patted her arm reassuringly. Then he turned to Elizabeth. "Okay, we have everything set. Nervous?"

Elizabeth Krause nodded once, her blond hair moving freely about her shoulders.

Hoyt nodded in agreement and filled a knapsack with clothing of differing shapes and colors. He seemed oblivious to the task at hand, his mind obviously kilometers away. Next to him, his father was slicing the bread to make sandwiches. He worked with an assured ease, having made countless meals during the tavern's life. Peter thought grimly that these would be the last such ones made in the building he knew as a second home. After a few minutes, Gerta arose and began filling a knapsack with various sandwiches and fruits, all wrapped tightly in wax paper. The older woman carefully laid each item atop a smattering of other belongings. Obviously, they could not escape with a great deal of personal effects, but they also would not try to go over empty-handed.

Wilhelm walked over to his wife, patted her shoulder, and nodded approvingly as she completed her task. She had finally stopped making negative noises, which were her only comments a day earlier. Gerta seemed particularly affected by the closing of the business and the forced relocation. Fortunately, she was a practical woman, something everyone liked about her, and Gerta set about organizing the Krauses' departure in addition to directing the packing of the bar.

While everyone bustled, Elizabeth noted her husband sat by the back of the building and brooded. He had planned their previous escape attempt and it had been dashed by the unexpected. Wolf had quickly grown fatalistic about their chances. Yet he remained determined to try again, if only so his wife saw the light of freedom. Her husband was perfectly willing to sacrifice his chances or his life so she could have the life they talked so much about since their marriage just three years earlier. She loved Wolf for it, but it also infuriated her, since he seemed willing to make his fears reality. They had argued late into the previous night and then slept fitfully in the back room. Their time alone together, of late, was rather limited and she regretted wasting it on a fight.

As they had done several times in the past, upon awakening, they kissed and cuddled, the fight forgotten. It was their devotion that began a series of discussions leading them to leave their home and journey to Berlin in an attempt to get past the security and be in the West. Such talking and planning was Wolf's way, Elizabeth knew, while she acted more impulsively. Their styles conflicted time and time again, but she knew that together they would compromise and find a common path. Teamwork had gotten them this far and nearly gotten them their freedom, so it was needed to work just one more time.

"Wolf? Sweetheart? Are you ready?"

The man unwrapped his arms from about his legs and turned around. His eyes cleared and he smiled faintly.

"Yes, Beth, I'm ready. Sorry to have been so little help, but I was lost in thought."

"Again," teased his wife, encouraging him.

"Again," echoed Peter, sealing the knapsack. He looked toward his mother as Gerta was completing her task. The knapsacks were gently placed on the ground next to Wolf's well-worn violin case.

"Hilda has borrowed a car from her brother so we must hurry. It'll take a while to make it over to the right place," Peter called. He clapped his hands together and rubbed them, anticipating getting under way. Elizabeth smiled, eager to get out of the building which had grown in her mind from refuge to prison. She walked over, tugged her husband's hand, and got him moving from the chair.

"I cannot thank you and your wife enough, Mr. Hoyt," she began. As she opened her mouth to say something else, she chose instead to throw her arms around him and hug, tears welling up all over again. "Thank you," she managed to whisper.

"You be careful, Elizabeth," Wilhelm said. "If you cannot get over, come back to us. We'll all start a new life here together and find some measure of happiness." He hugged her fiercely, and it briefly reminded Elizabeth of the hugs her father used to dispense with pleasing frequency.

She silently hugged Mrs. Hoyt while Wolf clasped hands with Wilhelm. He also said his thanks in a soft, quiet voice. Elizabeth couldn't read the emotion and allowed her concerns over his well-being to continue to grow.

Peter quickly kissed his parents good-bye and hefted the knapsacks in his hands, walking toward the entrance. Wolf opened the door, glanced about for the *Vopos*, found none and walked right out into the sunlight. Elizabeth followed, pausing briefly at the door to wave one final time to the Hoyts, realizing that if they were successful, she would never see them again. Swallowing back the emotions, she walked straight ahead.

Back in his suite, Kennedy beamed, happy with the way things were going. The more he thought about it, the more liberated he felt for having made the decision to destroy the Wall. He was convinced with each passing hour that history would find him doing the right thing, striking the right blow for democracy at the right time in history.

He hated the Wall and had hated it ever since Clifton arrived at his home in Hyannis Port, Massachusetts, on a beautiful summer day in August 1961 to break the news. It shattered the quietest month in the political year and began a series of events that brought him to Germany. He began to perceive this as his fate, and he was not one to deny the fates. Ever since his World War II experiences, there was a feeling he was toying with death, having cheated it once, and avoiding it at all costs. Last night was another example of that, although he was troubled over exactly why such an assassin would run. He thought he should know more about that but didn't. It nagged at him.

In the suite, controlled chaos had taken hold. Everyone seemed to be on the phone or typing memos or reports. Jacketed bellmen came and went with trays of beverages, and the noise level was steady. He paused to get some sense of what was happening and realized they were all doing his bidding. Although he had argued with them just a little while earlier, they were professionals and carrying out their orders.

O'Donnell turned to the President and gave him a half smile. Okay, they were doing his bidding and not too happy about it. He hoped they would change their minds when things happened the way he expected rather than the dire visions they entertained. What made them different was the anger that continued to fuel his mood.

"Where are we, Ken?"

Kennedy's old friend put down a phone, done with the call, and walked over. It seemed as if he regrew his daily beard stubble, but then Kennedy speculated O'Donnell hadn't bothered to shave at all. A little bit of a gray cast was along his chin line and made him seem older.

"Everyone is screaming. Everyone wants triple confirmations and we're handing them out pretty fast. Your Joint Chiefs of Staff are calling General Clay every fifteen minutes wondering if you've lost your mind. You haven't, have you?"

Kennedy smiled and shook his head.

"Well, Clay has everyone scrambling so you'll have your planes and missiles right on schedule. Sooner or later, someone will notice. What about the speech? Have you written your announcement yet?"

A negative shake had O'Donnell fall silent. Kennedy realized he had neatly considered how to phrase things, but they really needed to be written down. Glancing over, the secretary—Buford, was it?—was preparing some file folders when she noticed his gaze. She smiled at him, and he asked for the current draft of the speech. It was promptly handed over, with a pencil just in case. Kennedy took it, smiled his thanks, and began to walk back toward his bedroom, rereading the words he had struggled with just a day earlier.

"Eesh been . . . damn, I'll never get this right," Kennedy muttered. He tried the phonetic German phrase again and again, hearing some slight improvement with practice. Times like this he missed Jackie and began to wonder what she would think of his plan. Part of him hoped she would approve, but he suspected she would side with the others.

Reaching over, he picked up the phone from its cradle and asked for Chance's room. It rang four times and Kennedy was beginning to think she had checked out and moved on when he heard a click at the other end.

"Hello?" She sounded terrible, worn-out and exhausted. Maybe even scared.

"It's me," he said simply.

"How are you?" Angela started to sound more like herself.

"Fine, fine. Did you sleep at all?"

"No, not really. Too wired, I guess."

"Wired?"

"Hyped. Worried. I dunno."

"Will you be okay?" His voice carried genuine concern, not the professional veneer he had perfected as a politician in Massachusetts.

"I think so. Are . . . are you going ahead with your plans?"

"Yes, I am, Angela, and I think you, like the others, will see that I'm doing the right thing. I can't let Khrushchev think he can get away with insult after insult. I know I'm supposed to turn the other cheek, but I'm black-and-blue on both sides."

"You don't have to do this. Khrushchev won't last. They never do. . . ." She trailed off.

"Who never does?" He was slightly confused by her comments, worried about that wonderful mind being scarred by the incidents of the previous night. None of the spark or zest for life were evident in her voice.

"Don't worry about it, all right? So, when do you leave?"

"Just a few minutes. Listen, this isn't going very well. Why don't you come along like yesterday? I can have Ken set it up. Have you seen the Wall close up yet?"

"No, no I haven't."

"Well, then," he continued brightly, "come see it before it disappears. Meet Ken downstairs in five minutes." Hanging up, he smiled to himself and wondered if they'd have time for another encounter before he left the country. She certainly couldn't travel with the group, that would arouse too many suspicions, and the foreign journalists never exhibited the same restraint as the Americans. They were particularly rough in England, and the stop there could be dicey.

Looking over the speech, he began scribbling notes in the margins, adding phrases he needed to recall before standing at the Brandenburg Gate. He was running out of time. Then again, he considered happily, so was the Wall.

Angela was walking out of her bathroom, tossing aside a tissue marred with dark red lipstick, when there was a knock on the door. Thinking it was someone sent by Ken O'Donnell, she walked right over and opened the door.

It was Alan Spector.

"Oh, hi," she said, her voice betraying the tension and exhaustion she was feeling. "Come on in." He followed her into the small room, not even bothering to disguise the lame leg, and stood there, an expression of pain and concern on his face. She turned around and concluded this was a business meeting, nothing social about it.

"What happened?" His voice was fairly flat, without much emotion.

She shook her head and turned her back to the Temporal Warden. Walking toward the window and the seat she had curled in for so long, Chance wasn't sure what to say. Rather than fuss over phrasing, she sucked in a deep breath and then, suddenly in a rush, she told him everything since they'd last met.

His expression was unchanged as the story unfolded, and he nodded just once or twice as the tale was retold. Her student experience came in handy as she compressed events concisely, something that helped her during lectures. Was it just days ago she was in a lecture hall back home?

When she finished the long episode, Angela allowed herself another deep breath. Chance still felt uneasy about things, especially since nothing had gone as expected in the last forty-eight hours. Angela was completely uncertain of how things had unraveled so far so fast, but she also knew she was ill-equipped to fix things.

Spector finally unfolded his arms and took a few steps toward the window. Sunlight streamed through, reaching as far as the bed and brightening the room nicely. He remained silent, which began to worry Angela, who also knew she had to hurry if she was to meet the motorcade. Wow, motorcade. She had never ridden in one before this trip. Of course, they had pretty much stopped using such moving targets years before her birth, but it had figured so prominently in her studies that she'd often daydreamed about being a part of one.

Her thoughts were shattered when Spector finally spoke. His words were angry and harsh.

"This is just one lousy problem after another! Are you using anything?"

She was confused. "Narcotics, you mean?"

"Hell, no," he snapped. "Protection!"

"Oh, right," she replied. "Yes, the M-5 treatment. Perfectly fine."

"Good, then there's no chance for any little Kennedys to show up next year. Of course, that's just the beginning of a long list of temporal infractions, but we'll deal with all that when this is wrapped. What happened to Andropov?" His mind told him there were fewer than ten hours left to complete his task.

"I haven't a clue. The agents said he climbed a rope to another floor and vanished."

"Terrific. What are you doing now?"

"I've been invited to continue touring with him today and I'm late."

He stared at her with unbelieving eyes. "You're going? Are you nuts? Further contamination may escalate the time distortion! I haven't enough time for this! Don't go near him. Got it?"

She knew he was angry, especially with the alterations in time, but Angela was at a loss on how best to correct things. Of course, that was his job, but guilt was weighing heavily on her.

"This is a pivotal time in American politics which will influence the world," Angela said, her voice soft and without much emotion. She was as much speaking to herself as she was to her guest. As she continued, she seemed to ignore Spector and began to take slow steps around the hotel room.

"Kennedy was the first political media star, right? The camera loved him, loved Jackie and the children. At this

time, everyone could control what images would be recorded and it was all nicely manufactured. He could sleep
with a different woman every night of the week, and Walter
Cronkite would only report he handed out a citation to the
Boy Scouts. He was also young and a symbol to a new
generation of idealistic teenagers. His Peace Corps pro-
grams and the like were real stepping-stones for the major
generational changes unfolding across the country. And
what started in America would eventually sweep the world.
People like Adenauer and even Erhard would make way for
different leaders. You must know your German history, so
you know what these changes will eventually bring. It won't
be easy, God knows, but that Wall will come down and
these people will be united. And it all starts here. Today."

She paused, taking several breaths, and Spector studied
her. His own mind seemed to be working with her words,
and then he looked directly at her. With a little effort, he
drained the heat from his voice and said, "I admire
Kennedy, too. He's one of the major reasons I am here, in
this time. Although far from perfect, you'll agree, he was
the right president at the right time in America's develop-
ment. They had rested enough as a nation after World War
II, now they were ready to stand up and do something. It
leads them to the moon in another six years. I know all this.
And I agree, too, that Germany's current leaders will make
way for stronger voices. I like the fact that the German
people dismantled the Wall on their own and I want to
preserve that. That's why I need to change Kennedy's mind
and preserve history. This is what's right and I can't let it be
different. If I do, countless people will die in an unnecessary
nuclear war and the changes to the Earth may mean our time
is drastically altered, too. Trust me, Angela, I want to go
home someday. And when I do, it's to settle down and start
a life in my time. *My time*."

The emotions were suddenly turning to her own anger,
filling her stomach with a sudden flow of energy she hadn't
felt earlier. "I understand, but what can I do? He asked for
me and I want to be there. I can help him, Alan. I spared his
life once, and now with a killer on the loose, I might be able

to do it again. I'm responsible for this mess and I have to do something! I didn't ask for this to happen, right?"

"No?" Spector sounded exasperated. "Who bedded who? Of course you're responsible, and there'll be hell to pay one way or another."

"What do you mean? Can't I protect him while you fix things?"

"You can try," he conceded. "But your infraction, if unrepaired, will annihilate Earth and time as we know it. Even if I fix things, you're still liable for causing a temporal disruption. Inadvertent or not, these rules have been broken and you'll go uptime to answer for yourself."

Spector walked about the room, coiled anger in his step. She knew she had a convincing argument, and he was wrestling with ways to counterattack but was not coming up with anything he could plausibly use. Finally, he said, "You may think I have everything under control, but you are rather wrong, Miss Chance. You can stay with him, screw him again for all I care. I'll just run around Germany figuring out how to stop a squadron of fighters. Easy as pie. You bet."

The anger fled her and she felt some sympathy for the situation he was in. She walked over and placed a hand on his right forearm. They looked at each other, and she could see the anger seep out of his eyes. He was worried about his job, about the time stream, and the situation she helped put him in.

"I'm sorry, Alan," she said. "I screwed him and then screwed up."

12

Spector reached for the phone and called Urban at the UPI offices as Angela gathered up a handbag and rushed out the door to meet the motorcade. She certainly wasn't trained to figure out how to maneuver through an alien century during a crisis, Spector realized, and she was young enough to lack the experience required to do much good.

"United Press International, may I help you?" asked Katrina.

"Hi, Katrina," Spector said, trying to keep his voice bright. "Everything okay down there?"

"Sure, Spec," she replied. "Everyone is so excited about this parade, even Conrad is letting me off early to go hear the speech in person. Should be very exciting. Do you need something?"

"Has Conrad let Paul Urban out yet?"

"Nope, he's still pounding away in the back, hang on," she said. He heard the click as the line was paused, and he used the silence to let his mind race and consider his next steps after the call. No doubt there would be much ground to cover and he was without a car. On the other hand, most of Berlin's streets would be unappeasable given the security arrangements.

"Urban," came a familiar voice. In the background Spector could tell the Teletype was ticking off some other story so he knew exactly where his friend was in the office. It would be private enough for their needs.

"What's up?"

"The military radio bands are full of chatter," Urban began. "Fighter squadrons have been alerted, military units have been dispatched all along the Wall from one end to the next from the American sector. Not a word about protecting matters from the English or French sectors. Naval destroyers have been rerouted, and everyone is to keep radio contact to a minimum. They've got passwords galore and the new mission has already been dubbed Operation: London Bridge."

"I don't get it," Spector admitted.

"It's an old rhyme, I gather. 'London Bridge is falling down.' Not brilliant but serviceable and certainly not something the Communists would consider."

"This sounds too serious to be true, Paul."

"It's serious enough to scare the shit out of me," his friend agreed. There was a long pause. "Tell me you can fix this."

Spector was uncertain of how to answer the question. "I'm going to give this my best shot. It's all I can promise you. They didn't train me to fail, Paul, and I won't let Kennedy's name go down in history as the nuclear president. Okay, keep monitoring from the other room and I'll check back with you."

"I'm not too old to admit this really spooks me," Urban repeated. "Good luck, Alan."

Replacing the handset in its cradle, Spector looked out the window and could hear sirens in the distance, aware that the motorcade had started and the parade was officially under way. Being from the future had its advantages. Spector knew it would ultimately take four hours to traverse thirty-five miles, and the speech itself was nearly another quarter hour. So, with no more than six hours to go, he knew what his window of opportunity was. If only he had a clear idea of how best to convince the President, a man he had never met, to change his mind.

"Glorious day, isn't it?" Kennedy asked Lochner as the cars prepared to leave the curbside.

The President's spirits were strong and he wanted to commit each image and thought to memory, to preserve this day in glass and be able to look back on it as a highlight in a life filled with them. Seated in adjacent cars, the two men were parallel as the cars slowly followed the choreography that would take them from narrow side streets and straighten them out to a procession. White-jacketed German police were clearing roads, and a motorcycle escort was just ahead of the President.

In the car with him, as planned all along, were Mayor Willy Brandt and Chancellor Konrad Adenauer; the car behind him had Chancellor-elect Erhard, Lochner, and others. And behind them was the first of several buses filled with German diplomats and American representatives including Press Secretary Pierre Salinger, ranking U.S. diplomat Alan Lighter, Bundy, O'Donnell, Shriver, Jean Smith, and Chance. All in all, it was to make for a grand parade through Berlin's streets.

As Erhard's car pulled up, Kennedy and the soon-to-be chancellor had a moment to chat. "How do you handle these crowds?" he asked the President, through Lochner.

"They want to see you, and after all, they're the ones who ultimately elect you," Kennedy replied. "You soak up those good feelings and it'll empower you."

"We're not used to this sort of turnout," Erhard muttered darkly. He could hear the cheering in the near distance. "My arm will fall off before we make it to Brandenburg."

Kennedy chuckled and then reached out his left arm, bent at the elbow, hand stiff and swiveling only at the wrist. After a moment, he switched arms and repeated the motion with his right hand and arm. Erhard studied the motion, uncertain of the intent.

"See?" Kennedy asked. "You keep rotating arms so

neither one wears out. It also forces you to look out both sides of the car and no one gets ignored."

Erhard listened intently to Lochner's translation and then raised his right arm. He was stiffer than Kennedy but showed the right idea. Erhard repeated it with his left arm and cracked a smile. "I may have been wrong, Mr. President."

Kennedy laughed and then noted the cars were moving again; the parade was on.

Normally, Kennedy approved of the plans made by his staff, but today he was still slightly irritated to be alone in the car with Adenauer, the lame duck still clinging to power, and Mayor Brandt, with whom Kennedy had had periodic problems over the past two years. After the Wall went up, Brandt made the most noise in Berlin over the lack of U.S. response. He went so far as to correspond directly to Kennedy, rather than through the chancellor. To the American President, it seemed more that Brandt was grandstanding and trying to grab power from Adenauer. Instead, cooler heads prevailed, including foreign correspondent Maugerite Higgins.

When Kennedy was furiously belittling the efforts of Brandt to gain U.S. action in the days following the Wall's erection, Higgins demanded to see Brandt's own letters. "I must tell you frankly," he recalled her saying, "the suspicion is growing in Berlin that you're going to sell out the West Berliners." It was her interpretation of Brandt's correspondence that led him to believe the court of public opinion in West Germany was very different than the tepid one in Washington. It led to stronger support of the West Berlin people in the following weeks, culminating with Lyndon Johnson's trip later in the year. As a result, his opinion of Brandt softened and, although he chafed at being called a friend, Kennedy grew to respect the man. Still, two years later, he remained a bit uneasy around him, perhaps because he was as strong a political player in Germany as Kennedy was in America and like people don't always get along with one another.

And in the back of Kennedy's mind, he pictured jet

fighters looming larger with each passing moment. He tried to imagine which one would release the first bomb and whether or not that pilot should receive a medal. For a moment he tuned out Brandt's comments and tried to recall if the pilot of the *Enola Gay* was similarly decorated.

The thoughts were interrupted when the lead car rounded a corner and the motorcade reached the main route. Kennedy was caught off guard by the sea of people and the volume of their cheers. They must have been lined ten or twelve deep just to see the motorcade for a fleeting moment. He had just told Erhard that these were the real people of Germany and now here they were, close enough to touch.

Their smiles and cheers brought a large smile to the President's face, and he waved first to his left and then to his right.

"Hear that?"

"No, what?"

"In the distance, over the Wall. Sirens."

"*Ja,* so?"

"It has begun."

Elizabeth grabbed tightly to Wolf's hand and squeezed. She needed to draw strength from her husband, even though she knew they were both scared. The couple were following Peter out from between buildings along the outskirts of the new zone. Silence was prevalent, which proved unnerving after a while. She always imagined the city to have the sounds of life. East Berlin, this close to the Wall, had died. The new forbidden zone was another layer of cancer, eating away at the city's remaining vitality. From their vantage point, no one could see any guards in the vicinity. Border patrols, Peter assured them, took longer to cover the newly enlarged territory so slipping by wouldn't be a problem at first. Getting closer to the Wall would also mean increased scrutiny and chance for capture—and death.

Even after Peter called her attention to the far-off sound, she still could not discern it, which bothered her slightly. She usually had good enough hearing, but maybe her anxiety made her less aware than she should have been. That worried her anew.

"Look," Peter called, pointing an arm toward the watchtower to their right. Guards were clearly visible at the top, but their attention was turned to the growing throngs of people lining the streets and gathering near the Brandenburg Gate.

"If they're all so preoccupied, it'll be an ideal opportunity to get over," he announced.

Elizabeth hoped so but was uncertain.

Wolf looked around him and then shrugged his broad shoulders. "Which way?"

Peter and Elizabeth exchanged looks, and then Peter shrugged as well. "You pick, since I can't tell which way looks best."

With a grimace, Wolf Krause turned left and began hugging building after building as he led the trio along to the north. Silence was punctuated only by feet upon gravel or backpacks scraping against cement or brick. No one dared to say anything as they moved slowly, one building at a time. Then a block. After fifteen minutes, they were further from the watchtower, and breathing easier. No one passed them, no cars were heard in the zone. All was calm, eerily quiet.

The walking continued with great caution, although their speed increased with growing confidence. Elizabeth fretted over each building, wondering what had become of the occupants, their families, their friends. How many lives did the Wall disrupt or destroy? Would she and Wolf be another statistic of failure?

Finally, those fifteen minutes blossomed to an hour and the walking continued. No one dared say anything, but after clearing yet another block, Wolf raised a hand to slow the group to a stop. They were more than a kilometer, closer to two, from their starting point. On the other side of the Wall, a low hum of happy human voices permeated. Kennedy's appearance had obviously galvanized the Westerners and it made Elizabeth long to see something cheerful and good for a change. Not a single happy sight had greeted her and Wolf when they'd first arrived in East Berlin several days ago. A smile here or there, yes, but no one seemed to be enjoying their life. Cheerless lives were not at all what she had in mind when Wolf proposed, and she would do anything to find happiness again.

"This is pointless, Peter," Wolf said with resignation. "We've walked and walked and found nothing. Not a single opportunity. The Wall is solid, there are no ways over or under it that I can see. Did you spot anything?"

Hoyt slowly shook his head.

"I suppose we could try the other direction, toward the watchtower, but that will certainly be riskier and more than likely a waste of our time."

"Then what do we do, husband?" Elizabeth asked, frustration and fear evident in her voice.

"We keep going this way," Peter said, trying to sound firm.

Now Wolf shook his head, shoulders sagging in defeat.

"*Du bist doof.* I think not, Peter. We've come all this way and cannot cross over. We seem to be destined to live out our lives in East Germany. Come, I will buy us all a beer, and then Elizabeth and I will go back home. We'll try and restore some order to our lives and do what we can to make it a good one."

Stunned, Elizabeth shrieked, "Nooooo! You can't give up! Not after all this! We tried to be happy and couldn't. You were miserable, and we both won't let a new life into this part of the world! I want a family, Wolf; you promised me one. Don't make me go back! Don't!" As the words dissolved into sobs, she fell into Wolf's large, comforting arms. The hands stroked her blond hair and her back, containing the racking sobs as they shook her body.

She knew she had reached her limit and there was no energy left to fight. Her husband's embrace was the first truly good thing she had felt in a long time and she lingered, some small part of her enjoying his role as protector.

The sobbing ebbed after a few minutes and all was silent on the eastern side of the Wall once again. Peter had strolled a few hundred meters away, letting the couple have their privacy. He, in turn, seemed to be looking for alternatives. His expression told her that he wanted them to find their happiness as much as they themselves craved it.

When he returned, the look of despair in his eyes told her there were no alternatives left. Wolf was right. It was time to go home.

13

**Place: Checkpoint Charlie, American Sector,
West Berlin, West Germany
Time: 11:13 a.m., Wednesday, June 26, 1963**

The sun was warm and within minutes Spector began to
question the wisdom of wearing his black suit. He tried to
ignore the perspiration beginning to make him uncomfortable as he switched the small dark bag from one hand to the
other.

He was standing on line at the infamous Checkpoint
Charlie, waiting to cross into East Germany. With Kennedy
in the west, it was little surprise to the Temporal Warden that
the line was the shortest he had ever encountered it. Four
men and three women stood ahead of him, having their
papers and special passes scrupulously inspected by the
humorless *Vopos*. With the U.S. President nearby, the order
must have come down to do everything by the book, and
that meant scrupulous inspection of papers, bags, bulky
clothing, and the like.

Spector strained to recall if the itinerary included a stop
here, at one of the most infamous locales on the German
map. Daring escapes and tragic ends nested here in the

legend of the Wall, in just two short years. This was an
American checkpoint, run by the U.S. Army, but that did not
stop the *Vopos* from asserting themselves and rechecking
everything when people crossed over to their turf.

Passing the soldiers was no problem, and Spector even
surprised one with his flawless English. After matching the
photo on the pass with the person holding it, the soldier
began making a notation on a clipboard.

"Any word on Mantle's foot?" Spector asked idly.

The soldier seemed startled, and Spector was amused at
the thought that the language and question were nothing the
young man expected.

"I hear he'll be out until August," the American replied.
"You a Yankee fan?"

"Not really," Spector admitted. "I prefer the Red Sox,
since they have to try harder, but I'm also partial to the
Twins." After all, he had pitched several games for a
Minnesota team before signing with the Reds.

The soldier made a derisive noise. "All they have is
Killibrew and you don't win pennants with one hitter."

"Could be. Of course, teams have ridden one guy to the
top before. Look at Mays or Ruth."

The soldier smiled at the magic in the names. "Go on
through, dreamer," he said, waving Spector ahead.

Once across the American border, Spector walked down
a long pathway, noting the consistency of the concrete was
noticeably different between the two countries. The West
German material was smooth and well-worn after years of
existence as something previous. The East German stuff
was coarser and grittier, catching his polished loafer more
than once. It was newer and seemed to defy being worn into
anything resembling comfort.

The people ahead of him were obviously being put
through the drill all over again, where in previous visits,
they took a perfunctory look at the special passes and waved
them through. After all, no one ever tried to *break into* East
Germany. Today, though, the people shuffled with impa-
tience, and Spector cautiously glanced at his watch. The
motorcade was moving and there was little doubt that time

was being wasted. Still, he had few options and the one he was pursuing was the stuff of desperation—sort of like the manager calling for a suicide squeeze bunt with two out in the bottom of the ninth.

Finally, after fifteen irretrievable minutes, Spector was face-to-face with a forty-year-old *Vopo*. His boredom was evident as was the caution in his eyes. This was a career soldier, reduced to being a guard and obviously unhappy about it, Spector decided.

"Why are you coming to East Germany?"

"I have an appointment with Dr. Lazlo Kreizler, the famed psychologist."

"Never heard of him."

"Doesn't matter. I have, and we are consulting on a case. I must determine if my patient is suffering from a chemical imbalance or a serious mental deficiency. Since the patient can't come over, I'm bringing my information to him."

The solider gestured a gloved hand at the small bag in Spector's right hand. The Time Warden opened the bag and inside were a variety of authentic German medical supplies including some folded papers that were an actual case history he had stolen from a hospital some months ago.

The *Vopo* made an annoyed face, frustrated at never finding any interesting contraband—or was it an appealing bribe he sought?—and just waved him through.

Spector nodded in thanks and hurried ahead, making for the general direction of a medical center he had once visited but determined to get closer to the Wall and the real people of East Germany. Turning a corner, he stopped to gaze in wonder at the sight of East Berlin. The streets were empty for as far as he could see. Small one- and two-story homes dotted the perimeter of the new forbidden zone, and in at least two cases, he could see demolition work being done on these homes. From the construction materials piled up along the way, he concluded that the intent was to raze the homes in order to bolster the Wall.

In the last two years, the Wall had served as a visual aid to the world of what it was like to harbor a cancer in their own bodies. It began with thin razor-sharp rows of barbwire and quickly grew to become brick, mortars, and concrete. The work went fast in spots, so fast in fact that early portions of the Wall collapsed under its own weight. As people ignored the Wall and continued to meet and greet along the way, or simply step over the nuisance to leave East Germany, the army redoubled their efforts. Wire was replaced with thick stone, and suddenly neighbors and family could no longer touch. The Wall continued to extend its tendrils, threading its way through lakes, riverbeds, and fishing spots. The Wall consumed more and more man-hours; it demanded to be made bigger, thicker, stronger. Watchtowers were constructed and the checkpoints grew to just a handful, with the restrictions being tightened every few months. No one could see over it anymore from street level, no one could walk past it, nor could they swim under it.

The path of despair and destruction it carved was insidious and showed no signs of slowing its growth. In time, residents worried, the checkpoints themselves might have closed off entirely had it not been for the ever-changing Russian and German politics as well as the increasingly sophisticated world spotlight, in the form of television cameras. Pictures and reports from Germany made free citizens around the world howl in protest, and so the Russians kept the Wall up but the borders were, on occasion, grudgingly flexible.

The streets' silence unnerved Spector, for although he had studied the Wall and its bloody history, he had not spent all that much time on this side of it. Looking at the shuttered windows, abandoned cars, and piles of uncollected garbage, he sadly considered what it must have been like for people to suddenly find their lives turned upside down at the whim of a government more concerned with sending signals to presidents than in helping its people prosper.

He shook his head slowly, swallowed hard, and continued toward the Brandenburg Gate and his appointment with fate.

"Not very good, is it?" Kennedy asked repeatedly. He continued to refine his German pronunciation, reading and rereading his speech as time permitted. With each passing meter, Kennedy couldn't look at the rolled up papers at his side. Instead, he turned up the wattage of his smile and continued to acknowledge the outpouring of love and affection.

They had gone only a few kilometers and there seemed no end of heads, hands, signs, flowers. If anyone was protesting his appearance on German soil, Kennedy could not detect it.

"I'm not as bad as my brother Bobby," Kennedy confided to Adenauer. "I guess I ought to leave the foreign languages to Jackie."

Not sure of all the words, the Old One seemed to nod and then studied the crowds. In all his days as chancellor, he was assured not to have seen so many people gathered before to greet anyone—hometown hero or international statesman.

Satisfied, Kennedy looked out to the crowd, continuing to alternate arms and waves, soaking up the affection as much as the sunshine. At times his direct eye contact with people was broken unintentionally by the ultracautious Secret Service agents jogging alongside the car on both sides. Few wore hats in the summer heat, but most had dark sunglasses on, almost announcing who they were and why they were moving beside the President and chancellor. An endless stream of motorcycle-riding German police also buffered the traveling party from the people so even if Kennedy wanted to shake a hand or kiss a baby, he couldn't get close enough. The cyclists wore shiny helmets, goggles atop the brim; white-gloved hands staying on the handles; eyes straight ahead, making sure the approaching people posed no threat.

The President was used to the treatment and remained amused at the shocked expressions that wouldn't leave Adenauer's or Brandt's faces. Oh, yes, they loved the adulation being hurled at all three occupants and they beamed right back at their countrymen. Kennedy had earlier judged Brandt a political double, and he could tell Brandt would grow with such crowds while Adenauer seemed more aloof, not fully understanding why they were there. His time of leadership had definitely passed, and the American wondered what would happen if the world started to pass *him* by.

The cars had slowed to a crawl and finally stopped, as the drivers struggled to deal with the crowds. The politicians didn't seem to mind as they basked in the adulation. Automatically waving, one hand then the other, Kennedy's mind drifted from the here and now to just before this tedious procession had begun.

"Jack," a soft voice had called. Kennedy's mind lingered over the tone, the affection in his name. He turned and grinned when he spotted Angela approaching the procession. She smiled back in his memory, and they stepped toward one another, trying to get a moment's privacy amidst the cacophony surrounding them.

"Hi," he had said.

"Quite a show out there," she replied, but he knew there were things troubling her. For one, last night she couldn't take her eyes off his and today she wasn't meeting them.

"What's wrong? We don't have a lot of time for being coy," he insisted.

"Wrong?" She laughed hollowly. "You're taking the biggest risk of your life and you're asking me what's wrong?"

"My life has been full of risks. I almost didn't get elected, but I did. I took that risk, and I'm ready for this one."

"You risked everything in Cuba. Are you so certain this time? Then you had photos to support your goals and America believed you. What about this? You can't tell them what really happened last night."

Kennedy shook his head. "No, no I can't. But I can tell the world in a little while that America is tired of being ignored, tired of having bullies put barriers between families and neighbors. Absolutely, I can tell them that the Communists' day is over. When those planes shatter the Wall, Angela, it'll be like that folk song."

She looked at him blankly and shook her head. Nearby, Lochner had been starting toward them, pointedly looking at his watch.

"That folk song . . . hammer of justice, bell of freedom . . . you must know it. They sing the damned thing everywhere. Anyway, those missiles will be the hammer of justice and it has to be my hand swinging it. These people are looking to America for salvation and we've looked away long enough. So have you."

He had taken her face in his hands and given her a brief kiss. As Lochner finally approached, Kennedy's hands had dropped to his sides and he turned back to get in the car. She remained behind for a moment longer and then followed the others to her assigned bus.

That was nearly an hour ago, and Kennedy was still haunted by Angela's concern. The young woman seemed so earnest and she seemed to have more to say but never came out and said it. On the other hand, he was already involved back in Washington and could not possibly juggle one more intimate relationship. He'd have to break things off in Germany and make sure she knew not to contact him in America, much as he enjoyed her and her sharp intellect.

Kennedy wanted to make sure an aerial escort was ready to accompany Air Force One when it was leaving Germany. No doubt there would be a German or Russian response to the destruction of the Wall, but he had stared down Khrushchev once before. The blustering, bald Communist would not play the nuclear trump card. Kennedy was certain of it. The signals he had been receiving all along indicated that had he made a stand two years ago, the barbwire would never have metamorphosed into the monstrosity he was faced with today. Absolutely, he had to bring that Wall down and reassert his supremacy as leader of the Western World. Mentally, he flipped an obscene gesture at de Gaulle.

The suit was definitely a mistake, Spector concluded as he walked through the deserted streets. At least no one was there to catch the Time Warden in the forbidden zone. The eerie silence was oddly comforting to the agent as he walked along, considering his plan and weighing it against the others he had already rejected. And he rejected them all again. His plan was the only one that had some margin of success. Or so he thought.

The implant chronometer continued to rationally count down the minutes, and he was desperate to find out what was really going on. Again, he was fortunate not to be surrounded by people as his hands opened the faux medical bag and pulled out a small device, buried beneath the authentic tools of the trade. Placing the bag at his feet, Spector expertly extended the small antenna from the bottom of the device and pressed in two digits.

Within moments, the communications device had connected directly to the UPI offices, bouncing its powerful signal off a German weather satellite that had been launched the previous year. Since it was a signal no one had conceived of, no one could know to look for it and therefore it was as secure as any military channel.

"Urban. Spector, where the hell are you?"

"I'm in East Germany, near Otto Grote Wohl Street, heading toward the Gate."

"I'm stumped, why are you there?"

"No real time to get into it, Paul. I need the military update."

"The East Germans have figured out something is up and they're in a panic, from what I can tell. This happened without any warning whatsoever, and they even stood down from their normal alert status since no one thought Kennedy would turn out to be a lunatic. They're scrambling and might have planes in the air soon. Thing is, they won't be at the Wall in time and the debates on the open channels are fascinating. They don't know what's up or how to react."

"Any sense if the rest of the world is aware of all this?"

"Not yet. Even the West German army is just now getting the signal that something is up. By the time of that speech, the panic should be global. Now tell me again how you intend to stop this all by yourself?"

"Tell you as soon as I have it all figured out. I'll check back later."

He stuffed the device deep into the bag and resumed walking, deciding he needed a cool drink and a better sense of the East Berlin mood. All he needed was one good, populated street and he'd be set. Straining his ears, Spector tried to discern sounds that might mean a population center.

Hearing nothing, Spector shrugged and continued walking further away from the Wall, exiting the forbidden zone and entering East Berlin. He was determined to locate some place of note, and he felt the urgency make his legs move just a bit faster.

Finally, after another five minutes, he found people on the streets. Most were lined up in front of food shops or general stores, spending their hard-earned salaries on the basic necessities of life. Some children chased each other, their long hair flying freely and reflecting the sunshine. Others clustered by corners and chatted amongst themselves, ignoring the approaching Temporal Warden. He was surprised at how comforting the hubbub of human life was and how much more he preferred it to the desolation of the zone.

Walking along the street, he finally spied a sign signifying a tavern and decided to go in, get his drink, and figure out the next, crucial step.

The tavern was old, entirely constructed of dark wood that seemed to soak in the light. It was already smoky despite the early hour of the day, and the mix of cigarettes, cigars, and pipes was heady. Thick wooden tables lined three walls, and the fourth had the length of the bar attached. Taps were spaced evenly down the bar, and two bartenders worked the room, chatting along the way, usually bursting someone's joke by giving away the punch line. The bartenders chortled more than laughed, enjoying the mean fun they were having at their customers' expense.

About twenty-five men and seven women were in the tavern, most at tables and just a few at the bar itself. Spector smiled as he took all this in and enjoyed the comfortable feeling he sensed from the room. No one seemed to care about his arrival, which reassured him. These were the innocents, those the conflict was ultimately about, but none were invited to join in the political debate. Yet they were the ones taxed and overworked to feed the coffers of a government determined to make their lives even harder than they were a generation ago.

Moving toward the bar, Spector studied the faces at the various tables, absorbing some sense of who these people were. His eyes were drawn to a table near the far corner and the three people hunched over steins of beer and a plate with the remains of a single sandwich. Unlike most of the others, these three were talking only to each other and ignored the others around them. Looking at them further, Spector noted the ripped jacket of the man whose back was to him. The woman's blond hair, still pulled back, clinched it.

These were the people whose escape attempt he had ruined.

Spector broke into a smile and went to the bar, ordering up four beers. As the first two were drawn, Spector put down some coins he had in his suit coat and carried the beers to the rear.

Standing over the table, Spector said, "Excuse me, my friends. I owe you an apology."

Startled by the words, the woman's eyes grew wide and she shifted closer toward the wall. The other man looked up without comprehension. The man Spector addressed looked up, and his eyes narrowed as he recognized Spector.

Standing, the man seemed to be moving, getting ready to shake hands or make introductions, Spector thought.

Instead, a balled fist shot up and struck Spector square in the gut, knocking out air and making him grunt loudly.

He also fell against the wall and slipped to the floor, his medical bag dropping moments before his butt found the bottom.

14

**Place: Brandenburg Gate, West Berlin, West Germany
Time: 12:17 p.m., Wednesday, June 26, 1963**

The cars slowed and Kennedy craned his neck to get a better look at what lay ahead. There before him was the Brandenburg Gate, an immense structure that symbolized the division between the Berlins and Germanys.

More surprising was the throng of people flooding the *Platz*, or square by the Gate.

"I'll be damned," Kennedy muttered. He glanced to his left and saw similarly surprised expressions on his colleagues' faces.

There had to be thousands upon thousands of people crushed into the area. They were cheering and shouting, and only a small percentage could possibly see him. The motorcade had pulled in to the crowd's left, and the cheers went up in volume as the first motorcycles entered the area and continued to rise in volume as the presidential car pulled up.

"There are even more people by the Town Hall and you're not due there for another hour or so," Lochner commented, as he walked over toward the lead car.

Kennedy didn't acknowledge the comment but continued to stare at the Wall. His emotions were getting the better of him, and he felt the new surge of anger and adrenaline fill him with nervous energy. Despite his chronic back pain, he wanted to be closer, within spitting distance of the Wall itself. "Get me up there," he called out.

"Yes, sir," General Clifton responded. "The Wall itself also presents dual problems."

"What do you mean?" Kennedy asked, suddenly alert to Clifton's concerned tone.

"Once you survey the Wall, you can be a target to East or West sharpshooters."

"But," Kennedy replied, "the army has swept the area, right?"

"Affirmative. Sir, you'll have to go through the protocols," Clifton said.

"What do you mean?"

"To walk the Wall you need to be the Duty Officer."

Kennedy waved an impatient hand. "Whatever. Let's do it."

John Kennedy considered the Berlin Wall itself. He desperately wanted to see it and was willing to make himself a target, but his actions should not put others needlessly at risk. Turning about, he studied the entourage awaiting the signal to head up the stairs to the Gate. Clustered nearby were his sisters, Jean Kennedy Smith and Eunice Shriver, Angela, and Bundy. Elected or appointed representatives were one thing, civilians were another.

"Ted, I don't want Jean or Eunice coming up there."

Clifton nodded, obviously pleased with the command.

Kennedy looked once more at his sisters, his only family members along for the trip. His brothers Bobby and Ted had come to Germany a year earlier, which was one reason they'd missed this European swing, but he regretted not having their familiar counsel. He mused at whether or not they would agree. Bobby was more pragmatic than Ted, who was younger and more given to impulses like the President. He then zeroed in on Angela and reached out to grab the general's arm, drawing him closer.

"Don't let any woman go up there with me."

Clifton looked over and spotted Angela, knowing exactly what Kennedy meant. As it was, they lied to his sisters about who Angela was, but she was no fool. It was plainly obvious she was Kennedy's bedmate and companion—Smith had endured many of these over the years.

"Okay, let's go see the top," Kennedy said.

Paul Urban completed sending off a brief story, updating all on the presidential visit, and then switched off his goose-necked desk lamp. He was alone at the UPI offices and was uncertain if that was a good thing or not. After all, only he knew what was really happening around the country, and the thoughts continued to terrify him.

He swiveled around in his chair and straightened his rolled up shirtsleeves. With careful steps, he returned to the secret room and once more powered up the computer equipment that would provide him with amazing access to information that was short of the occult. Unlike his Tele-type, the computers purred more like a cat, and their lights signaled the work progressing.

A screen blinked to life and information immediately began scrolling across. Urban watched as first West German and then American armed forces were recorded. The information was not at all heartening.

He knew time was getting critical; there was still time to abort the mission but the closer the jets got to the Wall, the more likely they would be engaged by the East Germans. As he punched in a new instruction, the screen changed information streams and began spitting out facts from the East German military radio.

"They're still panicked," Urban said to himself. The army was still assembling but without marching orders. Nothing was going on with their naval forces, and they seemed to be waiting for direct communications from the Kremlin before sending a single plane into the air. There was no doubt that they wanted to be cautious and not start a war no one was prepared to wage.

With another few commands, hard copy information was

being silently printed to his right, all going into a file folder kept buried in his desk. If they ever survived the encounter, the information would make a great report for Spector's masters or a terrific book during Urban's retirement.

"How in the hell could they build that without our knowing about it in advance?"

Kennedy didn't look at Ted Clifton when he asked the question, and he hoped the general realized it was rhetorical. Atop the Wall, Kennedy used hands to shield his eyes as he scanned East Germany for the first time. Unfortunately, much of what he saw was red.

Three gigantic blood-red banners hung over the Brandenburg Gate, preventing Kennedy from getting a good look into East Germany. Or letting the East Germans get a peek at a potential savior.

"It's an offense against humanity," he muttered to those surrounding him.

Still, Kennedy could see glimpses of the other country and he was a little surprised to see that the buildings and streets seemed just like the ones here in West Berlin. He chided himself for expecting anything different, since it was just two short years ago that the Wall went up.

At the memory of that Sunday afternoon, Kennedy's anger flared anew.

The East Germans were not at all foolish, erecting the barbwire "wall" and closing all but thirteen of the eighty-eight pathways between the Berlins at one in the morning. Panicky communications between Berlin and Washington were slow and built up to a fever pitch as the sun first arose over Berlin and then, six hours later, over America's capital.

Kennedy's young hotshots, shaking up the status quo in formally Republican Washington, bungled the importance of the information. For example, Prime Minister Harold Macmillan knew within a few short hours and was already meeting with his advisors before Kennedy even woke up. At first, the intelligence officers discounted the panic, feeling the German mind-set had affected the Americans stationed there. That mind-set was simply that Berlin was the center of the universe.

They didn't want to trouble the President, knowing his penchant for keeping weekends trouble free. Kennedy, blissfully ignorant, went to Mass, ate a light lunch, and then joined his wife Jackie and father Joe on the cabin cruiser *Marlin*. It was just about one p.m. when the Secret Service agent aboard the cruiser received word they needed to turn around and come to shore. Fuming, Kennedy demanded to know what was so important. The word was handed to him by Clifton, dubbed "Watchman" by military protocol.

The one-page telex told Kennedy just enough but not the full story, and he was angry first at East Berlin and then at his own people for letting this fester. The Wall had gone up seventeen hours earlier, and he was only then getting the first news reports.

Upon further reflection, Kennedy also was amazed at the lack of urgency the Wall elicited from his own people. It opened his administration to worldwide charges of being soft on the Communists and their actions. That slowly began to fan the flame of anger that had finally erupted the night before. He also knew that his own strategists ignored warnings on file from as early as 1958 that the Wall was a serious East German option. It led him to bitterly complain much later, "Why, with all those plans, do you never have one for what happens?"

It was oddly comforting to have Clifton, his "Watchman" beside him at the Wall. They learned of it together and now witnessed it side by side. Kennedy remained rigid with anger and frustration, feeling mocked by the Wall. Again, he concluded he had made the right decision.

As acting Duty Officer, Kennedy walked up the wooden stairs which irritated the flaring pain and made him wince once or twice. It continued to feed the angry fire he felt in the pit of his stomach.

He was distracted when his attention was caught by something waving in the wind. Looking closer, he saw three women leaning out of a drab brick building, holding handkerchiefs.

Turning to General James Polke, the American military commander in Berlin, he asked, "Isn't that dangerous?"

"Yes, it is."

There was nothing left to see, nothing left to say. Kennedy sadly looked down and descended the stairs. At the bottom, Kennedy was cheered anew and he waved, flashing a smile that felt dishonest. He wasn't happy at that moment. He was frustrated that it had taken this long to act, frustrated that the Communists were openly mocking the Free World with this construct, and frustrated that he had to wait a few more hours to witness a new chapter for the history books.

As he strolled back to the car, winking at his sisters to prove he was safe and sound, a military guard approached him carrying a bouquet of flowers.

"What's this, Sergeant?" Kennedy asked, slowing down.

"This was passed over the Wall, from East Berlin, sir," the young man replied.

Kennedy hefted the flowers, trying to notice the fragrance, uncertain of which species they were. The bouquet moved him deeply, and he felt the symbol of hope they represented and what America meant to people on both sides of the Wall. There was no doubt left that the air strike was going to change the world. All he had to do was finish the tour and make the speech. The fighters should already be in the air.

Rubbing his face, Spector warily watched Wolf Krause down the last of his beer. Wiping a hand across his mouth, Wolf seemed a lot less angry and almost content. Reaching across the table, he helped himself to the untouched stein before the Time Warden and set it before himself.

"Forgive me yet?" Spector asked.

"No," Wolf said, a hard tone remaining in his voice.

"I didn't want to ruin your plan. I was too preoccupied with my own problems to notice yours until too late. I just didn't see a way around it," the Time Warden continued. He was suddenly alarmed at the thought bouncing again and again through his mind. His actions the other day had spoiled their escape attempt. What if they were destined to cross over? He needed their names and to have Basehart run them through the computer. Their destiny might be significant enough to help trigger the Priority Two alert, pushing the temporal wave faster. No question he had a moral imperative to aid them but he also had bigger factors pushing him to act.

"Who are you?" Peter demanded.

Spector smiled a little and signaled for a new round of beers. "My name is Alan Spector and I'm a reporter for United Press International."

"We used to see UPI stories all the time . . . before . . ." Elizabeth muttered.

"I understand," Spector said kindly. "I'm working on a special assignment and needed to be here for my work."

"So why the doctor bag, Mr. Reporter?" Wolf asked suspiciously.

"Give me a chance and I think I can make everything clear," Spector said calmly. He was working really hard to be friendly and reassuring. While taking their measure, he was considering how he could make things up to them, since the guilt was still with him from days earlier. If they could come to trust him, they might provide the answer to his needs and he had to decide soon. Talk was nice, but he was wasting precious minutes.

"Well, I'm Elizabeth Krause and this is my husband Wolf," she said, gesturing to the glaring man, who began drinking Spector's beer.

"This is our guardian angel, Peter Hoyt," Wolf grumbled. Hoyt nodded silently, suspiciously, watching.

"Why were you trying to leave your country?"

"We're Germans, Spector. Not East Germans or Communists or any of that shit. We're Germans and what we like about our country has been altered beyond recognition."

Spector remained silent, hoping Wolf would continue.

"We work longer hours, harder hours, and have less to show for it," Elizabeth offered. "I tried to be a primary teacher and I loved working with the children. But then, a while back, they started giving me revised textbooks. The information was wrong, distorting the facts, including facts from my own lifetime. I cannot lie to children. And I won't have any children in this poisoned land."

Spector nodded sympathetically, understanding the deep emotions behind the words.

"If I resigned in protest, they would hound me," Elizabeth added. "I couldn't do anything but just leave. My heart breaks when I think about those little faces I left behind. Without children of my own, they were all a little like my own."

There was an uncomfortable silence for several moments as the Time Warden allowed her to stem the tears gathering around her eyes. He averted his stare and turned his attention instead on her husband. "And you, Wolf?" Spector asked.

Krause stared back, keeping silent and sipping the beer. He remained uncertain, Spector decided, and didn't want to reveal his true, softer nature.

"I was a musician . . ." he began.

"He plays such a beautiful viola," his wife interjected.

Wolf glanced over at her, nodded in appreciation, and then turned his attention back to the reporter. "I'm with a state-controlled orchestra, playing in our home in Leipzig. Of course, with the state asserting itself, they chose what we could play. They chose everything for us. Our schedule, our clothing, our travel arrangements. Elizabeth could no longer come with me if school was not in session. I felt confined. The music was no longer sweet."

"It was killing him," she added.

"*Ja*, I suppose so. We never really traveled ourselves. We grew up in Leipzig and haven't seen much of our own country on our own. When we decided to try and leave for the West, we had to get help."

"That's where you came in?" Spector asked of Hoyt.

Peter nodded, keeping his own counsel and concentrating on his cigarette.

"His family grew up near us," Elizabeth said helpfully, having regained her self-control. "They came to Berlin about ten years ago, but we have kept in touch. Peter has come back to visit and is like a brother to us. He has been so good to us, as have his parents."

"I see," Spector said noncommittally. Things might work together rather elegantly—if only things remained calm until he could return to the West.

"Can you help us?" Elizabeth asked, fidgeting with her own stein, only half drained.

"He can help get you killed," Peter quipped, leaning back and lighting another cigarette.

"I might," Spector replied. "And then again, I might find a way to get you across and make things up to you."

The words settled over the wary trio, and only Elizabeth smiled at the thought. "Can you?"

"Maybe. I have need of some people for an important task, and if you're game, then I get your help and then afterward I can get you free."

"What do they do," Peter asked snidely, "pretend to be your prisoners? Just waltz up to the stinking *Vopos* and ask to be admitted?"

Spector chuckled and shook his head. "Nothing so simple. Let me explain as much as I can and we'll see if you're still willing. If you agree, and I get you over, I promise I will help set you up." He looked directly at Peter, sensing the suspicion from the family friend. "Will you be coming with us? You're not in my plans but I'm flexible."

Peter thought about the question and the obvious opportunity for something brand-new. "*Nein*," he finally replied. "They are my friends, my family. I will help you get them over, but I will stay here and help my parents start over."

It was a short while later when Spector signaled to the trio, huddled in a deep doorway of a quiet apartment building. People milled about, ignoring the three people, who tried gamely not to look like fugitives. They had traveled several blocks from the tavern and had remained relatively silent after Spector's plan was heard and approved.

To the Temporal Warden, it felt like the only plan, and he kept things moving, worrying about the time, worrying about the Krauses' resolve. Like any good baseball manager, he realized, there came a time when you trusted your instincts and your players. It made good managers great ones, like Stengel was or Hodges would be. He disliked the showboats or master strategists who moved his players around like checkers. Guys like Leo Durocher or Tony LaRussa were on that list, one Spector mentally tallied and revised as he continued to research players in his off-hours.

Right now, though, he had to be a player-manager and get moving. The *Vopos'* garage was usually undermanned, and he suspected that would be the case with increased activity along the Wall itself. His hope was to get a car, drive right over, and be done within half an hour. First came the car and that meant bypassing the guard.

No clever or convincing scheme came to mind so it meant taking the guard out as painlessly—and noiselessly—as possible. Spector walked toward the uniformed officer, noting his stocky build and greater height, measuring him up. In turn, the guard took notice of the approaching man and squinted in the sunlight. His expression was unchanged, but he kept studying the man.

"I'm sorry, I'm lost," Spector said in heavily accented French. The guard was taken by surprise by the foreign language and had trouble making out the words or intent. Spector stood as unassuming as possible, gingerly holding his medical bag, which would continue to act as a convincing prop.

"*Was?*" asked the guard, who took a step forward.

"I'm lost," Spector said again, this time in English. The guard didn't seem to know that language either and shook his head to express his incomprehension.

Spector shrugged and seemed to ponder what to do next. He inched closer to the guard, who made no move toward his holstered pistol. As the two men got closer, Spector suddenly lunged forward, driving both fists into the guard's midsection, and then clasped his hands and drove them hard against the back of the man's neck. A foot lashed out twice rapidly, and the guard was sprawled, senseless.

Sparing a moment to make sure his newfound colleagues had paid attention, he slipped a hand into the bag and removed a small vial, snapping off the plastic sealed top. The vial was one of several narcotics he had brought with him from the secret supply room he maintained back at the UPI. This particular substance was an airborne drug that would render any man unconscious for at least an hour, plenty of time to steal the car and get away before anyone noticed.

He glanced at his watch and then looked across the street at his friends. Lifting his right hand, fingers spread apart, he indicated a five-minute mark and then pointed in the direction of the checkpoint gate. Wolf and Elizabeth seemed uncertain about moving, but Peter waved in acknowledgment and gently pushed his friends into motion.

Something told Spector that Peter had seen some combat at some point. He was decisive, loyal, and understood the plan the first time he outlined it, asking incisive questions. Any question about his background was deflected, retaining his sense of privacy.

They moved off to complete their portion of the plan while he secured the transportation. What he needed was something small and simple that three people would look perfectly normal in. He reached down and relieved the unconscious guard of his keys, clipped to the wide leather belt. On the fourth try, he found the key to the garage door and Spector stepped inside.

The garage itself was a simple, open concrete space with racks of supplies and a repair bay to the right. Low lights dotted the room, casting pools of light, creating a lot of shadows that would make it tough to find people at night. He stepped back through the doorway and grasped the guard, dragging him into the building. It was a tougher task than imagined, given Spector's slighter frame and the deadweight of the slumbering guard. Spector moved him toward the repair bay and left him stuffed under a workbench so no one would find him easily.

Looking around once more, Spector was disappointed to note there were only huge, lumbering trucks inside. All the cars must have been pressed into use, moving the personnel to new spots. He mentally shrugged and decided he would have to make do. In some ways the truck would provide better protection, but he wondered what it would be like to drive one. He had practiced in Urban's car over the years, making sure he had the instincts right. The automobile was still one of the more fascinating changes to the world and something he was glad not to have missed. Driving uptime was too smooth and controlled for his taste. He liked having his hands on the wheel, the car totally at his command.

Against one wall was a rack with keys and license numbers written on bits of white tape. A quick scan told Spector which was the nearest truck, so he snatched a small key ring on the second row and headed toward it. On his way, though, he spotted a shortwave radio setup near the work bay. The Warden was not sure how he'd managed to miss that, but he was bent nearly double in order to move the guard. Figuring it would pay to tune in, he quickly went over and brought the machinery to life. As vacuum tubes warmed up, he continued to scan the vicinity in case he'd missed anything else of note. Vehicle requisitions, fuel supply reports, and other mundane matters were all he could find, but he gave up when he heard the static of a live channel come through a small speaker.

Tuning the radio carefully, Spector listened closely and heard the conflicting orders crisscross the radio. Whoever should have been in charge was doing a poor job of it, so opportunistic military officers barked orders to anyone who would listen. It brought a chuckle to Spector, who couldn't imagine a bureaucracy so inept existing back in his home time. He was disturbed to hear, though, orders to beef up the guards at all the checkpoints and to close them down at a moment's notice. Now, that would complicate things for Spector and company. His forged papers would help him, not the Krauses. He might have to revise his plan just a bit.

No doubt about it, he considered as he climbed into a green and black, mud-caked, nine-ton truck, he needed to get back across the Wall and reach Kennedy before the East Germans had their plans in place and could repel any West German attacks.

Kennedy was no doubt already giving the speech that had started this entire mission. The speech Angela Chance came back to hear.

15

Place: West Berlin, West Germany
Time: 12:43 p.m., Wednesday, June 26, 1963

The motorcade was practically crawling through the streets of Berlin. With the Wall to his left, Kennedy waved and smiled, enjoying the cheers. Adenauer and Brandt continued to seem overwhelmed by the experience but also grew to like soaking up the exposure next to the American President. It seemed as if every fifth person in the crowd had a banner or a camera. No doubt hundreds of amateur pictures were being snapped to record this historic day. Kennedy liked the idea of preserving things for the history books. A true scholar, he often imagined how the historians would interpret his collected speeches and written works. All of that was one reason he was so often accompanied by Ted Sorenson, sort of his personal biographer, and the one man Kennedy felt truly understood the context of his life and career.

Radio traffic between the cars and the motorcycle escort had been going on for a while and Kennedy grew curious. He wished he had Lochner in the car with him to translate, but protocol demanded otherwise. Finally, he tapped the driver's shoulder, hoping he understood English.

"Is there a problem?" the President asked impatiently.

Surprised that the American spoke to him, the driver seemed to stammer out an answer in halting English. "The crowds . . . they are so full . . . we have to go slower to get through the . . . streets," he said. "This will . . . take longer than . . . we thought."

Kennedy smiled his thanks, and patted the driver on the shoulder, and then returned to waving. His mind drifted off to consider the delays on his timing, and he prayed Clay and Clifton had realized the timetable was in need of adjustment.

A siren greeted Spector as he maneuvered the bulky, slow-moving truck through the narrow streets of East Berlin. He had difficulty figuring out the mechanisms at first but was gaining confidence. His mind, though, was mentally ticking off the minutes wasted and wondering if he would be back in the West with sufficient time to complete his work. A small voice began to whisper doubts about his preparedness, and he had to shout at it to go away so he could drive.

Kennedy looked to his left and saw the large platform set up for the speech, bunting ringing the roof. The space devoted to the platform was larger than Kennedy was used to, easily twenty feet off the ground and rather wide. A broad expanse of steps was in the center, and seats were awaiting the fortunate who would join the heads of state.

Army officers scurried out of a bus, one of several that parked behind the cars, and they rushed to make sure the setup was to their satisfaction. As it was, such public appearances were always causes for concern, and they seemed even jumpier than usual, probably because of Kennedy's instructions that morning. Generals Clay and Clifton talked it over with their underlings, the President noted, and then saw them check information with a uniformed German, perhaps their head of security.

He was eager to make the speech, look at the Wall close up, see the people eye to eye. Adrenaline began fueling his arms and legs, and he seemed on the verge of being jittery. Kennedy called out to Lochner, milling about near the lead bus, smoking a cigarette. "What are we waiting for?"

"Just the final details, Mr. President. This is a rather important moment for the people and no one wants it spoiled."

"I'm eager to get started."

After another couple of minutes, Kennedy finally was approached by Clifton, announcing that everything was ready. Gingerly getting out of the car, the President leaned close and said in a low voice, "What's with the air strike?"

"Everyone is ready and will get a final signal after the speech. You'll have to sign the executive order then," Clifton said without emotion.

"You still think this is a mistake, don't you?"

Clifton considered the question, and Kennedy realized how much he had come to trust the general over the past few years. He was a colorless, capable officer who always looked out for what was best for the Office of the President and the United States of America. As a result, his opinion often carried as much weight as Bundy's or Lyndon Johnson's.

"Your reasoning makes sense, but I think it remains hastily considered."

"Damn it, Ted," Kennedy said, getting hot, "they nearly killed me. America has been mocked long enough. You know that."

"Yes, sir," the career officer said noncommittally.

Kennedy looked out at the crowd, more convinced than ever that this was just what these people needed. A real tangible sign that America supported them. Respected them.

Adenauer meandered over toward the President and reached out to guide his peer up the stairs. Kennedy smiled, beamed in fact, which somewhat surprised the Old One, given how tired Kennedy had looked only a little while earlier. He never grasped the idea that Kennedy could put on a public face and practically perform for the public as if it were a high school production of *Camelot*.

As they made their way up the stairs, the roars of "Ken-nah-dy" were deafening. Adenauer passed a banal comment about the speaker system being loud enough for the crowd, which was estimated in the millions. One of the State Department aides speculated early on that nearly three fifths of West Berlin had turned out for the event. Such numbers were staggering to the leaders, Adenauer, Kennedy, and especially Brandt, the city's proud mayor. It was Brandt who greeted the President at the top of the stairs and escorted him toward a group of chairs arranged in neat rows to the side of the podium. Already milling about were Rusk, Bundy, Salinger, and Clifton.

"I want you to know," Brandt began, "this is unprecedented since the Third Reich. No one else in Germany has ever managed this amount of adulation."

Kennedy looked out from the new vantage point and just nodded his head. He was literally stunned into silence by the sight of human flesh. There were surely buildings behind them or concrete sidewalks they stood on, but he could see none of that. He saw smiles, sunglasses, fingers waggling, arms waving, and handkerchiefs brushing away tears of joy. Street to street, the *Platz* before Town Hall was a sea of happy, cheering German people.

Signs were dotting the crowd, mostly in English, cheering on the President. One even wished him and Jackie luck with their forthcoming child.

Windows were open and stuffed full of people of all ages, all classes. Everyone had their mouths open, and the sound rose up into the clear afternoon sky. No question, Ulbricht, all the way in East Germany, would hear the cheers.

If he harbored any final doubts about his actions, Kennedy banished them. This was his moment. This was Berlin's moment. He would not disappoint them. Dared not.

After a brief flurry of comments and short remarks, Brandt managed to get an introduction made, and the President of the United States of America strode forward and waved once to the crowd. Its volume rose even higher and resounded from building to building for a full minute. Patting the air, Kennedy finally got the noise level back under control and looked at the hasty scrawls in the margin of his final draft of the speech.

Behind him, his colleagues also had copies of the speech to keep track, taking note of how certain phrases of passages were received. Sorenson, his top speechwriter at the time, was near the front of the people, clustered in a roped-off area reserved for the American delegation. Even so, they were jostled, their backs were patted, and hands were shaken.

Kennedy looked out among the faces, returning their smiles. His gaze went toward the Americans and he winked at his sisters, hoping they would notice. It didn't hurt that Angela was also next to the Kennedy women, although they seemed to be pointedly ignoring her.

"I have been unexpectedly moved by the reception the German people have afforded me since I arrived here on Sunday," the President began extemporaneously.

Behind him, he could hear papers rustling: one of his colleagues checking for the remarks in the speech. No doubt these were men who had trouble ordering dinner if the menu was not directly before their eyes. Few seemed to grasp the necessity for tailoring comments for the temperature of the audience, adjusting it for maximum effect. He returned to his speech and continued. It was only about five hundred words, plenty of room for pauses, applause, and even a few additional comments.

The President was feeling the full effect of the crowd before him. It was as if each crowd before today had been a before-dinner cocktail and this was the banquet. A full seven-course meal solely consisting of wine which left him feeling almost drunk. With sharp memories of the Wall and the poor East Berliners behind it, he channeled that burning fury and continued.

"Two thousand years ago the proudest boast was, *'Civis Romanus sum.'* Today, in the world of freedom, the proudest boast is, *'Ich bin ein Berliner.'*

"There are many people in the world who really don't understand, or say they don't, what is the great issue between the Free World and the Communist world. Let them come to Berlin. There are some who say that Communism is the wave of the future. Let them come to Berlin.

And there are some who say in Europe and elsewhere we can work with the Communists. Let them come to Berlin. And there are even a few who say that it is true that Communism is an evil system, but it permits us to make economic progress. *Lassen sie nach Berlin kommen.* Let them come to Berlin." And the crowd went crazy.

Behind Kennedy, Pierre Salinger, the press secretary, turned in alarm to his colleagues. "Oh, Christ, he's nowhere near the text. What the hell's going on?"

"The President intends to rip down the Wall, and this is his beginning," McGeorge Bundy replied gravely.

"What he's saying flies in the face of his last public comments," Salinger protested, referring to a speech at Washington, D.C.'s American University, just two weeks prior to the European trip. There, he indicated a willingness to forge new links with Russia which would lead to the signing of a nuclear nonproliferation agreement.

"He's daring Russia to do something," Bundy added. "The line is about to be drawn in the sand, and by damn, they'll cross."

Kennedy continued to speak, savoring the enthusiastic reception the words were receiving. "All free men, wherever they may live, are citizens of Berlin and, therefore, as a free man, I take pride in the words, *'Ich bin ein Berliner.'*" The people continued to cheer, but there were mixed sounds that the President could not make out. It almost sounded like laughter.

In the roped American area, Angela's hands flew to her mouth to stifle the giggles that threatened to erupt. The action was noticed by Eunice Shriver, who turned and stared daggers at the younger, prettier woman.

"I'm sorry," Angela said through gasps. "But Jack is right, he's terrible with foreign languages. Just terrible."

Shriver glared again, this time joined by Jean Smith, also unamused and obviously unaware of what the President had just said to the people of Berlin.

Bundy buried his head in his hands.

"What's wrong?" Salinger asked. "It's a great line."

"But it's wrong," Bundy said after a moment. "It's *'Ich bin Berliner.'*"

"He said it."

A shake of his head. "No, he said, *'Ich bin ein Berliner.'*"

"Meaning?"

"The President of the United States just called himself a jelly doughnut."

Unaware of the gaffe, the President forged on, feeling the swell of emotions. "Freedom is indivisible, and when one man is enslaved, who are free? When all are free, then we can look forward to that day when this city will be joined as one and this great country and this great continent of Europe in a peaceful and hopeful globe. When that day finally comes, as it will, the people of West Berlin can take sober satisfaction in the fact that they were in the front lines for almost two decades."

The speech over, he waved once again to the people, and the cheers continued for several minutes. Kennedy basked in the praise and outpouring of affection as he was surrounded by people obviously looking to be photographed with him for posterity. The media platform, to his left and back over twenty-five meters, was in full swing with still and film cameras whirring away.

It was a damn fine speech, he mentally concluded, stuffing the written comments in his jacket pocket. He hated the original text, could never make it work to his satisfaction, and needed to give the people a tangible sign things were going to improve. Kennedy had almost declared the air strike but chose to reserve those blunt actions for later. Deciding he needed the people behind him, at the last minute Kennedy decided to signal the strike from Free University, his last scheduled stop in the country. The timing would be fine, calling in the bombers minutes before they actually struck the Wall. There would then be no way for the East Germans to repel the surprise attack.

• • •

"Great speech, great man," Stein concluded.

Back in the UPI offices, Stein and Katrina Beck sat in the chief's office. The black-and-white image on the just turned-on television was growing clearer slowly, enlarging to fill the fifteen inches of screen. When complete the image was a fairly static one of the platform and Kennedy's shoulders and head. It sufficed since the four microphones before him captured every syllable clearly. On occasion the roar of the crowd threatened to drown out the man, but he rose above it, making sure they heard him and the words' meaning.

"I thought his German was awful," Beck said mildly.

"Yeah, what was it he said?"

"I think he called himself a Danish . . . no, jelly dough-nut."

Stein chuckled and asked Beck to leave a note for Heinz to make sure that got into his story. The chief then ran a hand over his brushed-back short black hair and wondered aloud, "Do we have time for the American deadlines?"

Beck ran a mental calculation and replied, "It's early evening on the East Coast, so this can make their early editions if Heinz gets back and types like the devil."

"And what about Spec? He's out there getting reactions and we'll need that for the later editions. It may be a long day here, better order some sandwiches and coffee for those guys. Get something for yourself and Paul, no one's going anywhere." The pert young secretary nodded and stepped out of the office to begin preparations. This was nothing unusual for her, and if asked, she would admit to enjoying the extra excitement.

Elsewhere in the office, all was silent, even the Teletype, which was turned off to allow everyone to watch for a few minutes.

No one noticed Urban was not in the room. Instead, he was back by the computers, scanning military channels, charting flight patterns, and trying to keep from throwing up.

Rounding a corner, the truck knocked over a metal waste-basket, crushing it beneath the right front tire. Spector cursed loudly but didn't slow down, determined to make it to the meeting spot. He had just two blocks to go and then would be in position.

He'd been sweating heavily ever since he left the depot, and he was certain the *Vopos* would find him soon enough, ending his life in the wrong era, on the wrong side of the Wall.

Slowing finally, the dark metal behemoth crawled the final meters to the corner and then with a grinding of gears it stopped. The engine continued to run, and Spector spent a moment checking gauges to make sure there'd be enough fuel to accomplish his task. It must have been just filled up, since the needle was hard to the "F" side of the rectangular gauge.

After a few moments' wait, the trio crept around a corner, laden with brown paper bags in addition to their other belongings. Even Elizabeth seemed weighed down by the new purchases, and the three huffed and puffed their way to the rear of the truck. Without waiting for Alan to climb down from the cab, Peter and Wolf were unhitching the rear gate. As soon as it was down, they carefully placed the bags on the lip with Wolf climbing up and beginning to stow the bags more carefully. When that was done, he reached out a hand and helped his wife up, who in turn began receiving their belongings from Peter, who went about his work with a casual air.

Finally on the ground, Spector went to the rear and helped with the last few items, including Wolf's music case, which Elizabeth accepted with a genuine smile of gratitude. She seemed to finally be accepting the idea that the reporter was going to make good on his promise. He didn't feel as confident, but there was no way he was going to imply any such thing.

"I think that's it," Peter said as he relatched the gate. It made an unhappy noise as metal slammed into metal, indicating a need for lubrication. He fished out another cigarette and lit it, inhaling deeply.

"Come with us for the last act," Spector asked.

Hoyt shook his head. "No, I think I've done enough. Got to return the car to Hilda. I'll head back and help my parents."

"You got them this far, why don't you see it through with us? It'll be quite a sight."

Peter thought for a moment and smiled. "*Ja*, it will at that, won't it?"

With that, he scampered up the bumper and over the gate, practically falling into the happy Krause couple's arms.

16

Place: Town Hall, West Berlin, West Germany
Time: 2:20 p.m., Wednesday, June 26, 1963

"You've got to come to your senses!"

"Watch it, Dean."

"I'm sorry, Mr. President, but that speech just sent out all the wrong signals to Moscow."

The two men were arguing vigorously in a corner of a large room filled with American and German dignitaries. It was the scheduled luncheon between speeches, and Kennedy's last official meal in West Germany. Mayor Willy Brandt had spared nothing, and there was a sumptuous selection of German meats and fish in addition to salads, wines, and even good, old-fashioned dark beer. The gathering had begun several minutes earlier, and immediately the secretary of state had whisked his commander in chief to a private space. Robert Manning, one of the assistant secretaries on the trip, tried to block anyone from interrupting the conversation. His face a grim mask of determination, few approached.

"They will think you just did an about-face after your last speech and that won't win you any friends in Congress."

"Screw Congress," Kennedy said with heat. "And screw Moscow. That's the whole point. I want that Wall demolished and Khrushchev put on notice."

"It'll be war for sure, sir," Rusk added, knowing full well these points had been covered exhaustively since the wee hours of the day.

Kennedy was already tired and uncomfortable. Yes, German cars were wonders of engineering, but after the physical strain of the last few days—and nights—his back was threatening to shut him down for good. Mentally, he willed himself to put the pain aside, promising to relax soon. He knew a hot shower would help, that and about a half bottle of aspirin.

"I intend to summon that strike this afternoon and stand my ground," Kennedy said, beginning to move away and back to the gathering.

He stormed past the surprised Manning and headed for his heaping plate of food, gathered but untouched since they'd arrived. Once he grabbed the plate, his sharp eyes scanned the room, looking for a likely crowd he could blend in with for just a few peaceful minutes. A smile crossed his face as he spied Robert Lochner engaged in conversation with Ted Clifton and Angela Chance. Just what he needed, stimulating conversation without rancor.

"May I join you?" he asked casually. The three parted to create space for the President, who stuck a fork into a piece of sausage and began lunch at last.

"In all my years I've never seen a crowd like that," Lochner said complimentarily.

"Brandt compared it with a Hitler rally, and I can see what he meant," Kennedy said, agreeing. "Did you see that fervor? I swear, I could have asked them to rush the Wall and rip it down with their bare hands and I truly think they would have tried." The expression on his face was an odd mixture of awe and concern.

"Doesn't that please you?" Angela asked.

Kennedy paused in chewing for a moment, considering the question. Finally, he put down his fork and looked into

Angela's eyes, taking some small delight in her presence, knowing this was their last real time together.

"No, Angela," the Leader of the Free World said slowly. "In fact, it sort of scares me. These people are so desperate for someone to come to their aid that they're looking to me as a singular source of power. Today I could have asked them for anything, and they would have given themselves over freely. That's a tremendous responsibility, since you then have to watch what you say even more carefully. Had they rushed the Wall, the East German guards might have panicked and started opening fire. Before order could be restored, we'd have too many dead."

"It was unnerving, to be honest. I want to help them but . . ." He trailed off in some deep train of thought. Angela knew enough not to pursue the real issue, not with the unaware translator beside them.

"Had you asked, they would have stormed the Wall," Lochner agreed. "But these people may not be such a mystery to their mayor."

"Eh?" Kennedy looked momentarily confused.

"Brandt had armored troops and tanks a block or two away in case the crowd got out of hand. They were building to a fever pitch for days so he knew to be cautious."

Kennedy was surprised with the news but also pleased to see the mayor knew how to look after his people. It might be time, he thought, to reevaluate the man.

Lochner also seemed uncomfortable around Kennedy at the moment, probably because he was responsible for the man's latest bout of adultery. It did not faze the President at all; in fact he was grateful to his interpreter for finding someone as enchanting as Angela. After another moment or two, Lochner excused himself and headed for the bar at the room's opposite end.

"Mixed signals," she said, completing a thought he hadn't paid any attention to.

"Excuse me?"

She looked at him, surprised he couldn't follow her line of thought. Rather than repeat herself, she took a breath and tried again, looking more serious than last night when she nearly died. "You're taking a major risk with the entire world, you know. Russia was inching toward your nonproliferation pact, and everyone was urging you two to get close enough to sign it. I'm certain it could have happened. But now, after your speech, I'm sure Moscow will get nervous and they will react with even more alarm when you . . . complete your act this afternoon."

"Khrushchev could be simply playing me for a fool, dragging out the talks with no intention of actually signing," Kennedy countered.

She shook her head, hair barely moving in her solemnity. "No. He's scared to be the one to go into the history books as the man who started the first—and maybe last—atomic war. He'll sign."

Kennedy looked at her, forcing Angela to avert her eyes. She had come close to telling him what she knew. That pressure was building within her made longed-for exposure to the President quite surreal.

Before he could continue, a German parliamentary leader, his name totally lost on Kennedy, walked over and tried to begin a discussion over the damn chicken tariff again. Angela caught his eye and winked. He couldn't help but smile, which confused the politician.

"You'd better look at this."

Stein glanced up from his desk, ignoring the article before him, and gave a surprised look to Katrina. In her hand was a long roll of Teletype paper and a face that tried to equal its length. She rarely seemed so concerned, so he waved a hand, gesturing for the article. Beck handed it over, and rather than leave the office, she waited until he read it.

"Oh my God," he said under his breath. Then, turning up the volume, he bellowed for Heinz and Spector.

"Alan's still out," Katrina said.

"Why the hell isn't he here, meeting the deadline?"

"Can't tell you, sir," she answered, surprising him again.

Heinz by then had stepped into the office, notepad at the ready, a look of concern on his face. Stein waved him to a seat and handed him the printout. It took the political reporter a few moments to scan the piece, his eyes darting back and forth rapidly. He seemed to read it twice and then slumped in the chair, still holding the article.

Stein watched him for a beat, then two, and finally snapped his fingers to capture the man's wandering attention. Beck continued to remain in the room, a rather unusual stay for her, but the bureau chief didn't seem to mind.

"If this is true, then we've got something major shaping up. Is your article complete?"

"About fifteen minutes, sir."

"Okay, wrap it up and get it right to me. No mistakes so I won't waste time forcing you to rewrite. Check your quotes and official titles, you always manage to get one wrong. Then, get on the phone to the Ministry of Defense and see what's up. Call everyone you know who can be of help. If you have too many numbers, get help. Katrina will be fine for backup." The pretty young woman beamed a smile at both men, eager to get in on the action, absorbing the free-flowing adrenaline that was now pumping in the office.

"Katrina, have Urban keep an eye on the wire for more on this. If the East German tanks are really headed our way, we're in deep shit."

"But why?"

"That, my dear," Stein said, beginning to shoo her and Heinz from the office, "is for us journalists to uncover. This is news, major news, and we're expected to figure out the who, what, where, why, when, and how. Answer all that, and we have a story. Do it before the guy down the block and you're number one. I want to be number one."

"Hold on!"

The heavy truck rumbled and the engine seemed to growl in protest as the vehicle lumbered through the German streets. As they entered the forbidden zone, the Time Warden fully expected the *Vopos* to try to stop the truck. Instead, with its military markings, no one paid it any attention and they all allowed it to near the Wall, right by the famous American Checkpoint Charlie.

Spector looked in the rearview mirror and saw nothing but desolate streets, devoid of people or cars. Looking through the windshield, he saw the zigzagging Wall, with the inner barrier under construction by the American entrance. The entire Wall was supposed to have a secondary barrier erected to prevent even more people from escaping by some dastardly means. As it was, the concrete and brick structure was topped with barbwire, and guard towers lined the entire stretch of man-made barrier.

He had to find a spot for his plan, one that was hopefully just outside the reach of watchtower bullets. There would be only one chance for success and that meant he had to use all his courage to try, which would leave precious little left for him should something go wrong. Times like this, Spector desperately wished for some of the gear from uptime, tools that would enable him to practically disintegrate the Wall under cover of night, and slip in and out without ever being seen.

However, Time Wardens were trained to work with local equipment first. Should any device be accidentally discovered and examined, the Timeline would shatter and theoretical alternate timelines would sprout. Such temporal mechanics were Spector's weak suit, but he understood just enough to know that he alone might be responsible for a future that was bleaker than it should have been because of his carelessness. Not exactly the kind of thing one wants on their permanent record. Continuing that line of thought began to give him a headache, so he put his wishes aside and concentrated on trying to find the spot.

In the back, the three spectators huddled toward the right side of the cab and did not say a word. Even Hoyt had stopped smoking and sat, arms wrapped about his knees, trying to be compact. The Krauses hugged one another, and as the truck rocked, they gently banged into Hoyt as he remained unmoved.

Finally, Spector saw a stretch that seemed just right to him. It meant passing one final tower but they would care as little as the others, he considered, and pressed his foot gently against the gas pedal, forcing more fuel into the engine, urging the truck to accelerate. He could feel the increased energy being expended and liked the sense of power from beneath his feet. The truck's speedometer was edging past sixty kilometers per hour; too slow for highways but just a little bit too quick for these streets.

Glancing up for a brief moment, Spector noted that the guards were watching the truck with their own eyes, ignoring field glasses and keeping their guns to themselves. However, he felt uncomfortable under their attention and was afraid they'd try and signal him to stop. Instead, they merely watched, perhaps too bored to care about anything else.

Looking ahead again, Spector saw the great expanse of the slate-gray and dull red Wall grow larger. With every passing second, he tensed his hands on the wheel, keeping the course straight and true, coaxing just a little more speed out of the vehicle. Judging the distance became difficult with the increasing speed, so he was constantly recalculating in his mind, waiting until ten meters were left. A furtive glance about told him no other vehicles were in the area, and then he guessed it was time.

Goosing the gas pedal one final time, he made sure the wheel was straight, and then he turned and as rapidly as he knew how scrambled into the back of the vehicle, springing himself at the trio huddled to his left. The wheels crunching debris to powder made loud sounds as the Time Warden reached the others, stopping his flight by grabbing ahold of both Krauses. As he tried to scramble his legs around them, into a crash position, the truck reached the Wall.

The nine-ton monster smashed headfirst into the thick unlovable object, grinding wheels, collapsing metal, and forcing the engine to give up life with absolutely no warning. The impact threw everyone to the other side, head over heels, and then back to the center with loud thumps and a great deal of human moaning, which meshed rather nicely with the death throes of the nine-ton truck.

"What happened?"

"I don't know, but you'd better call an ambulance!"

As the first guard hurried to the other side for the emergency phone, the other guard, shaken out of his reverie by the sound of the impact, watched the truck. It smoked from the engine, but there was no explosion as so often happened in the movies. That fact alone made the guard curious, and he paid rapt attention to the scene, wondering how many people were in there, how many were still alive. What happened to them would be some cause for speculation but also cause for rejoicing. The Wall had withstood such a mighty impact and remained intact. Sure, some of the brickwork was destroyed, but it was still standing. The engineers had finally figured out how to make a Wall that would take such abuse and remain standing tall and proud.

The guard began thinking some more about the driver and how he didn't seem to be wearing a proper uniform when the truck passed beneath the tower. Something certainly odd about that.

17

"I'm empty."

Stein put a hand over the phone's mouthpiece as he glanced up, making angry eyes at Heinz. For the last half hour, both men had worked the phone hard, trying to find some additional information to the report found on their own news wire. Both men spoke to politicians, secretaries of politicians, fund-raisers for politicians, friends of friends, and even old sources from government stories. All the calls were polite, but no sense of panic was evident, no veiled clues were proffered. It was maddening.

"Me, too, but you don't have to broadcast it."

Heinz took a seat, lit a cigarette, and looked as if he had run a marathon rather than dial the phone over a dozen times.

Stein completed his call, yelling at the poor person on the other end, and then slammed the receiver into the cradle. He leaned back in the chair, cracked his knuckles, and stared at the ceiling.

"There's something going on. The East Germans don't start mobilizing T-34s and T-54s for no reason. If they did it first, we'd be screaming murder and accusing them of escalating tensions with Kennedy here. Meantime, we have a story confirming this from a chance flyby, and no one is saying a word. That in itself is remarkable."

"What do you make of it?" Heinz had obviously given up, deferring entirely to Stein's greater wisdom and experience. While this made Stein feel momentarily pleased, it also frustrated him because Heinz lacked the flair for finding new sources or ferreting out the information required by the rules of hard journalism. Times like this, Spector, with his uncanny skills, would have been preferable. Of course, no one had seen him in hours, so he could be on the case or in the tavern getting sloshed in celebration of the U.S. President's speech.

An hour ago, that was the big story. A thorough condemnation of Communism, total support for Berlin, and a rousing speech that would be repeated again and again. As it was, film of the speech was being readied for broadcast to television stations around Europe and even in America.

Forcing his mind back on the key issue, Stein thought about the reports from East Germany. If Ulbricht overreacted, Stein considered, then Brandt would surely match tank for tank—they were already in West Berlin—and someone might get nervous. For a change, he had no sage advice for the political reporter.

As the rattled Heinz left the office, Stein quietly picked up the phone, called his family, and suggested it might be a good time to go visit his mother in Hannover.

The taste of blood was the first thing Spector noticed.

It trickled from his nostril onto his lips, and the taste was bitter, unpleasant. However, it did make him focus his attentions and he began to stir. Nothing felt broken, but he also ached from head to toe.

Quickly, he looked around him and saw that his colleagues had also survived the terrific impact with the Wall. While the structure may have won the battle of wills, the

Krauses and Spector still had a chance to complete their plan. Spector reached over and brushed a rough canvas blanket off Elizabeth's shoulder. Peter Hoyt was already on his knees, brushing himself off and glancing over his shoulder, out the rear of the truck. Joining the gaze, the Time Warden did not see any *Vopos* coming their way, or anyone else for that matter. No question about it, when the East Berlin government said this was a forbidden zone, they meant it.

"I'm okay," Elizabeth said weakly.

"Good," her husband replied. Wolf was also beginning to stand, his left pant leg torn and a gash across the thigh. His elbow extended through the hole in his thick sweater, which must have caught on a sharp edge from the packing material that was already in the truck when they climbed in.

Wolf stood and uneasily moved toward Peter. Together, they began checking the fastenings on the packages they had brought with them. As they did this, Elizabeth also slowly rose and checked their baggage, including Wolf's music case. She smiled to see it had been thrown about but everything inside—viola, bow, rosin bag, cherished sheet music—was intact.

Spector's senses went off and he snapped his head around, making him momentarily dizzy. Straining his hearing, he caught the sound he awaited: an ambulance.

"Time to move," he announced. Even though they had no time to practice their plan, everyone did as expected and began emptying their purchases.

Within the guard tower, the two officers stared at the truck wreckage, imbedded, however slightly, in the Wall. No one could be seen moving within it, but neither one wanted to go down and look. That, they felt, was for the ambulance, already on its way.

Gunther, the guard who'd phoned for the ambulance, was the more senior officer and was the Watch Officer for this shift. He had personally been in a heightened state of alert given the reality of Kennedy and Adenauer being just a few kilometers away. His orders were specific: be alert, be vigilant, and shoot if anyone tries to escape. If Gunther were to fire, he was to be sure and make it a clean kill. The East German government was not at all interested in anyone getting over on this particular day.

He had been a *Vopo* guard for the last three years, assigned to the Wall only six months earlier and proud of his advancement. This was just a posting along a career path that he had been promised would ultimately lead to a brigade command by the time he was forty. At thirty-two, this seemed like a realistic and near enough goal to keep him interested in being the best soldier he could be.

Gunther's partner on the shift was a much younger soldier named Franz, and he was just in his first year with the army. Eager and quick to act, Franz was paired with Gunther because those in command felt the older soldier could mold Franz, make him a more exceptional officer, one who understood the chain of command and the importance of following specific orders.

"Ah, the ambulance comes already," Gunther said happily.

Franz looked at the truck again. He turned away for a moment, but something must have nagged at him because he abruptly turned again. The suddenness of the action had Gunther train his attention on the truck as well. Could it be, someone was alive?

The carriage seemed to shift from side to side, and it was too long after the accident for that to be the cause. Something was going on, so maybe Gunther had guessed wrong. Maybe there were survivors, and if he chose not to help them, could he be accused of letting his brethren die?

While Gunther mulled over those options, quickly praying the ambulance would arrive already, something stuck itself out of the truck's rear.

Several soft thuds sounded and Franz gestured mutely. Gunther looked at the small flares climbing into the sky, leaving behind small smoky trails. They were quickly followed by more sparks and smoke trails emerging from the truck. His first conclusion was that the engine had caught fire and the entire truck was going to go up in flames after all.

He was dead wrong.

Moments after that thought occurred to the veteran soldier, all hell seemed to break loose. Lights exploded all around the truck, none of them being remotely like flame. Yes, there were red, yellow, and orange, the expected colors of a fire, yet they were joined by blue, green, and purple.

Also, the explosions seemed to be of short duration and none near the truck.

"It's incredible," Franz exclaimed, a look of excitement on his young, clean-shaven face.

Gunther watched for another moment as more colorful bursts surrounded the vehicle. The lights began swirling in circles or spinning in an arc. So many, so fast, it was hard to watch them all. Then, in a moment, everything clicked into place.

"Fireworks," he simply said.

"*Ja*, and good ones," his partner agreed.

They watched the moving balls of light, neither questioning why the spectacular display happened to be loaded in that truck and what could possibly have set them off. As they watched, neither seemed to notice the dark-clad figure standing atop the truck's hood, tossing a rope ladder over the Wall. The man was at least six feet tall to start with, and with the truck another four feet off the ground, that gave him a good ten feet head start at this point in the Wall's construction.

When two more bodies stood on the hood, one began to climb, and that was when Franz took note of this new activity. He shrieked something Gunther could not make out but pointed at the Wall.

It took the senior officer a moment to see what was going on and shake the delight of the display from his mind. One hand reached out to sound the siren alarm while the other grabbed for a phone. He had to call in this escape attempt per instructions.

The siren sounded, loud and mournful, a warning to the other towers to go on high alert and to send cars along the

Wall's edge in search of trouble. Response time had been clocked at under two minutes. Gunther considered that, thought about the ambulance and the fireworks, and thought it might be closer to three before someone showed up.

Franz had not been given such orders, and he reached to the side wall and lifted a rifle from its rack. Turning with practiced ease, he took aim at the figures, trying to get a bead on the form that was now more than halfway up the ladder. The smoke from the fireworks and the bursting lights themselves proved an effective cover, and it was hard to get a single figure safely in the crosshairs.

"Wait," Gunther shouted, forcing Franz to look away from the target.

"What do you mean?"

"We were briefed this morning, remember? With so many journalists just on the other side, we did not want to do something that would reflect badly on the government."

"But," Franz protested, "these are people illegally trying to scale the Wall."

Gunther nodded in agreement, damning the fact that no one was picking up the other end of the call. "We can't start shooting without attracting the attention of the American army on the other side. They might fire back, and we don't want a war."

"But you want them to get over?"

"Not at all, but we can't start shooting through this mess. If you miss or hit the wrong target, then what?"

Franz hesitated then stopped. He thought for a moment, and Gunther considered that the training was going well.

Then Franz turned around, hefted the rifle, and continued to seek an accurate target in his sights.

18

Place: Berlin Wall, East Berlin, East Germany
Time: 3:23 p.m., Wednesday, June 26, 1963

"Let them try and get over the fence," Gunther shouted.

Instead, Franz continued to take aim, and finally, after what seemed an eternity to the older officer, the rifle fired. The sound was mostly muffled by the wail of the siren but its proximity made Gunther's ears hurt.

Placing his hands around his eyes, he squinted and tried to look through the haze from the fireworks. To his surprise, the man on the ladder tumbled backward, dangling from one rung held in place behind the knee. His arms waved frantically, proving he was still alive. The two figures below him moved erratically, and Gunther tried to imagine what they would do. Would they flee, try and rescue their comrade, fire back?

Franz lowered the rifle, grinning from ear to ear. "Good shooting, *ja?*"

"If he's dead, *du hasts gut*—you're lucky. If he's alive, we'll see," Gunther began. Then a sudden thought occurred to him, and he slammed a hand against the desk. "Of course this means we'll be filling out reports for the next week!

They'll want your version of what happened, then mine, then the autopsy if he's dead, detailed accounts of what happened every second since we went on duty. Your rifle will be stripped and studied if you miss. Your eyesight might be tested. So might my sanity if they decide I let you shoot knowing you couldn't hit your target the first time. A week easy."

This made both men slump their shoulders in imaginary defeat. Win or lose, the bureaucrats always seemed to come out on top.

Both men returned to their window and looked out at the truck. The fireworks had stopped, and the smoke was beginning to clear, rising above their station. If the two figures did anything it would happen shortly. The ambulance's siren—or was it the reinforcements?—grew louder, and Gunther assumed the people below could hear it.

The various responses replayed themselves in his mind once more as he watched, but nothing prepared him for the next act. A man sprung out of the truck's rear, brandishing a rifle and a pistol, both of which began spitting bullets toward the watchtower.

Gunther and Franz dove to the ground, surprised to see a fourth figure.

The rifle kept up a steady hail of bullets, some of which could be heard impacting against the tower's supports or the tower walls themselves. None made it into the post itself, so Gunther crawled toward his rifle. The time had come, he decided, to forget the rules and fight back for self-preservation. He'd worry about the reports later.

Slowly, carefully, Gunther motioned for Franz to remain still and then got up to a kneeling position, allowing him to look over the side of the post wall. The man was shouting something, but he was too far away to hear anything.

He afforded a quick glance at the Wall and saw one figure scrambling over the rope ladder, and over the treacherous, thick barbwire. Did the others already make it over? What about the man dangling from the ladder? No clear sign of anything.

Instead, Gunther concentrated his attention on the rifle,

one hand caressing the barrel. This had been his only rifle since joining the armed forces, and he was determined to only rely on one gun his entire career. He oiled it regularly and shot target practice weekly—just in case. With confidence, he took a poised stance, aiming carefully, and without hesitation squeezed off just one shot.

The figure below crumpled with impact.

Two police cars arrived just then on the scene, followed finally by the ambulance. The extra forces finally arrived, just as their need was erased.

Franz, who had watched in silence during the past minute, if that was all it truly was, reached over and silenced the siren.

The fireworks. Siren. Shouting. Gunfire. Escaping people. All gone. Vanished like a stage magician's final trick. There was a quiet to the air with only a tinge of something his tongue could hardly identify.

Once more his mind turned to consider the mountain of paperwork the day's actions would require. He sighed softly and lowered the rifle back into its place on the wall rack. It needed attention but it would have to wait until everything sorted itself out.

The barbs tore at everything. Skin, cloth, metal. The stings and pinches felt endless, and for Elizabeth it felt like the ordeal would never end. She wanted to scream loud and long, but the siren sounding off overhead drowned out any coherent thought, and she either followed the American's hand signals or worked entirely on instinct. Elizabeth hadn't realized her instincts extended to gunfire and mayhem, but they did, doing an admirable job of keeping her moving and alive.

All she knew was that her husband was sent up the ladder first, most of their meager belongings on his back. She watched him with some pride and more than a little terror as he scrambled up step by step. Suddenly, though, there was a new popping sound, one that didn't match the mirthful fireworks that were providing an unusual degree of camouflage. She glanced back toward the tower and then again at her husband who had stopped climbing. Then she discovered true terror.

Her husband was teetering, one hand still holding on to the rope while the other was waving aimlessly, dripping blood. The red spot on his leg began growing at a speed she thought unlikely, but then again she had never seen a bullet wound before so had no real frame of reference. Screaming Wolf's name over and over again, but unable to hear herself, Elizabeth stood still. It afforded her a chance to watch her husband, but then Spector had grabbed her from behind and dragged her to the ground, behind the truck and Wall, away from the guard tower and their guns. Still, she could see Wolf lose his grip and begin to fall, only to be saved from certain death by his right leg getting entangled in the rope. She couldn't hear the sound of his knapsack meeting the Wall or the agony emitting from his wide-open mouth, but her heart breaking was certainly loud enough in her own mind. It drowned out all other noise and seemed to isolate Elizabeth from the cacophony around her.

Wolf hung there for a few moments when her attention was torn away as Spector helped swivel her shoulders to see the next act in the drama unfold. To her utter amazement, her childhood friend Peter had burst from the truck and begun firing, using weapons stolen from the depot. Whatever he was shouting was lost on her, and she turned to ask Spector what was being yelled. The American was no longer at her side, but instead had scampered up the truck to the ladder, where he was already climbing. Within moments, as Peter's bullets kept the *Vopos* at bay, Spector, this odd stranger who'd managed to charm them into risking their lives, had managed to free Wolf and begin lowering him to the truck's top.

Elizabeth was by her husband's side in an instant and was relieved to hear ragged breathing. She tried to whisper encouraging words in his ear, but she couldn't find a word to say. Stunned into silence, Elizabeth was totally lost and on the verge of hysteria.

Perhaps sensing this, Spector had once more grabbed her shoulders and tried to get her up the ladder. He hissed instructions in her ear, practically shoving her to reach the ladder. Finally, as she was automatically climbing, the remainder of the belongings and music case strapped to her own back, her brain processed enough information to send a coherent signal.

Spector wanted her to climb and get to West Germany. He had made some sort of promise about helping Wolf, and she had no reason to either trust or suspect him but she just followed his orders. It was about all Elizabeth could do.

Atop the Wall, Spector handed Elizabeth another length of knotted rope that would be attached to the top, letting them climb down to freedom. For weeks, she imagined what her first view of freedom would be, what words she would say, when she could make love to her husband totally relaxed and unafraid. Instead, she looked directly down and the thought her brain processed was: *It looks no different than the East. Did I make a wrong turn?*

Then she was climbing down, feeling the weight on her back tug at her and weak muscles complain. Then there was another crack of a gun, and the steady tattoo of bullets vanished. Moments after that, the air itself turned off the volume control, and she could sense nothing but a slight ringing in her ears. Elizabeth Krause kept climbing down, confused by the events surrounding her and uncertain of what had just happened. The silence was annoying, almost maddening, and she was unable to turn her mind off, wild and random thoughts buffeting her.

The woman looked up and saw Spector scampering from one rope to the next, beginning his descent. Where was Wolf?

She screamed the question, finding her voice at last.

He said nothing but grew larger as he approached. It had become a desperate race down the ladder, and she was certain he would climb over her to touch ground first.

Instead, she continued to move, and with each step, things began to order themselves in her mind. First, she noticed tears on her cheeks, and she realized her husband was shot and wounded. Then she looked at Spector again and saw he climbed unencumbered; no Wolf. So, he was wounded, possibly dead, and on the wrong side of the cursed Wall. And then, one foot reached the ground and the word *safety* reached her mind. But it was obliterated instantly as a stronger thought impressed itself on her mind. Peter Hoyt had been shot and killed, protecting her chance to escape, letting her wish be fulfilled when he had no reason to do so.

The tears continued to flow as the other foot reached the ground, and then she fell to her knees with great racking sobs that seemed to cause her strained muscles to ache even more. It was totally unfair to come this far and be in West Berlin, be a free German woman, and be there without her mate.

The American had by then also reached the ground, and he hunkered down, resting on the balls of his feet, hands bracing his body, and merely waited her out.

A minute or two passed, and finally she seemed to run empty of tears and the sobs had stopped. She stood up, taking a moment to check herself over, and was pleased to see she was bloodied in many places but not seriously wounded. Elizabeth was safe, and the feeling of joy was tinged with great sorrow as she continued to think about Wolf and worry over his condition.

"I will bring Wolf back here," the American solemnly said.

Elizabeth didn't seem to acknowledge the words, so he repeated them and that made her turn around, still numb.

His expression was a combination of sympathy and grim determination. In his dark eyes, Elizabeth was sure she saw that he meant the words and would find a way. He had, after all, engineered their way over the Wall, but nothing was said about the price to be paid.

The enormity of the past hour finally impacted her every nerve ending, overloading her entirely, and she blacked out, beginning to fall before she lost sight. Her last image was of Spector already in motion, trying to protect her body before it was further injured.

"Get the fourth squadron in the air right now!"

"Heading?"

"Heading . . . patrol the Wall, all sectors. We'll get the seventh squadron up to join in the search."

"What do I tell them they are looking for?"

"They will know it when they see it."

The exchange both alarmed and amused Urban as he sat in the computer room, eavesdropping on the radio discussion between East German military leaders. They were in a high state of alert and with absolutely nothing to go on other than West German army movements. Such hair-trigger responses were alien to the traveler, and he began to wonder how Europe had survived the Cold War. Of course, if Spector failed, he would witness a rather different outcome.

Once more in the lengthy motorcade, John Kennedy was en route to his final stop, a speech at Free University. His prepared remarks were originally intended to sum up his visit to Germany, touching on the many issues between the countries. He had wanted to work in some of the themes from earlier in the day, encoring the performance before a newer audience, but he just couldn't manage to strike the right tone with pencil notations. There was no time for a serious rewrite during the luncheon, and he couldn't do it in the car, not with thousands more Germans waiting to catch his eye, wave, or flash a red, white, and blue flag. Perhaps there'd be time at the school itself.

The outpouring of emotion continued to deeply move the man and gave him the impression that his work was the right thing at the right time. In fact, he felt the time may have come to tell the Old One of the mission now under way. He tapped Lochner, now riding in the front next to the driver, on the shoulder.

"Chancellor, there's something important I must tell you and Mayor Brandt before we arrive at the University."

Both leaders gave the President their undivided attention, although Brandt had a suspicious glint to his stare. Adenauer continued to randomly wave, not looking at all at the people, still cheering at what seemed like the top of their lungs.

"The Wall is an atrocity, and after deep consideration, and many debates with my own staff, I have decided that this afternoon it will be stopped."

Brandt blinked once, then twice. "What will be stopped?"

"I have ordered an air strike that will begin demolishing the Wall along the American sector to signal to both East Germany and Moscow that we will not tolerate separating the German people." Kennedy paused to gesture toward the throngs on both sides of the slowly moving car. "They deserve better."

Adenauer seemed in shock while Brandt looked at first angry then uncertain. Neither said anything but Lochner, the translator, seized the moment. "Is this wise?" he asked in English.

"It's what I feel is required at this time," Kennedy simply said.

"What of the French and British sectors?" demanded Brandt.

Kennedy met his gaze with clear eyes and an almost relaxed expression on his face. "I hope the people demand they act in kind—or do it themselves."

"You must be pulling my leg," the Old One finally said. He looked past Kennedy, his hand finally lowering and no longer engaging the population.

"Have you lost your mind?" Brandt sputtered.

Kennedy shook his head, reengaged his ever-ready smile, and began absently waving to no one in particular. He knew there would be arguments, so he added that the strike was under way, the planes were coming, and the American forces were already on a high alert. Whatever East Germany tried to do, would be too little, too late, and the blow for democracy would stand tall.

"It'll be war," Brandt observed, anger creeping into his voice so the American President couldn't mistake the message during translation. "Had you moved in the troops when the Wall was a roll of barbwire, you could have ripped it down and Moscow would have blinked a second time. Instead, you do it now after all their man-hours. It invites some form of response. And if it's war, who's to say what level of weapon will be used."

Kennedy knew the nuclear option existed, and it had at first made him reconsider, but the white-hot anger of the assassination attempt remained in his mind. Slowly, with little detail, he made the events of the previous night clear to both men, explaining that if ever a line was crossed, that was it.

"Such a craven and cowardly act," Adenauer managed to say after a few moments.

Brandt and Lochner nodded in agreement, and Kennedy mused that the translator might have been feeling pangs of guilt since, after all, Angela had ended up in the room as a direct result of his being "helpful."

"There's no question that this deserves some form of response, but can't your vaunted CIA do something in kind?"

"Like what?" Kennedy snapped. "They can't even kill Castro, and he's just ninety miles away. Hell, I don't know if those spy jockeys can find their way out of their own headquarters. No, I must do something to stand above the cloak-and-dagger shenanigans. By God, Mayor, I want them to feel what righteous rage feels like. I want Khrushchev to quake in fear that if I can tear down the Wall, then I am capable of anything, and that will keep him in check."

"Or it might force his downfall and then who do you get? Better the devil you know . . ." Brandt countered.

"What about the people near the Wall? Are you willing to risk their lives?"

"No, Chancellor," Kennedy began slowly, forcing himself to calm down. "I am fortunate that the East Germans have such a wide clearance by the Wall on their side. Armed forces will clear the way about twenty minutes before the planes arrive and all should be secure. I'll have the Red Cross on alert, just in case."

"And what do we do?" Brandt asked, still angry. "Just stand by and let the mighty America do everything?"

"Actually, no," Kennedy replied. "I want your permission to have your military leaders talk with General Polke and get things organized. Those tanks and troops must still be nearby."

Brandt flashed a cold, knowing smile. "Heard about that, eh? Couldn't take chances. I've never seen the people so whipped into a frenzy."

"If we can't talk you out of this foolish act, then I want Germans involved in this operation," Adenauer announced, and even without the translation, Kennedy understood the tone. The Old One wanted his fellow countrymen to have a role, so his place in history remained strong. He needed to be recorded as a strong leader down to the end of his reign, be it tomorrow in a nuclear burst or in August when he was scheduled to step aside.

For a moment, Kennedy looked again at the cheering crowds as the car slowly moved through the city. A small voice asked if he was really that angry, but he pushed it deeper down in his mind and considered his own place in history, and prayed this was the right act at the right time.

Gunther ordered Franz to remain at his post while he joined the growing throng of people around the still form of Wolf Krause. After all, he was involved in keeping one third of the escapees in place. There were *Vopos*—both police and army—examining the truck, the Wall, the body. The ambulance attendants were kept away from the body until things seemed secure enough. Whether he lived or died didn't seem to matter to the men, who were following protocols printed on documents clipped to a board. In fact, he was amused to note how many had clipboards with them, all reading off the same documents and all checking things off almost in lockstep. If a man wasn't bleeding to death, he probably would have laughed.

A figure in a dark uniform and darker expression approached Gunther and, without introducing himself, began peppering him with questions about what had happened. The answers elicited more questions, asking exactly the same thing but phrased differently. Finally, Gunther couldn't stand the idiocy any further and interrupted a question about his training to ask, "Is anyone going to tend to that poor fool?"

The questioner glanced over his shoulder to note a man with a camera clicking off shots from a variety of angles.

"Not until we are done with the scene. Now, where did you train?"

Getting exasperated, Gunther snapped, "Does it matter? They tried to escape, we stopped them."

"No," the man answered, his voice dropping ten degrees in warmth, "you stopped one of four. One is dead, the other may be dead. This was not a huge success, and I am trying to determine if you or your commandant was flawed."

"Oh, and you would have done things differently," the guard sneered.

"Actually, yes. That truck would never have passed my tower without clearance."

Gunther cocked an eyebrow. "I see. And how would you have stopped it from twenty-five feet in the air?"

The man had no immediate answer, so he looked at the crowd once more. Gunther took some small satisfaction in confounding the pompous ass for a change but would not gloat. He recognized the man had enough power to have him busted in rank, imprisoned, or even drummed out of the service, and he had too much invested to let it all be destroyed for an angry comment. The veteran prayed he was smarter than that. "The photographer is done." With a simple gesture, he finally parted the sea of people and allowed the medical team to approach Krause.

They set about their work and stood, boots in blood, ripping clothes and tending to the leg wound. The fact that they worked quickly, passing materials back and forth, indicated the man was still alive, and Gunther was happy about that.

"What do we do now?"

Elizabeth was numb with fear, pain, and exhaustion, but she had been following Spector in silence for several minutes. They moved away from the Wall, trying to prevent any of the American or West German police from finding them. The crash and fireworks were certainly going to attract attention, so the intent was to move into the city and fade behind the throngs still filling the streets.

The reporter moved with purpose and an assurance that he knew where he was headed. His every act convinced the scared woman that her would-be savior was her best last chance at freedom. Not that she wanted to do it as a fairly young widow, but somehow his promise of retrieving Wolf consoled her. For the moment, she would trust him completely because she had no other alternative. After all, she knew no one in West Berlin or West Germany for that matter. With few East German marks, her prospects were grim, and Spector was her sole lifeline.

Turning down another street, he led her toward a small tavern that was not unlike the one the Hoyts ran just on the other side. Thinking about it hurt; Peter was dead because of her dreams, and she was afraid his sacrifice would haunt her.

Once inside, he brought her a hard liquor drink and told her to sip it while he headed off to find a phone. The glass was cool to the touch, and she was surprised to feel the dark liquid burn as it trickled down her throat. She wasn't familiar with much beyond beer and wine, so she couldn't even identify the drink. So here she was again, trusting Spector for everything. It couldn't last much longer.

"UPI," Katrina said as the line connected.

"It's Spec," he said.

"Where are you?" Surprise—and relief?—filled her voice.

"I'm at the Happy Bear on Glock Platz," he replied. "What's going on over there?"

"Stein wants your head for not checking in sooner," she confided. "All hell is breaking loose. The East German army is on the move, and no one on this side will admit to anything being wrong. Stein knows something's up and is going crazy trying to nail it down."

This panicked Spector for a moment, thinking he was out of time. Internally he knew he had fewer than five hours left. "How did the Kennedy speech go? Did he say something to provoke them?"

"Weren't you there? Never mind. He rattled the Communists and had the people frothing at the mouth. It was masterful but may have backfired."

"Not at all. He wants to rip that Wall down, I think."

"What? Are you kidding? How do you figure that?" She was sharp, he had to admit. In fact, she always had a drive and determination to be the best at her job that he rarely gave her credit for. At first, he thought he would ask Urban to abandon the UPI office and come help him in the field. That would have been a calculated risk. Instead, an entirely new plan occurred to him.

"I figure that the East German army is mobilizing to be ready in case Kennedy does something rash like call in an air strike. I haven't got anything confirmed, which is why I'm here in the field. Look, can Stein spare you?"

"Not really," she replied without hesitation.

"Think that through. Does he really need you or can you come help me here? It's vital I have some help, and you're the only one I trust at the moment."

There was a long pause and then Katrina asked him what was wrong. "Alan, what do you mean?"

"Never mind, I'll come there. Look, I'm bringing a friend with me who's in need of help. Please have some coffee brewed. And do you have an extra sweater?"

"A woman, huh?" Her voice sounded less than pleased. "Yes, I have something she can borrow. But what's up?"

"I'll explain as we go along. I'm about ten minutes away by car, if I can find one. Also, tell Urban I'm coming in and may need him as well."

Katrina sounded dubious, concerned, and confused but agreed to have everything ready, and Spector rang off. He returned to the table and noted with satisfaction that Elizabeth had finished her drink. The liquor would help for a short while and then the coffee would keep her going. She'd need to eat, though, so he found a passing waitress, ordered her a ham sandwich to go, and went out to find a taxi.

The ride was in silence as Elizabeth gazed out the window, studying her new homeland. The Temporal Warden could only guess how much longer she could keep absorbing new information and events before she hit overload and shut down—or broke down. He took that into account as he continued to consider his options, refining his latest crazy scheme. If he recalled his history right, the trick had worked at least once before and might work a second time, especially with everyone on heightened alert, which usually made things easier, not harder.

About fifteen minutes after hanging up, Spector walked

into the branch office and guided Elizabeth over to Katrina. With a brief introduction, he asked his friend to take care of Elizabeth while he gathered his things for the next part of his job. The woman looked curiously at Spector and proceeded to take over care of the obviously exhausted woman.

Before Spector could make it over to Urban for a complete update, his name resounded from wall to wall.

"Where in hell have you been? You know what a deadline is, right? It's the point beyond which your news is no longer new. Once you pass it, whatever you are working on is useless to me. I do not pay for useless. I pay for news. You have something for me to make me forget about the article I was expecting, oh, an hour or two ago?"

The part-time journalist let his bureau chief finish bellowing, a trick he had mastered by the second day of his employment with UPI. Then, taking a deep breath and composing himself, Spector began, "Actually, yes. Katrina tells me you need confirmation of what's happening. Well, I am onto something that may be bigger than Kennedy's speech."

"Do tell," the skeptical chief demanded.

"You know there were tanks in position while Kennedy spoke at Town Hall. Well, there are more tanks moving around the city's perimeter. It's spooked Ulbricht, and he's trying to react in kind. Things are escalating over some misunderstanding and, with Brandt accompanying the President, no one is talking to anyone else."

"Jesus," Stein muttered. "How'd you find all this out?"

"I was talking with General Clay when things broke. I've been tracking this down, trying to keep it all in perspective before we put out any panicky bulletins."

Stein nodded slowly, obviously absorbing the slightly fabricated story and assessing its implications. Then he noticed the strange woman being comforted by his secretary. Spector caught the look and launched into a new explanation before any question could be asked.

"Amazingly enough, that's our newest citizen. Elizabeth Krause. Just came over the Wall in a rather spectacular way. I found her and decided to help her in exchange for the exclusive story. Today's just a day for news."

"You never cease to amaze me, Spec," Stein began. "I love your exclusives, but sometimes your bullshit is too thick even for me. We'll sort *her* out later. Let's get this tank story nailed down. Do you have the contacts to follow this up?"

He shook his head. "I'm working on it but need to get back out. I want to be near Free University where everyone will be for Kennedy's last speech. If it all comes to a head, it'll be there." With that he turned and moved toward his desk, hoping Stein would retreat to his office, giving him a few minutes' freedom. He was rewarded with knowing his boss well enough to get those minutes.

Urban quickly met him at the desk and filled him in on the latest military radio traffic. Planes had been scrambled, and generals Clay and Polke were finally communicating with their West German counterparts. Questions were coming in from NATO allies, but all were being rebuffed, which seemed to exacerbate the situation rather than help. If things remained on track, the planes would be free to drop their loads at approximately five o'clock, an hour from now.

Spector absorbed that news, looked at the clock, and felt panic set in. Could he possibly rescue Wolf, change Kennedy's mind, and stop World War III?

"Have you spoken with Dianna Basehart?"

"They say nothing has changed yet and are just as nervous as me," Urban reported.

"I need you to get in touch with her and have her run the names Wolf and Elizabeth Krause through the temporal computer banks. I need to know if they do or did anything significant in either Germany. Add Peter Hoyt to the list."

Urban scratched the side of his head. "You mean, should they be here or there?"

"Exactly. Except Hoyt. They shot him on the other side."

"Uh-oh. Be a shame if you had to return them," the older man mused.

Spector's mind raced ahead, ordering the bits and pieces of his plan and screaming for him to get moving. Without realizing it, he ordered Urban into the computer room and to the rear panel that contained myriad supplies. A quick glance over to Katrina allowed him to guess her size, and he passed on the information to Urban. The Teletype operator blinked a lot as he memorized the list and then hustled off to the storeroom and the hidden spaces behind. How Stein never found them remained a testament to their discretion, and now was not the time to make a fatal error. There was precious little time for the Time Warden to preserve history.

Urban would be several minutes, which gave Spector time to convince Katrina to do the impossible. He walked over to the two women, noting that Elizabeth was wearing the brown tweed sweater, which did not match her outfit at all. The backpack and viola case were neatly stacked to the side of the desk, and she was nibbling at half the sandwich, a mug of coffee steaming beside her.

"Katrina, I really need your help and, as I said before, I have no one else I can trust," Spector began. "Elizabeth is too worn-out to do much else, and I have no time to find another ally."

The young woman looked up, appraising Spector, searching for the real meaning behind his words.

"What do you need?"

"I need you to play pretend with me and help rescue her husband," he said matter-of-factly.

Katrina blinked once, then twice.

"I don't have time to wait," Spector pressed on. "I need your help, your answer, now."

Katrina continued to consider the situation when Urban showed up with the supplies. She stared wide-eyed at the materials in his hand, looked again at Spector and had the realization that something bigger than reporting the news was unfolding. The Temporal Warden was hoping she would decide quickly and allow him to move out.

"Okay," she said in a small voice.

"Good," he said quickly. Grabbing at the white outfit in Urban's arms, he thrust it at her. "Go to the ladies' room, change quickly, and meet me out front. Paul, I'll need your car keys." Finally, the last desperate plan was being put into effect.

19

"Where on earth did you get this?"

Katrina felt the material stretch against her, just a little too tight across her hips and breasts. It was slightly starchy and itched.

She and Spector were in Urban's car, proceeding toward Checkpoint Charlie, hoping to get through as quickly as possible. He had said little as they drove away from the UPI offices, and she was truly confused as to what she was getting herself into. On the other hand, Spector had never asked her for anything previously and it was obvious he was desperate. In fact, she sensed that there was a great deal more to this entire day than he was admitting to. She hoped that he would finally open up, revealing the true Alan Spector to her, since after three years Katrina knew so little about him.

And yet she had always felt some attraction to him. He was handsome, yes, but so were a lot of the men she'd met since coming to work at UPI. She'd dated on occasion and had thought she had even fallen in love with one, a foreign diplomat, but it turned out he was already married and seeking a "friend" during his posting in Germany. That crushed her for quite some time, and she was slow to trust another man again. The subsequent relationship with Bianco also soured her on men. At her office, though, the men were all polite and friendly, surrounding her with people she could trust for much of her day. It helped smooth her frayed emotions, and only in the last few months had she begun to go out with men again.

Now this had happened and she tried to wait patiently, hoping she wasn't out to make a fool of herself or have her trust crushed once more.

"I have a large supply of costumes at my disposal. When this is all over, I may explain why."

"You don't like to wear these, do you?"

Spector glanced over at her and smiled. It was genuine and warm, which pleased her. "I'll let you guess for a while longer."

Looking down, Katrina smiled back. "It's tight enough on me; on you, it would split the seams."

"We're approaching Checkpoint Charlie. Ever been through before?"

"Actually, no," she said.

"Okay, here's the drill. We're doctor and nurse, with special permission to cross back and forth for the research and consulting we do with other doctors. You have been with me for three years and are trained in research medicine."

She nodded once and then idly picked up the special forged documents that got him through once today and would have to work again. There was no way he could have gotten these through normal channels, and they were so perfect, they couldn't be forgeries. How on earth could Spector have ever gotten such permission to cross without question? Just who was this man she had agreed to help?

"Have you ever acted before?" Spector inquired. His voice was calm, assessing information as if she were just another interview subject. In turn, she looked him over,

checking body language and making certain he was as calm
as he sounded.

"Not really," she admitted. "But this is simple, I guess.
Now, are you going to tell me what we're going to do or am
I just going to follow one instruction after another?"

"Well, if it will help you," Spector said with a small sigh.
"We're going to East Berlin in the hopes of finding Wolf
Krause, spirit him away from the authorities, and bring him
home. From there, I intend to get ahold of President
Kennedy and convince him not to bomb the Wall. All within
the hour."

"What? Who are you to try any of this? Explain yourself,
Alan," she demanded.

He sighed again, obviously weighing matters on his
mind. Before he could speak, though, the car was waved to
the gate and he had to hand over the documents. The
American guard was the youngest one she had seen yet, and
she wondered how young they were letting American men
serve. With troops around the world, and an increasing
number going to Vietnam, she wondered about the drain on
young men back home and how that might affect American
society.

The guard examined the documents carefully, checking
information against the ever-present clipboard. He took his
time staring at Katrina, which made her feel even more
self-conscious. "Kind of late to go over for a consultation,
Doctor," he said.

"I am needed! Why should you care if I gave up my opera
tickets to help save a life? A life! Time is being wasted,"
yelled Spector. Katrina noted the tone had a professional air
about it, so it proved he was a pretty decent actor. Another
facet to her mystery man.

The young man nodded and signed off on something,
returning the documents.

They were through.

Arriving at Free University, Kennedy got up and stretched,
trying to work the pain out of his back, knowing it would
fail. The day was proving to be longer than he had expected,

and the President was in agony, avoiding painkillers to stay sharp. In another hour or two he'd be back on Air Force One and could relax properly. In fact, he figured he would make his speech, demolish the Wall, and fly to Ireland to visit family and get the rest he craved so greatly.

It all sounded so simple, but people continued to buffet him with their doubts and fears. So much so, in fact, that the little voice continued to speak to him and he was unable to silence it completely. His own advisors were against it, and he could tell Brandt thought the President had lost his mind.

As with every other inch of the trip, Germans of all ages and sizes were awaiting him, waving flags and placards to welcome him or encourage him. The outpouring of emotion continued to bolster him, and he thrived with the feeling; it continued to convince him this was being done for them and they would approve. Wait until Brandt heard the ovation when he made his announcement.

Out of the car, Kennedy decided to soak up the feeling a little more intensely and walked over to one particular crowd and began shaking hands. The people rushed forward, straining against the barricades, forcing armed officers to rush over to contain the wall of people. Kennedy smiled, waved, shook more hands, and received the frequent kiss on the cheek. It felt like another campaign stop, one of countless such visits since he began political life nearly fifteen years earlier.

After a few more minutes of greeting the people, Kennedy backed away and walked over to O'Donnell, who was clustered with a group of Americans, including, to his pleasure, Chance. "What's the schedule, Ken?"

"You'll be meeting with the top faculty and administrators for a little while and then in about half an hour you will speak. As soon as you're done, we head back to the airport and leave. Dinner on the flight to save time."

Kennedy nodded, his eyes growing hard as obviously desired information was omitted. His friend caught the expression and then leaned in, hoping only the President would hear the following. "Okay, okay, we've got it timed so you speak and fifteen minutes later the bombs drop. We have coordinated troops on their way to the Wall, and the evacuation begins in about twenty minutes."

A smile broke through Kennedy's demeanor, and O'Donnell returned a grimace, clearly disliking the instructions he was carrying out. Another look among the Americans showed that O'Donnell was not alone. At least the military officers, even Clifton, were nowhere to be seen, obviously off running the operation.

The two men tried to make chitchat while waiting to enter the University's main building and meet the gray professors. It was strained so Kennedy turned to Angela, who tried to remain on the periphery of activity, a mere bystander.

"A little more than you bargained for?"

"Much. You know how I feel," she said. "The same as Ken and General Clifton and the others. Yes, you're angry, but you don't realize the enormity of your act.

"Mr. President, I feel somewhat responsible for this and get the idea you're doing this in part to salvage your ego. Don't. I'm not worth it. These people deserve better."

He looked at her, buoyed by the cheers he continued to hear. "You'll see, Angela. Everyone will see that this will be the dawn of a new chapter in history."

"And hopefully not the last one," she said under her breath.

Racing as quickly as possible through the East Berlin streets, Spector gestured with his right hand toward his second medical bag of the day. He asked Katrina to reach in to the very bottom, remove the false panel, and take out the equipment beneath it.

The woman obeyed, taking inventory of the various vials, packets of pills, gauze, tape, stethoscope, and capped syringes. His bag seemed ready for field medicine more than routine research. As her tapered fingers reached to the bottom of the bag, she wondered how he had acquired such a complete kit and why. The thoughts were wiped clear when the panel came loose and she removed a smooth metal rectangle. She studied it for a few moments, having never seen anything quite like it before. It was a steely silver, and there were thin seams to indicate sliding panels. Wherever he got it, she was certain Spector didn't buy it retail.

"Don't ask," he said, reaching over and grasping it with his right hand. With practiced ease, he slid open one panel, which was hinged from within and revealed a few lights and what looked to be the world's smallest speaker.

"Remote access, Spector," he said and seemed to wait for a response. A beep was quickly forthcoming, and she watched mutely as he spoke to the device. "Access East Berlin police and military radio bands. Seek information regarding wounded male who tried to escape over the Berlin Wall."

He placed it by his side as he drove with some determination. A finger waved her quiet, and she stewed, bursting with questions and concerns. Could Spector have been some sort of spy, planted at UPI to be activated at this crucial moment? Only spies and government agents would have gear others only dreamed about.

Two or three minutes passed in silence as the car maneuvered through the sparsely populated city streets. The direction seemed deliberate, not random, and Katrina used the time to study the face of the enemy. Pretty normal-looking people for Communists, she considered.

The odd device beeped once more and then flashed something across a screen that only Spector could make out. He nodded once, snapped the lid closed, and stuffed it in his pocket, while at the same time turning the wheel and gunning the accelerator.

"I know where Wolf Krause is and now we have to get him free from security and meddling doctors. I know, I know, you want to ask me about everything, but now's not the time, Katrina. Trust me a little while longer, then I'll explain everything."

"Am I risking my life?" she asked. It suddenly became important to figure out how much she could trust the reporter. His answer would tell her.

"A little, but not too much, I figure. If we can spirit him out of East Berlin without a single gun being drawn, we'll be fine. And you're not along for decoration. I will need you."

Okay, not a bad answer. He didn't dismiss the danger quotient, but he didn't seem perturbed by it either. "Are you a spy?"

"What, like Mata Hari? No, nothing of the sort."

That felt almost right, but the laugh seemed a trifle forced. She settled back in the seat and decided to go along for now. After all, without Spector, how could she possibly cross back home?

A few minutes later, the car pulled in front of a squat, square building that turned out to be the local hospital. Spector placed the car near a side entrance rather than the front and made certain all four doors were unlocked. "Remember," he said as they left it, "it's Paul's and we should try not to scratch anything."

She laughed a little and walked with him, side by side. His gait was assured, and he made himself look as if he belonged to the hospital. With the tight white uniform, she tried to feel as if she belonged beside him. Looking over, Katrina took note of the set jaw, the eyes looking straight ahead, and an attitude that seemed urgent but controlled. His face was handsome in profile, she mused, and she began reevaluating him all over again.

They passed through the side door and began walking to a fire door and the stairs beyond it. He took the stairs two at a time, not wasting a moment. She tried to keep up, but the heels made it difficult. As a result, he was up two floors and holding the door, impatiently waiting for her. With a little effort, she closed the distance and caught her breath. Spector was already moving down the hall, his bag swinging rather casually.

They made two right turns, then a left, and they came to an abrupt halt as they found two uniformed *Vopos* standing by wide, swinging doors. It was obvious the assignment bored them, and they didn't try to hide it from the staff. Beyond the doors, Katrina could see people bustling back and forth as if there was a great deal of activity to accomplish in a short amount of time.

"Your purpose, *Herr Doktor*?" one soldier asked.

"I am *Doktor* Spector, just summoned by your commandant," Alan replied with a no-nonsense tone.

"Why?"

"Why?" he repeated, his eyes bulging. "Because they want me to give him last rights. What do you mean, why? I am a doctor, there is a man with a bullet wound that needs my attention. Do I ask why you stand here with your gun holstered, costing you valuable time should he try and escape again?"

The soldier and his partner seemed flustered to be caught somewhat underprepared, by a doctor no less. They mumbled something unintelligible and let the pair pass through.

Katrina was amazed by Spector's bravado, but she began to assume that this was something he had done before and was comfortable with. More and more he was taking on a new persona, one she had never imagined existed, and it thrilled her to watch. It also concerned her, because this was getting more complicated than she'd ever imagined.

The medicinal smell was rather strong and made her eyes water at first. Someone in the back of the corridor was moaning in pain, but it couldn't be Krause; he had to be the one where the other *Vopo* stood guard. Spector walked right up to him and began to enter the room. The guard, a bit more alert than the two earlier, placed a firm grip on his arm. He slowed to a stop and Katrina slowed accordingly, doing her best not to bang into his back.

"Your business with the patient?"

"I was summoned to make an examination of the leg wound to ascertain the risk of nerve damage," Spector snapped off.

"And her?"

"She is my assistant. I work with a lot of equipment and someone has to record the information. I surely can't ask the patient to do it, now can I?"

The *Vopo*, a middle-aged man who obviously would never go beyond foot-soldier level, thought about the words but also the tone. He must have weighed it against the tone used by the other doctors in the last hour or two. Finally he stepped aside and silently allowed Spector to continue.

Inside the room, Wolf Krause was asleep in a small bed. His medical chart was open and on a wheeled table to the side. An IV tube was in his left arm, and no one else was in the room. Spector snapped open the bag and rummaged for the stethoscope. As he listened, his right hand reached in for the eerie device and snapped open a different panel. Katrina read as much as she could about the medical chart and volunteered, "The bullet was removed from the leg and he was given two units of blood. His vital statistics read okay, I guess."

"You guess?" Spector laughed a little, sounding amused. "Some nurse you'll make. Medicine has to be a very precise practice and guessing won't cut it. Watch." He waved the device over the wound and then took a long look at the open panel, reading the inside of the open piece. "He's out of danger, although there may be muscular damage. Moving him will be difficult but not impossible. It's a good thing they don't eat well here and he's not obese."

Spector then leaned over and whispered in the man's ear, calling his name over and over again. After a few moments, the eyes fluttered and the words grew more intense. Finally, Wolf looked around, and Katrina was pleased to see some recognition between the men.

"Don't talk, there's a guard outside the door. Elizabeth is safe in the West, and I promised her I'd come back and rescue you."

"What . . . about the . . . plan?"

Katrina frowned at the prospect of a new, unexplained wrinkle. The last thing she needed was to find out the Krauses and Spector were mixed up in something illegal and she was placing herself further in jeopardy.

"It's fine. I have just enough time to bring you over and then convince the President to stop a war. Nothing to worry about."

"What?" Katrina exclaimed. She was definitely in way over her head if this scheme involved President Kennedy. Quickly her mind reviewed the day's chaotic events, and a few pieces began to fit together in ways she'd never imagined. "Do you mean to tell me Wolf has something to do with the East German tanks and Kennedy?"

"Smart girl," Spector said, then busied himself checking Wolf's bandages. He looked around and spotted a folded wheelchair in the corner. He asked Beck to go and set it up, preparing to leave the hospital. Quickly, he found Wolf's ransacked backpack of clothes, but they had all been shredded by overzealous soldiers. Tossing them aside, he looked over at his bewildered friend. She was working as hard as she could to lock the collapsible pieces into place, having never done such a thing before. Yes, she had hoped the news business would be thrilling and she might get to meet interesting people or even travel, but doing it all in a matter of hours was a bit more than she'd imagined. In fact, she was starting to feel more overwhelmed than she imagined possible.

"I promise you," he continued as he began to disconnect Wolf from the IV, "this will make sense. However, we're on the clock and there isn't a lot of time left. Quickly, bring that over."

She wheeled the chair over, and Spector began helping Krause into it, placing a blanket over his bare legs. Katrina wished there was time to properly dress him, but the hospital gown would have to do until they were home—if they ever got there.

"How strong do you feel, Wolf?" Spector asked.

"Shaky," was the single reply, and the voice sounded world-weary.

"Okay, Katrina. The wheelchair comes with us. Grab my bag and let's get out of here. The elevator is around the corner, just past the wonder twins on the other side of the doors."

"Yes, *Doktor,*" she said, trying to put on a brave front. She knew better, though, her feeling of being overwhelmed was being replaced by a feeling of terror. One wrong move, with a prisoner of the East German army, and she was sure to be shot.

Spector opened the door and strolled past, with Katrina

pushing the wheelchair. She stopped and returned inside to get his medical chart. Returning to pushing, she reached the guard, who took attentive interest in her presence. First her tight uniform, which made her feel self-conscious, and then the patient.

"*Was*—" was all he said before Spector cut him off.

"I need X rays," Spector snapped. "Idiots never shot any, and they want me to give them qualified answers. Of course I can't, so it's going to cost me another hour. Idiots!" He continued ranting as he walked off toward the double doors.

Katrina looked over at the guard and shrugged. He smiled back at her, trying to look friendly but reminding her of too many leering men at taverns on her side of the Wall. She noted Spector was already haranguing the guards at the doors so she had to hurry.

"I don't know why I continue to sleep with such a man," she said as casually as she could, amazed at the topic that blurted from her mouth. The guard seemed equally surprised by the admission and just watched her as she briskly moved down the hall.

"Who . . . you?" Wolf asked, as she pushed the wheelchair.

"I'm Katrina Beck," she replied gently. "I work with Spec at UPI, and he convinced me to help you. I've met your wife and she is safe. Scared and worried about you, but safe. Now rest." God, she was beginning to sound as soothing as a nurse.

Fortunately, Spector's angry doctor act had the two soldiers actually holding the doors for her, so getting off the floor looked to pose no problem. Within a minute, it were at the elevator and she was beginning to feel her heart slow down. Maybe she'd take her own blood pressure in the car on the way home.

On the ground floor, it was a few turns until they were headed for the side door and the outside. Each milestone seemed of greater importance to Katrina than it should. She ticked off the ones that needed to be passed in order to reach home free. It was like a board game: leave the hospital security floor, leave the hospital, drive through the gate, deposit Wolf in Elizabeth's arms. If successful, she would get to the bonus round and watch Spector try to do something with President Kennedy.

"You there! Is that the prisoner?"

Spector and Katrina turned as one and saw a real doctor and a *Vopo* bear down on them. The soldier was better prepared and already had his gun out, and Katrina's heart slammed into overdrive while Spector grabbed the chair and pushed faster.

Thinking as quickly as he could, Spector reached the side door and hoisted Wolf into his arms. Spector's injured leg protested with a sharp stab of pain, but the Warden had to ignore it. He bellowed out an instruction to Beck and then was through the door.

Quickly, with trembling hands, she locked the wheels, turned the chair around, and shoved it down the hall where it quickly met up with the *Vopo*. He stumbled into and then over the chair, cursing loudly between the yelps of pain.

Great, she thought, now she was definitely an accomplice and was going to die. And Spector had said there was minimal chance for danger. If this was minimal, she hated to imagine what great or huge chances were like.

Outside, Spector was already hurrying to the car, and she ran after him, savoring the fresh air and sunshine in case they were her last moments. Instead, she found herself in the front seat, reaching over and adjusting the blankets around Wolf's body. His own breathing was a bit ragged, and she feared he was worse than the charts indicated.

Spector had put the car in gear and was tearing away from the hospital as the *Vopo* emerged from the door. He stopped running, took aim, and rapidly fired off three shots. Only one hit the car, in the rear fender, but Spector kept a tight hold of the wheel, swerved slightly, and straightened out as he sped up.

"I have to get to the gate before this can get out on the radio," Spector said aloud, more to himself than to Katrina. "That will be a few minutes so it's a real race. How's Wolf?"

"He looks unwell," she admitted.

"The scanner said the wound was serious but not deadly.

The rest, I suspect, is exhaustion. He's had a trying week."

"What do you mean?"

"He and Elizabeth tried to get over the Wall the other day and I fouled them up," Spector said matter-of-factly. "I sort of promised myself that I'd help them if I could, so when I saw them this morning, I knew they could help me with my plan."

"The plan involving Kennedy?"

"That one, yes."

She swallowed hard, trying to add the details to what she already knew. It frustrated her because she couldn't figure out how everything fit and what was missing. She barely knew which questions to ask so decided to ask for the whole story. "Are you going to tell me about it?"

"Soon, not now." He drove another block in silence, frequently turning around to check behind them.

Katrina shook her head dejectedly. "I know, I know. First we have to get out of danger. When will that be? When we cross the Gate?"

"Actually, after I stop Kennedy from tearing down the Wall."

Her eyes grew large, and she felt as if he'd punched her in the stomach. "What?"

"You say that a lot, you know."

His casual tone really annoyed her right then. Which led her to demand angrily, "Spec, tell me everything. Now. And none of this when we're out of danger stuff. I get the idea I'll be old and gray when that happens."

Spector nodded and seemed to seriously consider her demands.

20

**Place: Free University,
West Berlin, West Germany
Time: 4:39 p.m., Wednesday, June 26, 1963**

John Kennedy was anxiously pacing the room, having had his fill of niceties from the academicians. He wanted to get out before the cheering throngs and give them their hearts' desire. However, the German people had to follow their schedules, and the speech was to be delivered at five p.m. It was scheduled to be broadcast in Germany, and the word was going to spread far and wide—and rapidly.

The President noticed that his most trusted advisors were keeping their distance, either frustrated that they couldn't sway the man or concerned that the pacing meant he was ready to explode. He supposed he was ready to burst, wanting to share the news. Kennedy also noted that Adenauer, Brandt, and even Erhard were nowhere to be seen, no doubt coordinating efforts to keep the people clear from ground zero. That was fine by him, and a sign of their willingness to let the leader of the Free World lead.

However, even the delightful Angela was keeping away, staying in deep conversation with O'Donnell, and he wondered what they had to discuss. Her mind was filled with such interesting observations, he knew, so his old friend was no doubt captivated by her combination of brains and beauty. His own mind replayed her words, hearing her try to take responsibility for his anger. He knew the stakes were huge, but this was much more than a bruised ego. Wasn't it?

He glanced at his watch and wondered what he would do for twenty minutes other than continue to pace and anticipate the speech of a lifetime.

"We're going to die, right?"

"Not at all," Spector replied. "After all, we've accomplished so much in the last few hours that it would be a waste. Besides, I've never been to the World Series and want to do that once."

"How can you think of baseball now?"

He looked over to see that she continued to look annoyed. So far he had done a reasonable job of keeping her in the dark, but he had come to realize that the truth would have to come out. Still he was hoping to keep stringing Katrina along until he could explain himself in private. No need for all of Germany to know he was here to protect time from meddling visitors like Angela Chance.

"It calms me. Who do you think's the better pitcher, Sandy Koufax or Whitey Ford?"

She let out a strangled noise that was a manifestation of her frustration, and he realized he still needed her so he had better take things cautiously.

"Okay, let me tell you some of what's going on, just to make sure you're aware of the highlights. A KGB agent tried to assassinate President Kennedy and in nearly succeeding pushed the President over a line that made him decide the Berlin Wall had to come down. If that happens, the retaliation might plunge us all into World War III."

"Oh, my God," Katrina managed to whisper. Wolf, alert but still in the back, also let out a concerned noise which made both front seat passengers turn around.

"I explained only some of this to Wolf and Elizabeth,

enough to get them to agree to help me convince the President that this is the wrong path."

"But why you? You're just a reporter, aren't you?"

Spector shrugged a bit and then turned the car around a corner, leading them back to the gate at Checkpoint Charlie. The first gauntlet was about to be passed, with luck. If the *Vopo* back at the hospital got to a radio fast enough, they were going to be in deep, deep trouble.

"It's my job, which I'll happily explain later. Now, Katrina, I need you to help me."

"How?" She sounded confused.

"Unbutton the first two, no, three buttons of your top. Smile a lot and let them look to their hearts' delight."

"What are you talking about?" She stared at him, unmoving, definitely angry at him for even suggesting she do any such thing.

"If they stare at your . . . body, they won't notice a man in a hospital gown in the back. Trust me, it's worked before."

She looked at him with alarm. "You've done this before?"

"No, of course not," he hastily replied. "But I've read about other successful escapes, and this worked about a year ago in one of the other sectors. They were so embarrassed it didn't get much public attention."

"And yet you know."

"Because I'm a good reporter."

"Sure." She thought another moment and then unbuttoned the top of her outfit, which actually stopped feeling so constraining and almost felt comfortable. Normally she always dressed conservatively, so this was a look Spector was unfamiliar with and he paused to take a peek, figuring if everyone else was going to look, it wouldn't matter. However, she shot him such a look of disapproval that he returned his gaze to the approaching guard gate.

The same soldiers as before were at the gate, and they seemed to recognize the car or at least one of the occupants.

"A quick trip, *ja*?"

Spector handed over the documents once again and

nodded. As he hoped, the young guard from earlier walked around and leaned toward Katrina's now open window.

"Did the patient get better?"

"Actually, he was in surgery and the trip was a waste. We read his chart, talked to the doctor, and called it a day. How about you, when does your shift end?"

The guard leaned in a bit, avoiding eye contact—it was too high up for his tastes. "Oh, I finish at eight. What about you, when will you be back?"

Katrina shifted a little and the guard obviously approved as his smile widened a bit. Spector continued to wait for the return of his documents, praying the radio didn't squawk right then.

"We're expected tomorrow. Will you be on duty?"

"No, but I can be," the guard said happily.

"That would be real nice," she said sweetly. "We're expected at two and then are planning to be around through the doctor's dinner."

"So you might be free, *Fräulein*?"

"Free for dinner, anyway," came the reply and she smiled again. Spector thought she was being a little too obvious, but the guard was young and obviously unfamiliar with women who showed off as much "personality" as she did. It was definitely the stuff of barracks dreams.

"We'll see, we'll see," the guard said quickly. There were four cars suddenly backed up at the gate, and the furthest one honked repeatedly.

"We'll see you then," the smiling woman said and then looked forward. She was obviously expecting the gate to open at any moment.

The first guard had returned to the controls and allowed the gate to rise up, allowing the car to pass back to West German soil. The other guard walked back into position, the smile still on his face.

"That was one good-looking girl, eh?"

"I guess. You got lucky. I got the doc and the guy in the back."

The dreamy guard blinked once. "They came over, just two. What guy in back?"

"Uh-oh," the other guard said. Both men looked over and saw the taillights of the car moving further into the distance.

"That was great!"

Katrina was hurriedly rebuttoning her top, looking less than pleased. "Great, huh? It's the first time in my life I was ever shot at."

"I meant your act. They never once questioned Wolf."

"Nice . . . job," the passenger croaked out.

"Something to remember, right?" Spector added.

"Not one of the things I wanted to experience. Certainly no World Series."

"Okay, okay," Spector said. He negotiated the car back into West Germany and grabbed the least busy street he could find to get to Free University in time. A glance at his watch told him that there were ten minutes or so before the speech was to begin. He was certainly cutting things close, and for the better part of the last hour he had been out of touch with the big picture. Once more he pulled out his exotic device and flipped open a compartment.

"Paul, are you listening?"

After a moment or two, Paul Urban's voice returned, eliciting a look of shock from Katrina. "How are you doing that, Alan? I don't see a speaker."

His expression was one of annoyance, but it was there and gone in a flash. "Don't worry about it. Status."

"American planes from Austria are now in German airspace and will reach Berlin in seventeen minutes."

"Clever move. Kennedy starts speaking in ten, right?"

"Yeah, and the East Germans continue to move tanks with no clear idea of what's going on."

"What about West German forces?"

"Outer perimeter of West Berlin is the focus of the troops. Local police have started quietly moving people away from the Wall. No one suspects a thing. Alan, can you pull this off? Can you really convince Kennedy?"

"If the bombs fall, then you know I failed. Out."

Spector looked at Katrina's wide-eyed expression, asked her not to ask, and continued to drive. His mind raced ahead, reordering words he had practiced and trying out new phrases. He was hinging a lot on Angela's presence as well as Wolf's. If he calculated wrong, then he and the time stream were in for a rude shuffle.

The Free University was seen over the rooftops several blocks away. With the President and chancellor present, there would be increased security, but Spector prayed his special identification would get him past any security forces. Then he hoped Angela would still be with the presidential party to get him access to John Fitzgerald Kennedy. The enormity of the moment had yet to register with Spector; he couldn't allow it to interfere with his plans or his desperation. Later, when this was all over, he would stop to realize he had fulfilled a dream, albeit at a terrific price.

His mind moved on to the disposition of Angela when this was completed. There were very strict rules in place regarding such intimate contact with historic personages. The rules were written for men and women, with terrible penalties for anyone impregnating someone from the past or anyone bringing a baby upstream. Such rules were not in place when the Time Stations were first erected but were quickly added when someone brought home the son of William the Conqueror. It caused all sorts of political hell, and Spector was pleased to have been in training and missed the entire firestorm the act caused.

Angela may not be pregnant, but she had certainly consummated a relationship with Kennedy and that in itself was a violation. The act then causing the ripple in time was also another violation. If he failed to correct matters, he would share the blame with her, and he imagined she would be completing her senior thesis from an Edinburgh lockup. His failure would be a permanent black mark against him, and his Division Commander would send him to a low-risk Time Station such as Egypt at the time of Caesar and Cleopatra.

Since they didn't play baseball or have world leaders such as Kennedy in that era, Spector made a vow to himself not to fail.

That business complete, he wheeled the car into the first campus entrance he could find, only to be stopped by white-jacketed police officers. With a sigh for wasted time, Alan withdrew his press documentation and noted Katrina seemed to be getting into her vamp act just in case. With luck, they wouldn't need the encore.

The officer looked over the documentation carefully then returned it without comment and waved the car through, where another officer directed it to the left and the sight of the speech. Completing the turn, Spector cursed under his breath as he saw a fresh wave of humanity impede his progress.

"It'll have to be on foot, everyone. Are you up for it?" he asked Wolf.

The man in the back nodded once and got out of the car, weak but with a steady determination that bolstered the Time Warden's spirits. Katrina held his arm, partially for support and partially for show, which also pleased Spector.

The American began to push a path through the crowd; despite its mass the student body was pliant enough to allow them passage. Moving along steadily, Spector tried not to rush out of panic and made certain to study his surroundings. After all, if the Warden had to move, he needed to know where his best locations were. Training took over and he eyed everything as they continued to move slowly through the crowd, nearing the platform where Kennedy would momentarily take the stage.

After another moment or two, Spector finally managed to see the American delegation, milling about to the side of the platform, looking out of place in their severe American black and gray suits, white shirts, and almost uniform red ties. Even the women seemed to be in uniform with just-below-the-knee skirts in solid, somber colors with the sole exception of the official hostess, Eunice Shriver, looking rather conspicuous in pink with black trim, and a frilly hat that looked ridiculous on her. Further back in the crowd, the Warden finally spied Angela, not in such drab colors, but with a facial expression to make up for it.

Obviously she had not convinced Kennedy on her own and seemed to have given up hope.

He pointed out the crowd and destination. Katrina nodded. Wolf looked around and asked, "Where is Elizabeth?"

Katrina turned back for a brief moment, while Spector seemed to ignore the question of context. "Your wife is safe and back at our office, Wolf," she replied.

"I wish she could be here to help, but we'll have to do this on our own. Just a little further now," Spector said. And the group moved closer to the platform.

"If he doesn't recant his previous speech, the East will go nuts," O'Donnell remarked to Clifton, standing beside him near the doorway from which Kennedy was about to emerge. The President was completing some final conversation with Erhard, no doubt finally bringing him up to speed on the situation as it was developing.

Angela suspected the chancellor-elect was going to lose his mind upon hearing the country was to become ground zero in a new round of hostilities. Her words hadn't assuaged Kennedy's anger, and rational debate from his most trusted advisors seemed unable to turn him away from the action he'd ordered. As a result, she doubted Spector would be able to help, even if he ever arrived.

The University's administration had filed onto the platform, greeted by cheering and a handful of insults from the wave of students that had congregated hours earlier and fortified themselves with far too much lager. At least the sun was bright, the day comfortable, and the mood generally upbeat. No doubt few of the students had heard the earlier speech and had little clue that it was already perceived as a great personal moment for the American President, but a bad political opportunity for East-West relations.

Angela couldn't see Kennedy, Adenauer, or Erhard yet, so she hoped a last minute discussion was going on, hoping they could restore peace. Lochner must have been needed to translate since he, too, was nowhere in sight. She looked about further, momentarily making eye contact with Jean Smith and receiving a cold look of disgust in return. Finally, she noted to herself that General Clay was not in sight nor Polke, meaning the military was following through on their commander in chief's orders.

For a moment, she thought she heard her name and craned her neck to look back toward the entrance. No one was looking her way, so she turned around again and finally spotted a waving arm. It was Spector—with a nurse and a haggard-looking man. She was thankful to see him but was also filled with questions and a new wave of anxiety to suddenly realize that this was the very last chance to avert temporal disaster.

Angela moved toward the edge of the space reserved for the Americans and waved back to Spector, who was now ten feet away. Between her entreaties and Spector's press pass, the security guards finally allowed the trio to enter the area. She did note, however, that one of the German police officers was keeping an eye on Spector even after he entered the American "zone."

"Where's Kennedy?" Spector asked, his tone almost harsh and definitely urgent.

"He's still inside," she replied, still searching his eyes for help. "There will be some remarks from the University and Adenauer before he comes out."

"Get me inside. I must have some time with him if we hope to stop this disaster."

"Do you have a plan?"

"Mostly," he admitted in a rush. "Follow my lead once we're in."

Security would be tight, but at least Angela had gotten to know a few of the Secret Service agents over the last few hours of riding together on the bus. Also, she knew some of the key aides such as O'Donnell so she could definitely get inside.

Chase spotted two agents she knew (thanking her keen mind on conjuring up their names). They looked at Spector's credentials and gave him and Wolf a quick pat-down as extra insurance but evidently decided the nurse's hugging uniform couldn't conceal so much as a match. It took another few moments to poke through the medical bag, but everything looked routine to them and, of course, no one thought to look for hidden compartments or space-age tools.

Once inside, she spotted three more agents guarding a door where she suspected Kennedy was still meeting with the German government. Looking about, her suspicions were confirmed when she couldn't find Bundy or Lochner, so official business was proceeding. Others were scurrying back and forth, readying copies of the final speech in English and German for the media as well as clearing the remains of the afternoon reception. With such activity, the four people were not noticed, which was just as well.

Ken O'Donnell had entered the building right behind them and had been speaking with an American military officer off to the right. Angela watched the exchange and was not surprised to see the shake of O'Donnell's head, meaning Kennedy hadn't called the strike off. The old friend of the President turned when Angela called out his name.

He walked over and she separated herself from the group. Chance made sure she came across serious and with purpose, since O'Donnell was assured of getting her time with Kennedy. He leaned his head down toward her and gave her his full attention, which Angela appreciated.

"Kenny," she began, using the most intimate nickname, usually only used by Kennedy himself. "I saw you check in just now. The planes are still in the air, right?"

He nodded but moved a little closer to keep the conversation from carrying.

"I have someone with me that might be able to dissuade the President from carrying out his rash act. I know you've tried. So has everyone else, but I have a feeling this is the right man at the right time. With only minutes to go, the President must be having some final doubts, and maybe a fresh voice will succeed where we've failed. Those planes can still be called off, Kenny, and we can avert a guaranteed disaster. This man can be trusted as you trusted me." O'Donnell gave her a disapproving look, interrupting her.

"Okay, so I breezed in out of nowhere and got lucky. But you will admit he has come to trust me—okay, respect me, first. Trust may be too much to ask after two days. Still, I haven't misled the man or his office. I haven't asked for anything before and feel I deserve this chance to help save us all from a horrendous situation. We can't just let the President do this without a final chance. Alan Spector is that final chance."

The man was silent, his eyes searching hers. Her sincerity was there, he was certain, but was she right? She could read the emotions and thoughts running through his mind and noted his clear eyes periodically flicked over to where Spector, Wolf Krause, and Katrina Beck stood, trying their best not to be noticed by anyone. He also looked over to the locked door and checked to make sure Kennedy was still there.

Moments ticked by and Angela returned the gaze, deciding she had said what needed to be said, making her case.

Angela looked about, making contact with Spector, who seemed more anxious than she thought she felt. Her next thoughts were interrupted when a shuffling of feet caught her attention. Looking about, she saw the German diplomats cluster by the dark oak door as it opened and stone-faced Chancellor Adenauer and Mayor Brandt emerged. Neither said anything to their people but proceeded to yet another door where they entered and ensconced themselves, no doubt to talk amongst themselves. A few moments later, Erhard also left the room, but with an angry gait, and practically slammed the door when he joined his colleagues.

O'Donnell let out a heavy sigh and looked once more at Spector and company.

Angela waited anxiously, in silence, watching O'Donnell weigh facts against guesses against hopes. When the President didn't emerge after a minute, he took a deep breath and walked to the room. He entered it without knocking and there was silence.

A minute became two and Angela thought the worst was happening, that O'Donnell was trying to argue Kennedy out of the attack on his own, ignoring her pleas. Near the door, Secretary of State Rusk was looking impatient, aware that things were starting to slip behind schedule. Suddenly, Angela came to realize that there were at best ten minutes before the planes hit the Wall and time was running out. An odd thought for someone who traveled centuries to be there.

The door swung open a bit, and O'Donnell stuck his head out and whispered something to one of the Secret Service agents, one Angela did not know. He looked her way with an expressionless face and then walked slowly toward her.

"Please follow me," he said in a deep voice, without emotion. Angela smiled her thanks and wiggled a finger toward her colleagues. Within moments, the four people were ushered into the small, wood-paneled room that had two desks, three sitting chairs, no windows, and the President of the United States.

"Kenny, stick around," Kennedy said in a casual voice.

O'Donnell turned on his heel and returned to the room, standing in the back by the door. This told Angela he had done his part and everything else was going to ride on her. And Spector.

"Mr. President," she began, and he smiled at her with affection. Why did he have to go and make this so damn tough on her? He was about to blow up Germany and he was looking ready to take her back to bed. Instead, she quickly made her introductions and the President nodded his greeting to the people, not offering to shake hands. This was the more personal, quick-tempered, and impatient president. The public mask was tucked out of sight, and this was the last best opportunity for Alan.

"Alan needs just a few moments, sir, to explain some things which you may have forgotten in the haste of the last twenty-four hours," she said.

At the UPI headquarters, Urban was once again checking the radio waves, seeking new information and mentally checking flight information from the American jets against a map of Berlin. They were less than five minutes away and were asking for final confirmation from the commander in chief.

"Paul Urban, this is Temporal Warden Headquarters."

He quickly flipped the toggle that activated the view-screen. "This is Urban," he said, lighting another cigarette.

"We've completed a scan of those names Alan asked about and they check through clearly. Their role in the cosmic scheme of things is minor as is that of their offspring."

"I'll be sure to tell them," he cracked.

She glared at him and snapped, "Don't you dare! Hasn't Spector taught you the value of discretion?"

"Actually, yes, he has," Urban admitted a little sheepishly. "I was just being sarcastic. After all, if Spec doesn't complete his job, it won't matter what any of us are scheduled to do. Am I right?"

Basehart's attractive features faded for a moment, and she wouldn't meet his eyes. "You're right," she acknowledged, her voice barely above a whisper. She closed the connection.

A new crackle of static brought his attention to the East German bands, and, with a fiddle of a knob, he clearly heard. They had finally detected the approaching American jets, and their state of panic had notched up. Additional East German jets were scrambling, filling the three small air corridors the country maintained. Red alerts were ordered, and crisscrossing communiqués meant they were mobilizing for a counterattack. He was amazed that the Red Army thought the American jets were on their way to sneak attack East Germany itself and not the Wall. Still, the new tension was enough to make him break out in a sweat and once again pray Spector got to the American President in time.

Spector stepped forward, taking Wolf's arm to help steady him. They moved within five feet of the great man and stopped, sensing this was close enough without causing offense.

"Mr. President, I thank you for the opportunity—"

"You have three minutes so don't waste your time or mine," Kennedy said, cutting him off.

The Time Warden looked a bit surprised by the sharp voice but forged ahead, modulating his tone for respect and import. He switched his thoughts from German to English despite losing Wolf's participation in the matter. Katrina's

English was good, but she too might be lost. So be it. "Sir, this man is Wolf Krause—"

"I know, Angela already did the introductions."

This was not going to be easy, Spector realized. Still, he had to try and swing for the fences.

"Wolf Krause is a musician. He plays viola for an East German orchestra. His wife Elizabeth is a schoolteacher. Together, they represent the people you are trying to help."

Kennedy looked away from the speaker toward Krause, who tried to look fit and proud, rather than weak and injured.

"You see, they have tried all this week to find some way around, over, or through the Berlin Wall. That's how I encountered them and heard their story. It meant giving up their home and even their future to try and find freedom in the West."

"I understand you know what I am planning," Kennedy said, not at all hiding his annoyance at the fact. "This will help people like Wolf."

"No, sir, it will not," Spector countered. "Wolf is currently an unwilling victim of Communism. It is not a government he chose or has any say in. By crushing the Wall, you invite an armed response that will turn Wolf either into an unwilling soldier or a casualty. Elizabeth becomes a widow."

Kennedy flicked his eyes once again at Wolf. The man stood still, silent, and just returned the steady gaze. Katrina stood just as quietly by him, a hand still helping steady the musician.

"Wolf and Elizabeth are not alone. I understand you could not see much beyond the Gate earlier, but you know full well that there are millions of people over there. Millions separated from their families, kept apart from friends or careers. None of that was asked for but given to them by a government scared of their own people. All they can do is act like the neighborhood bully.

"Yes, those are all good reasons for the Berlin Wall to come down. It must come down, there is little argument about that. But not by you and not by America. Instead, it must be done by the people of Germany—East and West. They must rise up against that bully and reclaim the land for themselves. Only when the people demand it, can Germany be unified. If America intervenes today, it puts the entire incident on a global scale, and that will mean you and Khrushchev will try to one-up each other after Cuba.

The President walked closer to Wolf, Katrina, Angela, and Alan, obviously weighing several matters. The conflicting emotions were not visible on his face, but Spector could recognize them from the minute shifts of his eyes and folds of skin around them. He was clearly conflicted and wavering, which was good.

Kennedy moved directly to Wolf's side and studied the bandages from the leg wound, the dried blood spoiling the pristine white. The President also ignored Katrina entirely, focusing just on him. "How did this happen?"

Angela quickly translated the question, and Wolf first looked at Spector for clearance to speak. The Warden nodded just once, praying the words would be enough.

"I was shot trying to climb over the Wall. They fired from a gun tower."

"Your own countrymen would shoot you? And freedom meant that much to you?"

Wolf nodded in agreement upon the near simultaneous translation from the attractive woman. "*Ja*, our life was an unhappy one in the East and would not improve. We wanted a better life here, with the opportunity to bring children into a land of love, not oppression."

"Should I destroy the Wall and let everyone else have a similar chance?"

The East German paused, understanding the importance of Kennedy asking him the question and the timing of it. Minutes were trickling past, and the jets would fire on the structure soon enough. "*Nein*. The Wall is an abomination, but it is a German wall and a German problem."

Spector jumped right in, hoping to seal the argument. "You have every right to be teed off at the Communists. What they tried last night was horrible and must be responded to. But not this way. What they tried was something personal, but what you want to do now is something that will affect millions of Wolfs and Elizabeths. You'll snatch away their chance for happiness and could plunge the entire world into a new dark age."

Angela moved closer, speaking up in a firm voice, one filled with conviction. A conviction usually gained through education and lost sometime after graduation. "Your Doomsday Clock is at seven minutes, right? Seven minutes from Doomsday can tick away overnight."

"The lessons from World War II should not be forgotten, sir," Angela added in a soft voice. She moved even closer to the group, noticing Kennedy had allowed the distance between them to dwindle. "The untold millions that died from the Holocaust, the exterminations in Russia, the Allied forces that gave up their lives. It was all to stop one man from overrunning the world. That same threat no longer exists. Instead, there's a nuclear issue to contend with, and you're still studying the effects of those blasts on Japan. You're witnessing what the radiation has done to the survivors and their children. That was just two cities with crude atomic bombs. What you have and they have inside the silos are far more effective, and the residual radiation could make much of Europe, Asia, or America uninhabitable for centuries."

"Is your ego so great that you're willing to punish so many for a failed assassination attempt?"

Kennedy stared, obviously moved, but still showed no clear answer. Spector couldn't read any change in his decision, and he grew depressed.

"Very persuasive, Mr. Spector," the President said. The tone told the Warden that the gambit had failed.

He realized there was one final truth, one final gamble. He reached deep into his medical bag and withdrew the DA. Walking closer to the President, he gestured toward the furthest corner of the room.

"What is that?"

"Proof, I hope, that what I'm about to tell you is the truth."

The two men walked away from the others and settled on

the opposite side of the small room. As soon as they stopped moving, Spector activated the device and contacted Urban. As the man's voice came clear, Kennedy looked amazed and then cracked a wide smile at such a marvel.

"Urban. Things are going crazy."

"Explain."

"I have President Kennedy with me." That should have been caution enough for Urban to watch how much he revealed.

"The American jets are on course and on target. The German police have begun evacuating the Wall all along the American sector. British and French officials have been stonewalled by General Polke, so they're getting nervous, contacting home for instructions. The East Germany skies are cluttered with jets just looking for an excuse to do something. Their radios haven't quieted down, and everyone is nearing panic, uncertain what the West is up to."

Kennedy's eyes grew wide during the report and then they narrowed as he looked at the gleaming, smooth DA. "How the hell does he know all that?"

"Because he's sitting in a computer monitoring room listening in on all radio traffic. He's using an incredibly sophisticated computer that is linked to my hand-held device."

"Who are you?"

"A loyal American from Ohio. I was selected by . . . fate maybe . . . to be here today and preserve us all from a terrible mistake."

Kennedy continued to look at the device.

"Mr. President, I come from a time and place that is the stuff of fiction. This is all I have to prove to you that this is all wrong."

"The future," Kennedy said, more to himself than to the Warden. "It's crazy but it's the only way this could all exist."

"Perhaps."

Kennedy tore his stare from the DA and looked directly into Spector's eyes. "I believe this is not a trick. I even think you may be from sometime after today."

"Perhaps," Spector replied, but this time his expression

betrayed him and Kennedy caught it, getting the confirmation he sought.

"What will happen to me? To Jackie?"

For a moment, hopefully too brief to be caught, Spector's eyes grew sad as he reflected on the last five months of Kennedy's life. His third child would be born premature and die in just two months. He faced increasing troubles at home over race and in international politics as Vietnam escalated. Then there was the fateful trip to Dallas in November and the sudden image of John Junior, three, saluting the coffin of his father.

Kennedy took in a sudden breath, and Spector knew Kennedy read the expression, understood the sadness. He was always said to be fatalistic, believing that his life was a series of obstacles to overcome, but he hoped for something less than tragedy.

The President slowly walked over to O'Donnell, the friend who was a mute witness to the entire exchange and remained steadfast by the door. He had watched the entire drama unfold but stayed out of the discussion and Spector respected that.

"Kenny?"

"Yes, Mr. President?" Despite the years, there was enough professionalism between them to keep to the protocols the office of President demanded of all.

"Get Ted in here, call it off. The order is: stand down."

Spector broke into a smile, and that was signal enough to Wolf to also smile, although he had a tear in his eye. Katrina hugged West Germany's newest citizen as Angela gave Spector a quick victory hug. The student then looked over at Kennedy, who seemed rather shaken by the events of the past day. She walked over to the man, waiting just long enough for O'Donnell to leave the room and spread the new command. The Time Warden watched her and hoped the worst was over.

"Are you okay, sir?" she asked gently.

Kennedy looked at her with haunted eyes and the look

disturbed her. She thought about the studies she had made of this era and this man.

"Let's see," Kennedy began in the same soft tones. "I'm exhausted, my back is killing me, I can't get to Ireland quickly enough, and I still have one more damned speech to make. Now I'll have to revise the text on the fly, revising what I said just hours ago. The American press is going to love that."

She squeezed his left arm, taking just enough liberty to imply the intimacy they'd shared less than a day earlier, but with enough respect for the man being in plain view of others.

Spector stood and watched, without being able to hear what was being said. It was okay, since this was a moment for them alone. He turned his attentions to Wolf and saw the man smile with relief.

"Mr. Spector . . ."

"Alan, please."

"Alan. When may I see Elizabeth?" The hope and anticipation were evident, and Spector wished he had someone similar to cherish.

"Would you like to stay and hear the speech? It's not as history-making as the one he just made, but it's a good one."

Wolf considered the words and the opportunity they presented. Instead, he shook his head. "I do not feel as good as I may look. I'd rather find my wife and lie down somewhere."

"Did you and Elizabeth ever make plans for once you arrived in the West?"

He shook his head and flashed a sheepish smile. "*Nein*, we never really talked much about it. All we focused on was the Wall and getting past it. I don't know if we ever really believed we'd find a way here."

Spector smiled sadly at the man, realizing his new life was not going to be an easier one at first. Still, he made a promise to help him get over and didn't stop to consider what would happen next. There was no question that he would use his resources to help the two get settled. After all, it was his scheme that got the man shot; the least he could do was find them a place to stay.

"Okay, we'll go back."

"Alan, things have been going rather quickly, but I think I understand everything that went on here today. But tell me, whatever happened to the assassin? The one Angela mentioned."

Spector went rigid, as if hit by lightning. His eyes went wide and he was suddenly in motion. He waved Katrina over and asked her to return him to UPI headquarters in Urban's car. Then the Warden briskly walked over to the President, a hand extended.

"Mr. President, thank you for letting me help. I just realized I still have one more job to do so I must leave. Good luck with your speech."

Kennedy eyed the man carefully, obviously unsure of what to make of him. After all, the President was used to being the one to end meetings, not his visitors. Angela also caught Spector's expression, and she seemed to recognize the need for urgency. She opened the door for him, and the man was through it as if the starter's gun just went off.

21

Place: Free University, West Berlin, West Germany
Time: 5:10 p.m., Wednesday, June 26, 1963

The scene in the halls was similar to New Year's. People shook hands, clapped each other on the back, and broke out fresh cigarettes. After all, a war had just been averted and sanity restored to the President's mission. All the military people were on phones or walkie-talkies. The Secret Service agents were also in motion, readying the path from the room Kennedy was still in to the platform. All the opening remarks were under way, and Kennedy was due at the podium in just a few moments.

Spector cursed himself for being sloppy. He was so busy running back and forth to East Berlin that he never once stopped to consider that the KGB assassin, Gregor Andropov, was still loose. His original studies showed that the man had been apprehended, just a minor footnote in history. Free, he had the chance to change history by completing his mission.

Something told the trained agent that the open-air platform and hundreds of German students would allow Andropov a perfect opportunity.

Without being rude, he moved his group of happy people out of the building and back to their car. In short sentences he told Angela his fears and insisted she come with him. The woman seemed torn, wanting to linger near Kennedy, but acquiesced.

"Where would he attack from?"

"Katrina, he's a skilled assassin. It could be from anywhere on the campus. Have you been here before?"

"Not in a few years," she replied.

"Well, think, where would you be if you wanted to kill the President?"

"Don't forget, the security is even tighter than you might imagine after what happened the other night," Angela observed.

"He'd shoot, no knives," Spector muttered. "He'd have to be in a building, not on top of one." As they neared the building, he seemed to have settled a plan in his mind. Thumbing on the DA, he spoke quickly to Urban.

"Fire up the Beamer and call up a map of Free University. We have to think like an assassin and pick his likely spot."

"I'm on it, but Stein is beginning to think I have the bladder of a newborn."

"After today's news, he won't remember a thing about it, now move!" Spector knew the President would now be anxious to make his speech and leave the country, so he mentally readjusted how much time he had left. At best, it was twenty minutes.

With a slight screech, they stopped in front of the UPI building, and as Katrina and Angela helped Wolf out, Spector dashed into the offices. Ignoring Stein's shout, he made a quick dash toward the back of the offices and the secret room. Within, Urban was marking a screen, highlighting six buildings that surrounded the open space, which today was crammed with admiring students.

"What do you have?" he asked without preamble.

"These six dormitories are the most likely spots," Urban explained. He gestured toward the two furthest from the square and said, "I don't like these much considering the angle and the ways to escape. I'm starting you instead on the most likely one."

"Got it," Spector said, as he checked the charge on his uptime pistol. He stuffed it in his pants pocket, removed his jacket, and nodded in readiness.

"I'm setting you down six minutes ago and will bring you back in ten minutes. You'll have to act quickly."

"Agreed. Let's do it."

As Urban's practiced hands activated the time machine, he said, "Good luck."

Spector didn't feel lucky as he moved through the glowing rip in the air.

Time: 5:19 p.m.

The machine deposited Spector inside the dormitory, near a staircase. He appreciated Urban's efforts but wished he'd ended up on the roof, since it would be easier on his leg to go down stairs than up. However, he had no time for such thoughts and began heading up, figuring the third floor would be the best place to start.

His conditioning made it easy the first two floors, but the sweat coated his body by the third floor and he was uncomfortable. Standing atop the landing, he listened carefully, trying to discern a clue. Otherwise, he'd have to go room by room which might take a lot of time.

Already the speeches to introduce the President had begun as Chancellor Adenauer prepared to introduce Kennedy one final time.

Urging himself forward, Spector decided to try the left side of the floor first. On the way, he heard nothing, figuring just about everyone was partying out in the square. It certainly seemed packed enough for everyone enrolled at the school plus their friends.

His thoughts were interrupted when he heard a muffled sound twenty feet ahead of him. Withdrawing the gun, he ran the short distance and stood before a nondescript door. The sound was definitely one of pain, so maybe Andropov had taken a hostage for a precaution. He never had read a complete dossier on the man and now regretted it.

With his good leg, he kicked at the door to surprise the assassin. The wood splintered easily, the door swinging into the room, and Spector followed, gun thrust forward.

The heavyset woman was stark naked, straddling a scruffy-looking student who was tied to the posts holding the metal bed off the floor. Both shrieked as they saw first the gun, then Spector.

"Uh, sorry . . . carry on . . ." Spector said sheepishly as he backed out of the room, trying to force the broken door to remain closed.

Time: 5:17 p.m.

This time he instructed Urban to set him in front of the second building and to give him a little more time. He was already tired and after bracing himself on the bad leg, it throbbed, reminding him of how personal this had become between him and the Russian killer.

He stood in the shadows, as the sun began to set, and was fortunate no one was looking his way. Stepping back from the building, he craned his neck and searched the windows. The crowd applauded as Chancellor Adenauer was introduced and launched into his remarks.

The lowering sun flickered off something on the fourth floor, but Spector couldn't make out the item. Instead, he limped into the building and forced his body up the four flights of steps as quickly as possible. His breathing was labored by the second floor this time, and the throbbing became a steady stabbing pain by the third.

On the fourth floor he withdrew the pistol and tried to quietly move toward the room. He counted doors to match the windows he noted outside. At the eighth door, he decided to try a subtler approach and gripped the door handle. It was not locked and turned soundlessly. With the door open a few inches, Spector looked through and saw a figure, back to the door, leaning halfway out the window. It was a male's body, wider than he imagined, but it made little difference to the Warden.

"Slow and steady, Andropov, move back," Spector said, summoning as much authority as he could muster given his weakened condition.

The body moved back and turned quickly, something in his hands.

Spector lowered the gun to take aim but then saw the young student proffering the camera his way.

"It's the only thing of value I have, take it," the student said.

"I'm not a thief, son," Spector said in an embarrassed voice. Again, he turned and left the building. As he limped downstairs to return forward in time, Spector checked his chronometer and figured he had less than two real hours left to him.

Time: 5:16 p.m.

This time, Spector paused long enough to have a drink of water and wipe the sweat from his hands, head, and neck. Urban tried to be encouraging, but Spector didn't want to hear it.

Instead, he had to calculate the odds of what he was about to attempt. In going back to Free University a third time, he would have to deal with the fact that he would be there four times. At the moment of arrival he would be at both Free University and just walking into the UPI offices. A minute later, his third self would arrive just a building away to bother an amateur shutterbug. A minute after that, his fourth body would turn up to interrupt a passionate moment between students. Should any of the bodies meet, there could be serious consequences.

"Set my return for twenty-five minutes," he instructed. "By then the first two trips will be over, and I'll be just me when I get back. If not, I'll still have time for the next two buildings."

Urban was tapping in the instructions, nodding at the logic.

Before stepping through, Spector decided to fill his pockets with three small black balls, stun grenades that would work at a distance. Given how his leg felt, he wasn't sure if he could handle Andropov up close and personal.

Again, the weary Time Warden was deposited before a dormitory, and he once more looked up. His angle was different and the sun was a minute higher in the sky, so the light worked differently and nothing reflected. Some final announcements were being made, and Spector knew he had to move inside in a moment before he materialized in front of the building next door. He had yet to meet himself in this way and knew Wardens did this in only the most dire of circumstances. While this may be dire, it was not necessary to spook himself.

Just as he walked to the building's wide entrance, he glanced up and saw something thin and long emerge from a fourth floor window at the far side of the building. Now that was no camera lens, he said to himself.

With renewed vigor, he hustled up the four flights of steps, taking careful note of the sounds outside. Adenauer was speaking now, and in a few more moments, Kennedy would speak. If he were an assassin, he would use the moment of the welcoming ovation to fire off the shots, masking the direction. Time was getting more precious by the second.

Trying to ignore the injured leg, he picked up his pace and made it to the fourth floor. Taking deep breaths at the top of the stairs, he listened for the sound of any other students nearby. It was silent inside the structure, loud just beyond the walls.

Spector took one final deep breath, withdrew the pistol, and moved down the hall. It was empty, lit by lightbulbs even in daytime, and was dotted with doors on both sides, with the occasional crowded bulletin board. He moved in the proper direction, noting janitor's closet, rooms, bathroom, fire stairs, and the rest of the layout.

The crowd cheering rose to a new level, and it was evident the President had been introduced. If he were Andropov, he would fire while the man was being cheered, hoping the sound was drowned out by human voices. That meant it was now or never.

Limping the last few yards, he gained enough momentum to kick at the wooden door, forcing it in, hoping to distract the KGB agent.

Wood splintered once more, and Spector was suddenly face-to-face with Gregor Andropov.

As expected, the man had set up a rifle on a tripod and was obviously kneeling to take aim. The gun's barrel was in the window frame itself, so it could not swivel and be used against Spector. The room had two twin beds, a pair of dressers, two closets, a small mirror, and lots of laundry scattering the floor. Whoever lived here was not present, which left just two men to struggle in a tight space.

"It ends here and now, Andropov!"

The Russian seemed startled to hear his name, but it was momentary, and ignoring the pistol aimed at him, he flattened and grabbed a hunting knife hanging from a sheath draped over one of the beds.

In the distance, Kennedy's amplified voice could be heard, but the words were not distinct and were mixed with occasional cheers from the crowd.

Spector backed up a step and then ducked down to avoid the thrown knife. It hurtled directly over his left shoulder and imbedded itself well into the splintered door. He noted the strength required for such a throw and adjusted his strategy accordingly. After the struggles of the day, there was little doubt he was more fatigued than the Russian, so he would have to outthink him. That in itself would be difficult, given the record on what a cunning strategist Andropov was.

Taking aim, Spector leveled the gun at the sprawled Russian, but suddenly he grabbed the sheath and hurled it at the American. As Spector moved, spoiling his aim, Andropov got to his feet and was charging across the room.

The two men clashed, bodies banging into one another with force. Andropov's hands went for Spector's pistol while the Time Warden tried to throw his opponent off balance. They bumped and strained against one another until the Russian was backed against the other bed and was momentarily off balance.

Spector got off one good punch to the jaw, hurting his hand in the process. The other hand, with pistol still attached, broke free at that moment and he used it as a club. Andropov moved at the last moment, taking the blow on his shoulder rather than his head.

A knee went into Spector's belly, forcing air out of his lungs and making him back up. This gave Andropov a chance to get back to his feet and renew his efforts to dislodge the gun from the American's grasp. Instead, the Time Warden swung the arm around, breaking the grip and once again letting the gun club the Russian. The blow made Andropov stagger back, but in so doing, he dropped backward to the bed and brought his legs up, double-kicking Spector across the room.

The American's head banged on the opposite wall as he tumbled atop the bed, and suddenly Andropov was on him. His breath was pretty horrid, Spector noted, as the two tussled, arms wrapped around each other. Neither man had a clear advantage as they rocked back and forth. Andropov began to use the momentum and forced Spector's head back into the wall. It was enough for him to break free.

Expecting the fight to continue, Spector struggled to his feet to discover the room was empty. The Warden heard footsteps and a few screams, imagining the rushing Russian on the run. Would he go down and over the fence? Would he go down a floor and hide? Or would he go up?

Spector got his bearings and limped to the fire steps and listened as he moved. Footsteps were clearly moving up, so it was off to the roof.

As he moved upward, Spector tried to clear his mind and gather his wits. Why up? he wondered, taking deep breaths to get control over his overtaxed body. And why give up the struggle and flee? Andropov was a trained KGB killer, which meant he knew how to kill with weapons or his bare hands.

He strained his ears and made out the sound of a heavy

metal door, which indicated the roof. So the man was fleeing with some unsuspected escape route at the ready.

At the top step, he steadied his gun, then his breathing. With one hand on the knob, he turned the handle and eased the door open, fully expecting Andropov to be ready for more. Instead, there was no resistance, no sound.

Spector carefully stepped onto the roof and saw Andropov in mid-flight, leaping from one building to the next where a fresh rifle and tripod were set up. Of course! Not only would the assassin have alternate escape routes, he would have multiple murder sites. Rather than aim at Kennedy, though, the Russian had reached the rifle and swiveled it in Spector's direction.

Dropping to one knee, he used his left hand to steady his right arm as he took aim, knowing he'd have one shot, maybe two.

Andropov was similarly taking aim but was working more out of reflex and experience; he fired first.

Spector hit the rough gravel surface of the roof and heard the bullet fly overhead. Rolling to his right, he tried to present a moving target. At the same time, the Time Warden heard a second shot.

This one smashed into his good leg, forcing a loud scream from the American. Wounded, he knew Andropov could finish him off at any time. The next shot would be to kill, he reasoned, and then the Russian would be free to kill Kennedy.

Dragging himself to stay in motion, he reached into a pocket and withdrew a stun grenade. It had slightly more heft than the baseball he threw in another lifetime, but the size was nearly the same. There'd be no time for anything fancy, no tricky curves.

It had to be pure heat.

He hadn't pitched anything other than wadded up paper balls since the train wreck, but he'd studied pitchers and read everything there was on the subject. Gripping the grenade, his index finger triggered the device which had a three-second fuse. Winding up, he saw Andropov try to take aim but pause at the unexpected motion.

The hand was coming overhead now. The grenade, hard and heavy, flew from slick fingers at the height of his ear. He grunted with the effort but watched with satisfaction.

Andropov was standing firm, holding his gun steady, ready to fire. The device arrived faster than he imagined possible; Spector could tell from Andropov's surprised reaction.

With a muffled thump, the grenade released a concussive force that blew Andropov off his feet. He landed hard on the rooftop but still held on to the rifle.

Spector hadn't waited. He had already gone into his windup and threw the second grenade.

It, too, found its target, and the explosive release pushed the Russian toward the edge of the roof.

The third and final grenade pushed him right over the edge.

Gregor Andropov fell nearly five stories to a messy end on the pavement before the dorm building. American Secret Service and German police saw something and were already running toward the body to investigate.

The Time Warden was breathing hard and fighting to stay conscious just to make sure the job was done. He could hear Kennedy's voice over the loudspeakers, clarifying his statements of earlier in the day. The President did not order the Wall's destruction. A sound overhead distracted him, and he looked toward the sky.

Spector glanced up to see in the distance four jet fighters do a flyby and roll in salute of the President, which was far preferable to the volley of missiles originally scheduled for their sortie.

He tried to control his breathing and nerves, waiting the several minutes he had left before the Beamer brought him home.

He practically crawled out of the Beamer when the device finally plucked him out of whatever strand of time he was operating in. Thinking about it started to make his head swim, so he concentrated on business first.

"What happened to you?" Urban rushed over to help his

colleague up. He gasped when he saw the blood-soaked pant leg and the small pool of blood marring the pristine floor.

"I stopped Andropov. He's dead and Kennedy didn't call in the strike. We . . . won."

Urban nodded as he ripped the pants, trying to see the extent of the damage. Worry filled his eyes, and he began working on cleaning the wound. In short bursts, he explained, "The Proximity Alarm shut off a few seconds ago, and Dianna Basehart has called to confirm the catastrophe is over. It got rocky throughout time, she said, but everyone everywhere will manage."

"Good, good," Spector murmured.

"Just one other thing," Urban said gravely. He began binding the wound with gauze and adhesive tape, figuring it would hold until a real doctor could examine it. "The computers finally kicked out the information that Andropov was manipulated into doing his work. A traveler is working at the Kremlin, and Bill Mason wants you to track him down."

"Sure," Spector said with a harsh laugh. "Give me an hour and I'm off."

"You know, they could send in someone else. That Basehart for example."

"Maybe, but I gather whatever the traveler wanted was spoiled by me so it can keep." He looked around the room suddenly. "The alarm is off, right?"

"Sure. Now let's get you some fresh pants from the costumes and finish this up."

A ragged and worn Spector managed to make his way from the secret room to the front offices of UPI. Everyone was working full tilt with Katrina, back in her normal outfit, rushing from Stein's office to Urban's station, clutching blue-marked papers. Heinz was tapping away, and in a corner, Wolf was hugging Elizabeth. The words "happy ending" occurred to the Time Warden as he scanned the office, but he knew there were still lingering odds and ends to be sorted out.

"Spec! Are you done for the day?"

Without looking up, Spector waved a weary hand in

Stein's direction. "Yeah, I'm done," he replied, his voice rough.

"You look like hell. What happened to you this time?"

"Digging deeper than usual for my story," he wearily replied. Fortunately, he had paused to wrap the leg, noting the bullet had passed through it so he should heal with minimal fuss.

"Well, that's nice," Stein said, his voice dripping sarcasm. "Have any news for us? You do recall that's what we pay you for."

Slumping at his desk, Spector emptied his pockets of odds and ends, carefully tucking the "magic" papers in a drawer. His right hand grasped a steno pad, and he took a dramatic look at it, for Stein's benefit. "Of course, Herr Director," he said. "After all, I have brought UPI the exclusive and dramatic escape of two East Berlin citizens on the day Kennedy proclaimed his love for Germany. Try finding that on the Reuters ticker tonight."

The bureau chief looked across the office, watching Wolf and Elizabeth Krause chatting quietly with Katrina and Peter Heinz. His expression softened a notch and then he scowled. "Where the hell is Gruber? This story is worthless without art to back it up!"

"He's in the darkroom," the ever-ready Beck replied. She stood to go and retrieve him.

In a few moments, Katrina completed her task and stole over to Spector, who seemed to sit at his desk in a slight daze. "What happened?"

"I . . . I stopped Andropov and left it to General Clifton and Ken O'Donnell to clean up the mess. Obviously, none of this will be officially revealed or released. After all, how could the American government acknowledge two threats to the President, one caused by a grad student and one prevented by a mere reporter?"

"You owe me a lot of explanations, Alan," Katrina said. She seemed both angry and sympathetic, aware of how much he had risked these past few hours.

"Yeah, I do," he admitted. A smile spread across his sweat-stained face. "I owe you much more than that."

"What?"

"You say that a lot, you know."

She laughed, relief in her eyes. "Yeah, I do."

He looked around for a moment, realizing Angela Chance was not in the room. Katrina caught the look and answered the question before it left his lips.

"She's at Tegel, seeing Kennedy off. There was a call, from one of them, I guess, inviting her over. What will happen to your girlfriend?"

"Believe it or not, when you understand everything—and I will finally explain all very shortly—she will be sent home and punished for her interference with the day's events."

Katrina merely blinked, clearly confused by the unexpected answer. Spector smiled at her, imagining the countless unasked questions and actually looked forward to explaining himself. After all, she trusted him when he needed it most, so it was time to trust her. Let her into his life and perhaps she would be the companion he had longed for. She was strong, cute, and very good at what she did. Yes, maybe there was some leeway in his rules to allow such a mature relationship to develop, especially if she had full knowledge of his role.

These last three years were tougher than they needed to be, relying just on Urban. Mason was right, Spector worked best in a team situation. On the other hand, he concluded that every point that required a Warden probably required a Warden with a team, even if it was just one other. They'd have to have some talks about that when his tour of duty was over.

First, he needed to complete his tour of duty. As soon as he healed, he would have to track down the traveler who'd unleashed Andropov. And then, Spector had many options to reconsider, and one involved asking for an assignment in a nearby time zone, just a few years upstream. One with a team setting, of course. Perhaps someone had to be around in, say, 1969. After all, someone might try and scuttle the Apollo 11 mission, and it would certainly allow him the ability to protect that historic moment. And being around for the Miracle Mets in that year's World Series would be a nice bonus.

Best of all, if things actually clicked with Katrina, she would still be there. He'd have to work on her English, though, but there were a few years in which to get ready.

22

Place: Tegel Airport, West Berlin, West Germany
Time: 7:43 p.m., Wednesday, June 26, 1963

The plane taxied along the ground, gaining momentum, threatening to lift off from Tegel Airport at any moment. Kennedy was reclining, clearly exhausted to all who could see him. The American press had already been told by Press Secretary Salinger that the President would be unavailable until the morning. Clifton, O'Donnell, and Sorenson were seated nearby in the well-appointed living quarters.

If he had to travel around the world, Kennedy at least appreciated the comforts offered by Air Force One. Looking out the window, the sun was already setting and West Berlin's lights were twinkling into existence, transforming the city into a European jewel. There was little doubt that he needed a lot of sleep and the restfulness of visiting Ireland and seeing his ancestral home. Damn the critics, he considered, he needed a vacation stop along the way. Germany was far more taxing than expected, and then there was still Rome and England to consider. It would be a fruitful trip overall, but he recognized the toll it was taking on his body.

The pain was constant and refused to diminish despite

exercise and painkillers. He had to be careful with his movements, and all that sitting and waving certainly didn't help. Nor did the sex with Angela, good as it was.

She was an unexpected dividend on this trip, despite the admonishing comments and glances he received from his sisters Jean and Eunice. While his entourage generally accepted his extracurricular activities, his family never approved. And yet most engaged in similar dalliances on their own.

Angela was witty and intelligent, passionate and comforting, much unlike many of the women he had spent time with over the years. There was something special about her, almost too good for his time and place, he mused. As a result, he was less than thrilled when they had to say good-bye. However, he had a wife and mistress back in Washington; there was no room for anyone else. And she couldn't accompany him further since it would provide the press a chance to criticize him. While the American media might behave and play along as they had repeatedly before, the British press would be less merciful. After all, the sexually tinged Profumo scandal was still fresh on everyone's mind over there, and they would pounce on Kennedy in a minute.

Chance seemed to understand all that before he could articulate any of it when they were alone for the last time. Bob Lochner and Ted Clifton had organized the five-minute meeting in a pilot's ready room at Tegel, without either principal asking for the chance. Kennedy appreciated the gesture on behalf of his staff and wouldn't forget it.

Angela was already in the room when Kennedy was escorted in by Clifton. He tipped his hat to the woman, smiled, and backed out, gently closing the door. She was wearing a new dress, something royal blue with a knee-length skirt and high scoop neck, hiding her breasts, as if trying to be slightly less attractive and therefore less tempting. Her eyes were slightly red-rimmed, and he presumed she had been crying before he arrived.

"Mr. President," she said once the door was closed.

"Angela, it's Jack," he replied. Their voices were quiet, soft and filled with emotion.

"No, you're the President of the United States. Me, I'm just a grad student who kind of got in over her head. I never should have . . ."

He embraced her in a tight hug, which was more to comfort himself than her. "It was wonderful," he murmured. "You should have and I'm thankful. Besides, without you, it might have been a dull political day."

She tried to laugh but a sob caught in her throat. "I nearly got you killed, nearly caused you to start a war, and you're laughing about it?"

"I'm too tired to do anything else, Angela. It's over and the world is blissfully unaware. Oh, a few of my staff know what went on, but not even they fully understand what transpired. I think you might be the only one."

She shook her head, stepping back with enough effort to break the embrace. "No, Alan Spector is the only one who knows what happened today. He was running around Berlin—both Berlins—while I rode in the bus."

"Resourceful man," Kennedy admitted. "He's obviously a loyal American."

"More loyal than you realize, sir," she answered. "He risked a great deal to put things right today, and you may never understand that." She seemed on the verge of crying all over again.

"The plane is waiting, and you know my staff, they like to keep things on schedule. Please don't cry and spoil this. I want to remember the fun, smart Angela."

At that, she tried to smile and blink through the tears. One rolled down her cheek, and Kennedy caught it with his left forefinger. He stroked her cheek one final time and kissed her forehead.

Without another word, he turned and left the room.

As the plane climbed into the early evening summer sky, Kennedy recalled the expression on her face. It was one of inordinate sadness, and he couldn't imagine what could cause such deep emotions after just a few days together. And not even exclusively together, since she had to share him with the Old One, the Fat One, most of West Berlin, and a KGB killer.

Spector's expression haunted him. Those eyes were filled with sadness and sympathy, and he wanted to question the mystery man extensively. Obviously America survived to reach some glorious future, and he wondered what his contribution would be. There was much to accomplish, and it convinced him to work even harder to get reelected so he had the full eight years to leave his mark on America.

The thoughts were interrupted when he caught O'Donnell and Clifton discussing the crowds and their reaction, almost uniform praise and adulation for days. He listened to their observations and tried to put things into perspective. The Germany he had visited was nothing like the one he'd imagined after listening to his brothers Bobby and young Ted discuss it after their visit the previous year.

"Why didn't you tell me it was going to be like South Boston?" the President asked.

O'Donnell laughed a bit at the comparison, and the men launched into a discussion of the visit. They tried to put the entire thing into some sort of political perspective. Kennedy listened and considered the images in his mind of the crowds waving German and American flags, the handkerchiefs being waved by the brave souls in East Berlin, the hands he shook.

Before the conversation broke and Kennedy tried to nap a bit to combat the pain, he turned to Sorenson and commented, "We'll never have another day like this one as long as we live."

Epilogue

Place: East Berlin, East Germany
Time: 1 p.m., Friday, June 28, 1963

On the pretext of honoring Walter Ulbricht on his birthday, Soviet Premier Nikita Khrushchev came to East Berlin. He was truly there, UPI's Peter Heinz reported that afternoon, to counter Kennedy having just visited the other side of the Wall. It was a futile political gesture, and the populace on the Eastern side let him know that.

As the Premier toured the Wall, no one on the Western side waved so much as a handkerchief or a single flower. The sounds of the people lining the streets were muted while observers swore the chants of "Ken-nah-dy" still echoed along the concrete and wire monstrosity. When he chose to speak to the public, a mere two hundred and fifty thousand were counted, compared to three fifths of the West Berlin population for the American.

Where the President proudly proclaimed himself a Berliner in identification with the German people, Khrushchev bluntly spoke of the Wall and not the people it intimidated. "The Wall? I like it just fine. The hole was filled so that no wolf can break into the German Democratic Republic. Is this bad? No, it is good!"

Shortly after Kennedy returned to America, he prepared an envelope and slipped it into his desk drawer within the Oval Office. In his sprawling hand, he marked the envelope, "To be opened at a time of some discouragement." It was intended for any successor to his office and as a legacy to be passed on.

It was revealed sometime later that the paper inside the envelope had just three words printed:

"Go to Germany."

In the two years since the Wall had gone up, a West German report two months later estimated 16,456 people had escaped from East to West. None had escaped in the reverse direction. For all those who made the attempt, a known fifty-four were dead and countless others had been arrested or thwarted.

It would stand as a tangible symbol of the Cold War until the German people finally chose to rip it down themselves on November 9, 1989. The Berlin Wall lasted twenty-eight years, two months, and twenty-six days; its destruction by all Germans finally signaled the conclusion of the Cold War and the beginning of a new era for the world.